THE SECRETS BETWEEN US

CYAN MICHAELS

INKUBATOR
BOOKS

Published by Inkubator Books
www.inkubatorbooks.com

Copyright © 2025 by Cyan Michaels

Cyan Michaels has asserted her right to be identified as the author of this work.

ISBN (eBook): 978-1-83756-626-6
ISBN (Paperback): 978-1-83756-627-3
ISBN (Hardback): 978-1-83756-628-0

FIVE WEEKS AGO

My black leather glove skims slowly across the trunk of a silver luxury car.

I love this moment.

No, it's more than love. It's adoration. Reverence.

With a drop of curiosity, if I'm being honest. No matter how much I plan everything down to the tiniest detail, I can never predict how they will react.

She'll be awake by now. Time for a peek.

The second I open the trunk, a slim calf kicks out, flashing a scuffed Louboutin. Restricted by a tight pencil skirt, it does not make contact with my shin.

They always try to fight, even when they know it's pointless.

A pale face peers out of the shadowed space. Streaked mascara. Smudged lipstick. Torn sleeves where her designer shirt meets the handcuffs.

Aww. The little princess is all disheveled.

I can barely control my smile at her utter helplessness.

"Please don't hurt me." Her voice is hoarse as she chokes, "You can take whatever you want."

Oh, I will. I always do.

1

AMY

THURSDAY

The needle pierces over and over in a steady rhythm. It's almost in time with the song playing quietly in the background. Then the music's tempo picks up and surges ahead, while my fingers remain steady. Watching sharpened steel forcing itself through leather is tranquil to me. A ritual. Something I've devoted my life to. It's impossible to know if each person has a true calling, but this is definitely mine.

My dad taught me when I was very small. Mom often thought I was in the basement rec room doing my homework when I was actually in the workshop. That's where Dad did his leatherwork, and other crafty things, while I tried to absorb every drop of wisdom. From sewing to molding to occasionally using superglue to solve truly desperate problems, Dad showed me how to fix any situation.

I work methodically, turning the piece slightly, following the angle. Lost in the sensation of zoning out completely. It's nearly a trance. Nothing exists but the hum of the motor, the pull of the thread. It's like a mental shield between myself and anything that stresses me out.

Which, being a modern woman in today's crazy world, is obviously a *lot*.

It's always something – drumming up enough business for my shop, balancing work with my son, my husband, and our small home. This weekend, I should finally be able to focus on just one thing – it's my pre-autumn work weekend.

Sure, I guess I'm sort of a nerd when it comes to my work, but I can't wait.

A tinkle from the old-fashioned bell over the door breaks the spell as I stop the industrial sewing machine. Rolling back my shoulders, I can feel a few familiar soft creaks. How long have I been hunched over?

Looking up from my workspace, I call out, "Hello?" I jump to my feet, smoothing down my lumpy old sweater and checking how much hair has escaped my ponytail. There's a line between comfortable craftsperson and looking down-right frumpy – a line I tiptoe on the edge of a bit too often.

There's no telling who might come in the door and what sort of mood they'll be in. Being ready for anything always makes life easier.

A familiar brunette waves as she approaches. "Hi, Amy!"

My smile blooms the instant I recognize her. Of all of the personal assistants who are sent to my shop, Megan is one of the friendliest. Like most of them, she's wearing a low-key designer shirt and black pants outfit with chunky high-heeled boots. It's like their uniform – chic enough to shadow their bosses at glamorous events, but casual enough to run errands.

One of these days I'll be bold enough to ask how they all get their hair so abnormally glossy.

"Just one second." I step back and punch in the security code for the storeroom. Following the long row of stark industrial metal shelving, I find a bright teal handbag loosely wrapped in clear plastic. Kicking the door shut tightly behind me, I hold up the bag on the way to the front counter. Megan's shoulders drop and she nods with relief as I unwrap it, pointing out the nearly invisible repair. "A few of these newer brands have weak handles," I explain. "You see right here? I mix a few strands of superstrong clear nylon into the thread when I restitch these. It's just a pinch thicker, and normal people will never notice."

She laughs lightly. "That's incredible. I can barely tell the difference, even when you point it out. Thanks, Amy. You're a life saver. I didn't want to face Olivia if it didn't turn out."

My hands move in a familiar dance as I remove the protective layer of plastic and run a microfiber cloth over the clasps to make sure they shine. Then I drop one of my custom-made lavender mint sachets into the bottom so the bag will smell fresh and dreamy when opened. I wrap it in soft pink tissue and slip it into a *Pristine Purses* shopping bag. I want my customers to have the 'brand new purse' experience all over again.

Megan swipes her boss's black credit card, flashing a perfectly whitened grin. "I told three of my colleagues about you at a party last week."

"Thank you!" I grab three business cards and write *"Megan's Friend - 5% discount"* on the backs.

"Amazing." She slips them into her own purse, noticing my frown as I examine it. "I know, I know. I need a much better bag if I'm working for *the* Olivia Rhodes. Like I could ask for a raise."

"No, I'm worried about that zipper that's starting to rip

out. May I take a look?" She hands over the worn black purse for me to examine. "Just give me two minutes. Grab a sparkling water from the fridge if you like."

"Oh, no, you really don't have to–"

Ignoring her protests, I head to the sewing machine that's already loaded with black thread. After fixing and reinforcing the zipper that's starting to break free, I also give the handle edges a quick once-over. Then I take a microfiber cloth to quickly scrub the metal hardware, flashing a grin as I return to the front counter. "I know this is just your everyday purse, but there's no reason for a solid bag to fall apart before its time."

Megan gives me a sheepish smile. "Thanks. How much?"

My hands fly up to wave her away. "Don't be silly! The worker bees need to stick together, right?"

"Wow. Thanks, Amy. I really appreciate it." Her phone buzzes and she instantly frowns.

"Your queen bee?" I snicker. We've had several entertaining and occasionally catty chats about her employer, Olivia Rhodes. On the surface, she's another early twenties trust fund princess with delusions of grandeur and supremely high style.

I once looked up her family, and was hit with a deep pang of sadness. Her parents both seem business-obsessed and ice-cold. No wonder a young lady is going to seek the approval of strangers. I'd bet my sewing machine that the poor girl wasn't hugged enough as a child. No wonder I've seen Olivia be both incredibly kind and wildly mean. She lives in a volatile world of extremes. I genuinely feel sorry for young women like that, who have no true life's purpose.

"Yup. Thanks, gotta run. Making moves and paying bills, right?"

"Right. Have a great weekend."

"You too." Megan waves from the door. "Especially since you have the weekend off!"

"I'm sorry?"

Her thumb jerks to the window. "This street is being closed. There are signs out front about a broken water main being torn out." Her phone buzzes again. "Gotta go. I'll be back in a few weeks with some belts. Thanks again!"

Megan dashes out the door, and I'm left staring at the backward image of my logo on the glass: *Pristine Purses – designer leather repair, cleaning, and conditioning.* I walk past the open shelves containing samples and repair diagrams to peer out at the street.

Workmen are spray-painting neon pink and yellow markings on the sidewalk out front, turning this quiet stretch of Barrett Street into a horrible graffiti nightmare. All cars have been cleared from this end. Trucks and excavators are rolling into the nearby parking lot.

Well. This *sucks.*

Mr. Laskaris, the older gentleman who runs the café next door, sees me through the window and shrugs dramatically. I return the gesture, watching as he looks around in dismay before going back inside. Poor guy. He relies on foot traffic and people driving by. How much business will he lose this weekend?

I had the next three days blocked out to get ahead of work. Existing orders, plus new samples, cleaning out my extensive customer database, and deep-cleaning the storeroom. I do this twice a year to make sure everything is kept as pristine as the name claims.

When I can't work, I become antsy. When schedules are changed at the last minute, I get jumpy. If I don't know precisely what's going on, my mind races and I feel unstable.

My hand flutters to my throat to find I'm already flushed from nerves.

It's times like these I wish I had access to my husband more than three days a week.

2

AMY

Great. Just freaking great. My heart sinks as I stare out at the utter chaos outside my shop. I guess it's Murphy's Law of Timing that the street would be blocked off on the one weekend I truly had my heart set on working long hours.

Referrals maintain my business, and my clients expect me to be open during regular hours. The women who spend thousands upon thousands of dollars on designer handbags usually come from old-money families. Their mothers have spoken to these young ladies about the value of taking care of their luxury items and having a good repair person on hand.

As a general rule, wealthy people always want to "know a guy". They like to be prepared, because they're always planning for the future. I'm more than happy to be "the guy" who can fix almost anything. To continue being their top contact for every leather item that requires attention.

Which means I can't ever drop the ball, and have to kiss their asses at all times. I should stock up on special lip balm for those occasions.

Racing to the shop laptop, I check this weekend's pickups. There's only one scheduled for Saturday afternoon, but I happen to know that Casey Lowell is in Europe for at least a month. Yes, I skim the social media pages of my clients to keep an eye on what's going on with them, and in the fashion world. Although most of them are only slightly younger than I am, I don't want to lose touch with today's styles in their age group.

It's also handy to see what they're up to. I mean, everyone needs a tiny drop of drama in their lives. That is, beyond being semi-addicted to true-crime podcasts, of course.

I send an email to Casey's personal assistant to explain the situation, asking if she could come late next week instead. My shop is open Wednesday through Saturday, then for two hours Sunday afternoon, so that my son can come with me and "help" by organizing leather swatches and coloring at my workbench. It also gives me Monday free to do housework and errands, and Tuesday to spend completely with my husband, Craig.

This tight schedule has been holding me together. I'm one of those weirdos who adore routines. Things running like clockwork. It makes me feel like I'm in control.

"Control is a tricky balance," Dad often reminded me. *"You can't control everything, pumpkin. Be prepared, but you'll need to pivot and improvise when things inevitably go sideways."*

I send a quick email to all of my customers, apologizing for closing suddenly this weekend, but it's out of my hands. If nothing else, it's an excuse to remind them that I exist if they haven't been by lately.

It's kind of a pathetic reason to reach out to my clientele, but at least it's for their convenience, instead of being salesy. Every small business article says that I should have an official email list and be providing branded content weekly, *blah blah blah*. That feels like an annoyance. I don't ever want my name to be associated with that feeling.

Instantly, I get auto-responses that two of my regulars aren't in the country this week – Alexandra and Piper. Even though I doubt they've ever met since they live in different cities, they're both loaded and are both super-malicious. I'll bet they'll be returning to in-boxes overstuffed with fancy party invitations and thousands of social media responses.

Marketing and social media are definitely my weak points, since I'm not a pushy person. Honestly, what introverted craftsperson is? I'd rather let the work speak for itself, and work off referrals as much as possible.

Yet I also need more money to pay for the latest shop rent increase, and saving for the future. Namely, my son.

My fingers drum restlessly on the worn wooden desk. Rent is going up again at the end of the year. Quite a bit this time. Mr. and Mrs. Narvaez have already warned me about it, thank goodness. It's a lovely building, and they've just updated the front windows and installed benches and planters in front of each shop in the row. The increase is pretty fair, actually. It's just going to stretch things thinner than I'd like.

If I had a bigger house in a good neighborhood with a large front room, I could work at home again. Then I wouldn't need a babysitter to take care of Asher after school three days a week.

Yet having a storefront makes the business seem much more established. Plus, there's the security aspect. Having people know where I live is dicey. According to Mom, every single man on the planet has the potential to be a mugger. She drilled that into my head until I finally listened to her pleas to not have strangers come around the house. Yet these days, people have cameras everywhere. With visible lenses pointed at the doors, I'm positive I'd be safe.

If I had a real budget to create a proper workshop somewhat separate from the house, I would love to work from home again now that I've boosted my clientele so much over the past few years.

Luckily, Asher absolutely adores his babysitter Penny, and Sundays in the shop with me, so he's the happiest five-year-old I know. Okay, so he's the only five-year-old I know well. Plus, I'm likely biased, since one smile from my little man makes my heart sing.

Of course, every caring mother is obsessed with her children. Yet I know in my heart that my son is a gift. He's always even-tempered, always ready to help. What toddler asks if he's putting his toys away correctly?

Sure, I see him through rose-colored glasses, but it's the cutest thing in the world when he lines his stuffies up neatly in a row on top of his blocks. Like he's putting his fluffy shark, bear and puppy on pedestals.

I rush to make a handwritten sign for the front door, just in case a customer makes it over the planks and torn-up sidewalk this weekend. Then I tidy up the shop as I do my routine checks before closing for the night.

It's a shame that Penny has been sick so much lately. Some kind of stomach bug for the past few weeks. She's been bravely fighting it, but needs some real time off. I had to take Asher to my mother's this morning, so they can spend a long weekend together and I can get ahead of work. Now I won't even be able to get into my shop.

Which means I'll have the weekend completely to myself for the first time in... I can't even remember how long. I am not the kind of person to believe in signs. Yet maybe this is a clear sign I need to recharge with an utterly relaxing long weekend.

My vision fills with images of a leisurely bubble bath and a glass of wine before ordering dinner just for myself, without having to think of anyone else for once. Wives and mothers should be allowed to be totally selfish once in a while, right?

I drop my phone and notebook into my shoulder bag, double-check that the back door and storage vault are locked, then I set the security alarm and lock the front door behind me as I leave.

It takes a bit of negotiation with the workmen to drive my car out of the quickly growing zone of utter destruction. Having this much chaos around my shop makes me nervous. What if the windows are smashed, or the freshly painted trim is nicked? It's impossible not to take every detail personally when I've poured my heart and soul into my business over the past several years.

My hand flutters to my throat. I can already feel my skin growing warm. Stress-induced flushing. When it gets really bad, I break out in hives. Geez – I could never play poker professionally with this condition, unless I threw on a silk scarf as camouflage.

Several blocks away, I pull into a mini-mall with my dry cleaner and grocery store. An odd, prickling restlessness creeps across the back of my shoulders. Is it bizarre that I don't know what to do with myself when I suddenly have free time?

Maybe I just miss Craig.

Sure, it's strange that I only see my husband all day Tuesday, then Wednesday and Thursday evenings. His job takes him all over the place, with a bunch of high-tech internet security projects. But this entire week he's been in Las Vegas at a giant tech conference.

We've always made the most of our short time together each week, but lately I feel like he's been pulling away. It's starting to make me unsettled. Heck, I was actually jealous for a split second when I came home last Wednesday night and Craig was on the floor playing blocks with Asher and Penny.

Maybe we're just both tired from working so hard and need to plan a date night. It's been a while since we've spent an entire evening alone, talking about anything other than work and Asher.

As soon as Penny is feeling better, I'll see if she can stay late on a Thursday and I can take Craig out to dinner. Maybe to a tiki place for those fancy fruity drinks we both love.

A naughty little thought tiptoes through the back of my mind. Maybe I should take him to a cheap motel for the night so we could really be alone? We've always been totally in sync in the bedroom. That's one area we can't afford to let slide. Since we can't spend all of our time together, our emotional closeness comes from phone calls and texting. Our physical closeness is condensed into the time we have.

Even though he's been distant, he was extra-fiery about three weeks ago. I could use some more of that. I'd been worried that things had been starting to fade a bit over the last couple of months. But I won't see him until Tuesday, and have no idea if I'll be able to contact him before then.

Twisting to reach into the back seat, I grab a couple of dresses and two of Craig's jackets, and go into the dry cleaner. The owner smooths down her pale blue smock and greets me with a huge smile. "How many today?"

"Four."

As always, she spreads everything out on the counter, quickly checking for loose buttons or zippers. I appreciate how thorough she always is, which is why I come here. She checks that the dresses don't have pockets, because of course not. Then she goes through Craig's jackets. One is black, one is charcoal.

I often joke that he's some sort of superspy, wearing clothing so bland that nobody can remember what he looks like. His dazzling hazel eyes always sparkle when I tease him.

"Ahh," she grins, pulling out a piece of paper and handing it to me. "There's always something."

"Thanks." I stash the dry-cleaning ticket in my purse, then go outside with the paper in my hand. Craig's work is apparently so top secret that I wonder if I should tear it up and throw it in the trash. Or take it home to shred it properly. On the other hand, he's never brought a scrap of paper related to his job home, as far as I've ever seen.

It only takes three more seconds of wavering before I unfold it. Then I blink hard, not sure if I'm reading it correctly. It's a pickup slip for first-grade school photos from St. Mary's Elementary.

Our son goes to kindergarten at Westfield Elementary.

Yet the slightly smudged, low-resolution, black-and-white photo on the page looks *exactly* like Asher.

3

AMY

It's taking all of my focus to put one foot in front of the other.
Get food, get home. That's all that matters for the moment.

It's some sort of weird mistake, obviously. All I need to do
is get home so that I can eat and take a breath. There's no
need to feel rattled even though my work weekend has
suddenly been cancelled and Craig has apparently gone to a
school he claims to hate, to take Asher for photos.

The grocery store is relatively empty as I pick up some
staples and easy meals that won't waste my energy. The
cashier doesn't seem to notice that my hands are trembling.

As soon as I get back in the car, I attempt a few deep,
slow breaths from the bottom of my diaphragm, rolling my
shoulders back as I try to release my tight trapezius muscles.
It doesn't calm this sick, heavy feeling in my stomach as if I'd
swallowed a stone. No, it's a handful of sharp rocks, and
they're all jostling around.

It must be some sort of weird mistake. But how? Why on
earth would Craig have a receipt and instructions on how to
download photos from a different school? We've only been

together for six years, but we covered things like previous relationships on our first amazing date. He didn't mention any other children. That's the kind of thing that comes up naturally.

I check my phone and see there's a voicemail from Craig. *"Hey, honey. I miss you so much already. This conference is incredibly dull, even with the bright lights of Vegas in the background."* It sounds like he's walking around as he speaks. *"Tell Asher that I hope his baseball game the other day went well, and I..."* There's a pause. *"Sorry. I just walked by a baseball poster here in the hotel lobby. Please tell Asher I hope his soccer game went well. No matter how it turned out, I'm incredibly proud of him."* He chuckles. *"We cooked up one fabulous kid, didn't we, honey? I hope you don't work too hard this weekend, and take some time for yourself."* There's a strange noise in the background that I swear sounds like a crow. *"Love you. I'll talk to you tomorrow."*

I rewind the call partway to listen to that section again. It definitely sounds like a crow. I don't think they go as far south as southern Nevada. What would a crow be doing in downtown Las Vegas? They're supersmart birds – maybe they've figured out the slot machines.

Las Vegas has a ton of attractions, and Craig could be walking by absolutely anything. But there was no sound of other people. No slot machines, no traffic, no hotel murmur, nothing else whatsoever. His phone has an incredible microphone, and I'm always begging him to go somewhere quieter before he calls me because it picks up everything.

This time, it picked up a breeze and a bird call. Definitely not the busy hotel he claimed to be in.

Not to mention, Craig sounded seriously distracted. He's

been to Asher's soccer games. We've laughed endlessly about how adorable five-year-olds are when they run around chasing each other as much as chasing the ball.

It was important to me that Asher start meeting kids outside of his kindergarten class. His school doesn't have a decent sports program, but I feel that team sports are helpful at that age as long as they aren't competitive. Luckily, his team has a great coach who is only focused on playing a bit better every single time. I didn't want to let him play baseball until he's older, with better hand-eye coordination, and Craig agreed.

My breath starts coming a bit too fast, and my left finger begins to twitch. My palm lands at the base of my throat – already flushed. The traffic drifting by the parking lot seems slow, so I focus on starting the car and driving home.

For the first time in our entire relationship, I have the crystal-clear feeling that my husband just lied to me.

The drive home is an exercise in deep breathing and attempting to recall every anti-stress tip Dad ever taught me. While recalling his life lessons, I can always hear his voice in my mind as clearly as if he were standing beside me.

"When we're feeling fear, that's processed in the amygdala, a part of the brain that's very primitive and therefore doesn't process language. If we speak our fear into words, it pulls the focus into the prefrontal cortex – the logical processing system. Then we can work on our problems, and it turns the fear response down a bit."

"I am confused." The steering wheel seems unconcerned by my declaration. "I hate when I don't know what's going on. I am freaked out by that school photo form. I hate that Craig is away so much and I don't understand his job. I can't stand that he can't tell me the details of what he does. I hate that I can't catch up on work this weekend and I feel totally out of place."

Wow. Easing my foot off the gas since I was starting to speed, I clear my mind with several minutes of deep breathing. Maybe that actually helped.

Looking around at the traffic on the smaller streets, I can see cars pulling into driveways. Husbands and wives waving from the car or front door. Kids running out, excited that a parent is home.

It's frustrating that I only have half a husband, in a way. Three days a week is better than partners who are deployed overseas, or go on year-long research missions. Yet life seems to be set up in a weekly format, and I only get forty-three percent of a week with my darling husband. No wonder I'm panicking over a single stupid receipt that has to be some sort of mistake.

It doesn't feel like a mistake. It feels like another sign.

Like the broken water main on a weekend when Asher was already staying with my mother. A weekend I don't have any important pickups.

I suddenly have the time to think, and that's not a good idea right now.

Because all I'll be able to do is dwell on the fact that I know in my guts that Craig is keeping something from me.

Something big.

4

BECCA

I didn't imagine it would be like this. Every vision board, every plan. Life goals and grand fantasies. Not a single one turned out precisely the way I expected.

Even though I'm sitting in the white and lavender office in my gorgeous home, puttering on my laptop while a clay face mask sinks into my pores and green tea steams beside me. The home life parts of my dream boards and goal lists are coming along quite nicely.

Especially since the pale pink tulips are opening in the vase beside me, and my personal chef is available this Sunday evening for a special pizza night. Another great weekend of shooting family content.

My fingers tense slightly while scrolling through countless photos, searching for yesterday's shot of my breakfast. It's the perfect photo for a blog post about the importance of nutrition plus comfort in the mornings, when our true consciousness is beginning to activate.

This is what I get for being a dreamer.

My focus is usually on details like aspirational lifestyle

photos and inspirational quotes. Not the exhausting bits like figuring out whether to splurge on a visually stunning vacation, or a stunningly curated backyard glamping weekend that might be more in line with my elevated earth mother image.

It always comes down to money. Until it's rolling in, I'll have to keep faking it. Which is incredibly annoying. This stress has been weighing me down for the past few months. Even my yoga instructor has noticed it in my shoulders.

Those extra jobs had better pay off so that I can hire an assistant sooner rather than later.

My eyebrows lift as I find the photo I've been looking for. Then I try to keep them gently lifted, to avoid squint lines. Yikes, when is the last time I did my face yoga videos? I need to make time for that before I lose any more definition in my jawline.

Many momfluencers have switched to purely videos, yet I prefer scrolling slowly through photos and text for at least half of my content. More like an elegant magazine than a quick TV show. Timelessness is one of my brand keywords, and I take that stuff seriously.

When I hire an assistant, they can make a database to save time. Then I'll need a design team to make everything more cohesive and change my colors every season. A manager to wrangle better brand deals. Real ones, not the ones I've been faking for the past year.

A team of people is something every influencer aspires to. This would allow me to live freely, creating content while others process it.

Until then, as always, a woman has to do everything herself.

5

AMY

By the time I'm sitting at my kitchen table with the groceries put away and a cup of tea in front of me, I have not calmed down. I am focused. Well, kind of. My hands are still shaking slightly as I open my laptop, setting the photo form beside it on the kitchen table.

Do I want to look into it? Of course. Am I mentally equipped yet? Maybe I should wait until I've mellowed out a bit more. Turning the page over, I set it under the fruit bowl – as if that will stop the information in its tracks for the moment.

Instead, I check my email. I've lost touch with many of my friends since most of us have been so busy with work and motherhood. It's time to start forcing myself to do social things where I'll meet other parents. It's annoying that strangers drain my social battery so quickly. I've usually got one solid hour before the excuses start flying out of my mouth in my quest to get back home.

There's an email from Westfield Elementary, reminding me of tonight's school board event. One of those self-congratulatory shindigs where people are given kudos for simply doing their jobs. But it's for all three elementary schools in this area. Including St. Mary's.

The school I desperately want to get Asher into. The school that Craig said was too far away. Where apparently he has a photo download code.

Which must be some bizarre mistake.

I mean... my mind blanks for a solid dozen blinks. I honestly cannot think of any decent reason he'd have that.

Maybe my inner radar is off kilter at the moment because I'm so sure that Craig was lying to me in that voicemail.

Not to mention... I check in the drawer of the dining room sideboard where I keep important flyers. There was one about tonight's school board event that came in a few weeks ago. Wasn't there? It was green, I think. But it's not there now.

It's possible that I'm mistaken, yet it gives me another strange, prickly feeling.

I jump to my feet, my autopilot kicking in as I do a quick tidy of the space while I get my bearings. The kitchen is furnished with a sturdy second-hand wooden table and chairs, framed prints of botanical vegetable drawings, and a cheerful frog print booster seat for Asher. Nobody would know that I found the booster seat at a thrift store. Or those picture frames were found in Mom's attic.

Everything here is modest. Functional. Some people use the term "essentialism" but I've always thought of my lifestyle as "enoughism". The basics are all we need. All of us Taylors have been this way – Mom made recycling clothing into an art form, and could make leftovers last for a week. My Dad... well, he would get any job done with whatever he had on hand. *"Living small can help prepare you for anything,"* he used to say.

That's great for me, but not enough for my son. Sure, he has a huge laundry basket full of toys here in the living room, and another upstairs in his bedroom. But when I've taken him on play dates, all of the other kids have five times as much.

Ugh. None of this reminiscing is going to sort out what to do about Craig's photo code.

This restlessness is going to drive me nuts. I check the mail on the hall table, and the pizza promotions, real estate flyers and endless roofing discounts land right into the recycling bin. My gaze settles on a bright blue flyer for tonight's school meeting. Wow, they're extra enthusiastic about getting parents to attend. Maybe St. Mary's wants to show off their new facilities.

Putting Asher on the right scholastic track has been weighing heavily on my mind. He's gone to Westfield Elementary for junior kindergarten, yet by all accounts, that school is garbage. I've never been a snob on my own behalf, but for my child... There's nothing I wouldn't do for him. Every time he looks up at me, those big, hazel eyes looking so much like Craig's, I know I'd go to the ends of the earth to set him up with a wonderful life.

The large class sizes at Westfield prevent my son from getting individual attention, which is crucial to help children grasp basic concepts at the right pace. St. Mary's classes are roughly half the size. That in itself is a huge reason for me to be anxious about moving him.

Even though we're in the Westfield district, if I plead my case to St. Mary's, Asher could be switched. Our address is right on the edge of the district, so it's enough of a gray area that nobody would notice.

It was shocking to me that Craig thought it was a terrible idea. As if staying in a crowded school with a crumbling library and a ratty old playground was good enough for our son, just because it's a bit closer. Our boy isn't worth a few more minutes of driving time? That's crazy.

Maybe that's why he had a St. Mary's paper in his jacket? Could he have been looking into the school and wanted to surprise me?

Screw it. I have to know.

I bring my laptop to the dining room and plug it in. Pulling the sheet of paper out from under the fruit bowl leaves a smear across the table. The page is soaked. Asher must have been playing with the textured glass bowl again, dripping pear juice that slides under the bottom. I can't make out the download code, and the photo is now a blob that doesn't even look human.

Maybe that's for the best. I mean, did that tiny blurry photo really look like my son? It's entirely possible that I was seeing something disturbing because I was flustered.

A sharp, loud knock at the door makes me leap to my feet, dropping the sweet-smelling paper back onto the table with a plop. The sound is followed by the vigorous rattle of the doorknob as someone tries to barge right in.

Mom knows to knock quietly. Craig taps lightly, then uses his keys.

Which means it's Fiona. *Ugh.* Not now.

I open the door, smiling politely at the woman whom I should think of as a sister by now. Yet with her gaudy makeup, blaring voice, and utterly in-your-face personality, it's clear that my old friend and I have outgrown each other years ago.

Clear to everyone but Fiona.

"I saw your car – you're home early," she chirps, lounging her dark rose tracksuit against the door frame. "What's up?"

I hate lying. I really do. But this time, I'm going to justify it by mentally claiming it's self-defense. Casually scratching my throat before she notices I'm about to flush, I smile and sigh. "Just getting ready to go out."

"Yeah? Craig's not actually putting you ahead of his precious work and taking you on a date, is he?" She laughs as if her statement were a killer punchline.

Fiona has no internal filter. Zero. It's no secret she detests my 'half a husband' situation. It's very clear that she thinks I deserve more. It gets exhausting to explain things over and over. It's also exhausting that she pops up at the strangest times.

I have to admit, her spontaneous drop-ins have saved me on a few occasions. Like in the middle of a date that was going terribly wrong. And the time she brought my important package in from the rain when the delivery guy chucked it in the hedges. Her heart really is in the right place. But now is not the time for a girl chat with someone I can't trust to keep a secret until I'm ready to share it.

If I don't think of a valid excuse immediately, she's going to invite herself in and find out that Asher is with Mom this weekend. Then she'll insist on a girls' weekend of wine, takeout and endless true crime documentaries.

Fiona is positively obsessed with killers. What makes them tick. How their unstable childhoods make them completely lack empathy. Personally, I think it's whiplash from her own boring upbringing, and now she's trying to think of ways to make herself seem interesting. Everyone needs a hobby.

She's the hobby queen – falling headfirst into a new one every few years. At least this one doesn't leave me searching for places to display the new freeform candle sculpture or the plant pot with googly eyes. Her silversmithing phase was interesting, at least. It resulted in the lucky key necklace she never takes off, and a charming bracelet she gave me that I still wear sometimes.

I'm utterly fascinated by those true crime killer shows too, to be honest. It's oddly intense to learn about what severely damaged people are capable of. Just not when I'm already dealing with Craig's potential lying, which is throwing me off balance.

The thought of loafing with her for the weekend would have been a blast eight years ago. Now, the thought makes me prickly when I'm already stressed.

If watching a certain kind of show is the singular thing we have in common anymore, and I dread every time she appears unannounced, I'm going to eventually have to find a way to tell her I need to turn down our friendship.

My eyes land on the blue flyer in my hand. "I'm going to a school event tonight. Comparing the facilities and getting to know the board. That kind of thing."

Fiona tolerates Asher, but in general, avoids children at all costs. Thankfully, she's already backing away, twirling her key necklace in one hand. "Oh. Well, have fun with that. You said that Asher is with your Mom this weekend, didn't you?"

Oh crap. I may have accidentally mentioned that a few days ago. "Yes, he'll have more fun there than hanging out with me over my work catch-up weekend."

"Sure. But maybe you'll be done earlier and we could do something. Call me tomorrow?"

"I'll try, but I really have a ton on my plate. I might be out of touch until next week. Sorry."

She rolls her eyes, showing off the blue sparkles of her eye shadow. "You know you work too hard."

"That's who I am."

"Yeah, yeah. And I love ya. Have a good one!" Thankfully, she walks away at top speed. Her house is only a twenty-three-minute walk away, and yes, she's timed it.

Now I really have to go to this event. Deal with strangers. And ignore the unsettling feeling that keeps washing over me every time I remember I'm pretty sure my husband lied to me.

No. Not pretty sure. Certain.

6

AMY

I've never had a proper ritual.

Every other woman seems to have a defined process for preparing to meet strangers. Maybe if I had a system, it would be less aggravating.

I make myself a sandwich, then get into the shower, using an extra few minutes to properly condition my dark, wavy hair. Now is not the time for it to be out of control. I need to look extra polished. I'm going to have to chat with strangers, which has never been a strong suit unless they're customers and I'm explaining something.

I went to one of these multi-district primary school events a few months ago and walked back out after about twenty minutes. Everyone else knew each other already, and I quickly became uncomfortable. Not to mention, I'd come straight from work, and a few of those women looked like they came straight from a runway. How does a working mom have the time to do model-perfect makeup and a blowout? It's totally intimidating.

Putting on my makeup carefully, I'm thankful my hands

are steadier. This time I'll be calm and collected. Look the part of the concerned, friendly mom. Pretend that I'm not shy around groups of new people. Make new acquaintances. Figure out how to get Asher into St. Mary's.

Basically, I need to be the strong, clear-minded version of myself. That version usually shows up when I really need her.

I select a dark, midnight blue dress. Although it isn't very trendy, it's definitely flattering. One thing about being so busy all the time is that I'm always moving, which keeps my figure... well, fine. I'm strong and healthy, even if a few spots are rounder than I'd like.

I switch my earrings to the green zircon teardrops that almost look like emeralds. I've always secretly wanted the real thing, but jewels are a definite waste of money.

Something clicks in the back of my mind. The first time I tried to go to one of these events, there was a glamorous woman who was acting like everyone knew her. Someone murmured that her name was Becca – a famous mom blogger, or social media guru or something. A few of the other women had seemed quite starstruck. I tried to get them to chat about the enviable St. Mary's music program, hoping she would join the conversation. Then Becca was dragged away by a friend or a fan, and I didn't see her again.

Although I hadn't had the nerve to go chat to her, she was definitely giving me a few strange looks. Possibly because I looked like a church mouse compared to most of the other women.

I add a bit more eyeliner and the good mascara, then open a deep closet drawer filled with my semi-secret stash of a handful of fancy luxury handbags. Three of them have been scavenged from second-hand stores. Two of them were used to barter for repairs on larger bags. One of them was a repair that wasn't claimed after three years, and according to my paperwork, more than two years means they forfeit the item.

Walking in with a pristine ivory vintage Lola Q's of London handbag might grab people's attention – a possible conversation starter.

I'm ready early, so I sit at my laptop and look up this Becca woman. Do influencers really influence anyone? Maybe she has some influence over the St. Mary's board. She might at least be able to help introduce me to the right people. The well-off people I meet through my business all love being treated like experts. Like they're deeply "in the know".

There aren't many mom bloggers in this area, so Becca is easy to find. Holy geez... The woman has a ton of videos, blog, and photo posts on several platforms. She's some sort of lifestyle and parenting guru. And clearly a fashionista, of sorts.

Wow. The more I scroll through her perfectly lit and curated photos, the more I'm awestruck. Every woman dreams of being this put-together. Effortlessly flawless. Although I'm struck by another round of nerves, I can't let it get to me this time.

Scrolling quickly through her endless photos, I jump to the logo again. "Becca Roberts – Mom, Dreamer, Inspiration Conduit."

Thank goodness I've finished my tea, or I might spit-laugh all over the front of my dress. This woman actually uses terms like "MomtasticBombastic" and "BakeBreak". She hosts "SitFit" sessions for women who need to work out at their desk.

My hand flutters over my mouth. People are actually buying her mini-courses in "Mommy-Calmy"? It doesn't even rhyme correctly. From the tons of comments, it seems like a lot of people really look up to her.

Leaning in, I take note of the names flying by. Evans-Mom07. LoganHouseMouse. TamingTwinz. The same people are commenting several times on every post. They must be superfans. Or, stalking this woman is their only hobby.

From her lavish lifestyle, I assume she has millions of followers... then I actually look at the numbers. Hmm. Less than a tenth of what I would have expected from the way she speaks to her "Morning Brew Crew" as if thousands were hanging on her every word.

I've never paid much attention to social media beyond a quick check of local restaurants so I know how fancy they are. And of course, my own pathetic attempt to post at least one before-and-after repair per month on my shop website.

It seems like most young women aren't able to eat lunch or drink a cocktail without posting about it. Which I've always considered a security risk, but apparently that's an outdated concept these days.

Scrolling along, I find these bright colors and immaculate white interiors kind of addictive. I could see why people would want to keep skimming along, and...

What?

My vision freezes on a photo of Becca and her son in front of St. Mary's Elementary.

He looks remarkably similar to my Asher.

And this photo is crystal clear.

Is it... could it be possible that Craig has another son?

7

AMY

My mind is blank. I need to think, yet... it's like the wheels are spinning but not catching hold, like back tires on an ice patch.

Maybe I'm just seeing Asher's likeness in this similar boy because I won't have my son around for a few days, and some weird primal part of me misses him already? That's crap. Why am I looking for excuses? I need facts. There's a notepad and pen in front of me. I should be taking notes. That always untangles things. Craig is the one obsessed with writing everything down and seeing things in a visual way. It helps him process any problem or puzzle.

That's the only truly weird thing about my straight-laced, always calm husband – his obsession with puzzles. He's absolutely normal in every other way, to the point where I tease him for it. One night a week, usually Wednesdays, Craig takes Asher out to the garage for them to have "father-son time". They make wooden toys and do their puzzles. He claims there's no brain teaser that could possibly beat him once he puts his mind to it.

I always laugh, assuming that it's some spill-over from the stressful problems he has to solve at work. Asher is extremely smart, so learning problem-solving skills is likely going to serve him well. Since Craig has an unbelievable memory, hopefully that will be passed along too.

It came in handy when we were naming our son, since Craig seemed to know the meaning of every name. I liked Nicholas, after my grandfather, but Craig said that it meant "the victory of the people". He didn't want our son to be successful due to other people, or some nonsense. I also liked Jace, which means "healer".

But Craig insisted on Asher, which means "happy or fortunate". Which our son has been from the moment he arrived.

My eyes are tearing up. Why am I forcing myself to be calm when the right thing to do is freak out? Craig might be having an affair. That's the easiest, most logical explanation.

It's the kind of thing we read about online and don't think it could ever happen to us. A man with two families in different cities. Truck drivers who have three wives in three different states. Is there any possible way Craig could have two children in two different school districts?

I don't... can't... don't want to think that is even possible. It's utterly insane.

Maybe... a lot of little boys look similar at that age? Maybe Craig has relatives that he didn't tell me about, and it's his cousin's son?

I know what it sounds like. I'm making excuses already, when I have zero facts, only a bucket of questions. Part of my brain is definitely leaping to conclusions.

Logically, I can see that I may have been an idiot for not knowing Craig better before we got married. That a four-month courtship, then getting married and pregnant immediately, was foolish. Yet we were so in love that it felt right.

Well, now it feels right to dig up as many answers as I can. Instead of freaking out, I choose to focus on the things that I can control in the moment, just like Dad hammered into my head for years.

This school business will distract me from the fact that Craig and I are going to have a long, uncomfortable talk next week about why he had a photo receipt from St. Mary's in his jacket. Especially since every time I brought it up, he seemed to hate that school. Along with figuring out what is up with this Becca woman and her son.

Maybe this explains why he was so against Asher going to St. Mary's. Well, his opinion is no longer valid, since he's not here and basically had a smoking gun in his dry cleaning.

My fingers dart across the keyboard as I'm looking up St. Mary's. I see that Becca woman's photo in the group shot of the PTA moms. She is undoubtedly one of those people who loves being in charge of everything. Loves the attention. She wants the camera trained on her at all times.

Her son looks maybe a year or so older than mine, but they could honestly be brothers. Craig having a second family would certainly explain our weird half-week living situation.

I don't want to think about it for fear of throwing up my turkey sandwich. Tonight's purpose is my own son and my own sanity. And hopefully a lot more answers.

Looking down, I see my hands are clenched into fists, fingers pure white with reddening knuckles. No, I'm not stupid. I'm just going to leave the mental door open that there *could* be a tiny chance of there being an innocent and rational explanation. One that won't tear my marriage and life apart.

I wouldn't bet money on it, though.

Okay. Stick to the mission. Gather information about how to get my son into a better school. That's all that matters for tonight.

Purse, coat, shoes. I force myself to march out the door and get in the car. Then I take a deep, slow breath, remembering how Dad said to never drive angry or exhausted. It leads to bad choices. Which leads to bad results.

Driving is always a great time to catch up on WBLW. Our local radio has news every fifteen minutes to "keep Lakevillians in the constant loop". Benny and Trish are great at sharing the most important news quickly, without any nerve-scrambling loud ads or sound effects.

At the moment, I'm just hoping for a bit of amusing drama to distract myself from my own for a solid two minutes.

I tune in to a bouncy summer pop hit that sounds like it was designed by engineers with the sole focus of making my chin bounce along to the beat. I'm almost ticked off that it works so effectively, but at least it makes me laugh out loud, breaking the tension.

"Thank you for listening to WBLW — concentrated local news highlights three times a day. We'll be covering the mess down on Barrett Street, where crews are repairing a nasty broken water main that might take several days to repair. We'll also have our buddy Chad warn us about the volatile weather this weekend. But first, police are questioning the public about a missing twenty-one-year-old woman over at—"

I snap it off. This is not the time to put anything creepy or negative into my already scrambled brain.

Tonight's meeting about consolidating educational fundraisers will be a cross between a social event and fact-finding mission to switch Asher's school. At the very least, it's an excuse to get out of the house, avoid Fiona's wine-soaked cackling, and do some detective work on what the heck is going on with that Becca woman.

Mostly, I hope it's a distraction to keep my mind from wandering down terrible rabbit holes about my husband's possible affair and probable second son.

Although it feels like the rabbit is already digging deeper.

8

AMY

The thought of another version of my son walking around in the world is absolutely insane. But thinking he might have some connection to Craig? Madness.

More than madness. That photo looked just like Craig's son. I've always been relatively good at compartmentalizing, so I lock that into the back of my mind. All I have to do is get through an hour of this event, meet some people, and get some information.

It's hard to drive with crossed fingers, so I simply make the motion with my mind.

Please don't let Becca Roberts be there. Please.

Of course, I need to check her out in person. I'm torn between needing to know the truth about her and wanting to put my own son first. I can only compartmentalize so many things at once. If I dump a truckload of stress into a shoebox, it's going to spill.

Wait. No. I've been trained for this.

Blowing out all of my air, I visualize a brick wall in my mind, pushing all thoughts behind it. Then I carefully take out just the things I need to get through tonight. The rest can wait until I get home.

Dad took it upon himself to teach me anatomy when I was eleven, then moved on to psychology when I was twelve. I didn't realize at the time that he was preparing me for the day he left.

"You control your own mind, pumpkin. You can allow yourself to be stressed, or you can set a thought aside as if it were a coffee mug you don't need at the moment. The human mind is capable of much more than you could ever believe, if you trust in it. Just breathe and focus. You can get through absolutely anything smoothly if you remember those two things."

By the time I arrive at the brand new St. Mary's gym about ten minutes later, I'm not exactly calm, but I'm relatively clear-minded.

It smells more like a country club than a school gymnasium. The resonant clicking of high heels on the basketball-lined hardwood floor sounds like a woodpecker convention. The crowd is at least ninety percent women, and half of them are holding glasses of white wine.

Perhaps this is an excuse for many moms to get out of the house on their own? One parent has to go, and kids aren't welcome. So this is one of the few instances where mothers could insist on a night out. That's kind of sad. But I get it. If it weren't for Penny and my own mother, there have been a few times when Asher's erratic energy might have driven me to use any excuse to take off as well.

I help myself to a glass of sparkling lemon water, then survey the crowd. The only person I've spoken to before is Laura, one of the Westfield moms. I think all we chatted about was the weather and our kids. Good enough for small talk. After a few moments, the man she's speaking to walks away, so I sidle on over.

"Amy Taylor!" she exclaims, squeezing my elbow. "So good to see you."

"You too, Laura." Crap. I can't remember her last name. How strange that I can remember the full names of all of my clients, their fashion sense, their assistants, and most of their friends and associates, yet not people out here in the real world. Maybe I do prioritize my business over everything else.

"What are you up to this weekend?" I ask brightly.

Laura rambles for a bit about it being her turn to host her mother's birthday party, and how nervous she is to cook a full turkey for the first time on her own.

"That's exciting." I smile warmly. "No matter how it turns out, you're going to be completely relieved that you finally got through it all by yourself."

She nods emphatically. "Thank you. Yes, even if it's not as good as Mom's, it'll be..." Her voice drops to a whisper. "Oh my goodness – Becca Roberts is coming over!"

An icy shiver zips up my spine, and I set down my water on a nearby table before it splashes. I turn and smile, forcing my shoulders to lower and appear relaxed.

There she is, in person. Staring straight at me. Becca's gaze is a laser beam, inspecting me from head to toe as if scanning my frame like in a spy movie. I felt less scrutinized during my last physical.

"Do you know her?" Laura hisses. I shake my head. "She's an up-and-coming social media superstar. Perfect parenting, modern lifestyle, plus some crunchy granola stuff."

When Becca reaches us, a faint waft of vanilla and sage drifts past. Wow – she's not just pretty. There's a hint of that movie star radiance. A glow. She holds out a perfectly dusty rose manicured hand to Laura. "So nice of you to come and meet us at St. Mary's," she says sweetly. "I'm Becca."

"Laura Jones. Lovely to meet you. And this is Amy Taylor, also from Westfield."

Becca shakes my hand lightly, her skin feeling soft and well-moisturized. Just enough pressure and length for her handshake to be warm and friendly. I can't stop staring into her deep blue eyes. The whites are a bit too bright, as if eye drops are part of her grooming schedule. Her makeup is red carpet flawless. Every deep chestnut hair is perfectly waved into place. Even the subtle freckle above her necklace simply draws attention to her elegant collarbones.

She's almost too perfect. Except there's something in her eyes. An intensity that triggers a weird spot deep in my guts.

It's a... darkness. Like there's a shadow over her soul.

More likely, I'm just jealous. Mothers don't walk around looking like this. It's unnatural. She looks like she would never tolerate a child in her presence for fear of getting sticky fingerprints on her artfully draped smoke-gray dress.

I'd bet fifty bucks that her son would never use her face cream as tanning lotion on his wrestling action figure.

"So nice to meet you," I say, as she releases my hand.

"Amy." Her head cocks slightly to the side, showing off a dangling earring that I guarantee features a real emerald. Suddenly, I feel cheap and tacky. My accessories don't belong in the same room as hers, except for my purse. "Have I seen you here before?"

"I was at another school meeting a few months ago, but couldn't stay long."

Becca smiles, nodding sweetly. "Yes, we always put our families and our work first, don't we?" As she shifts slightly, I notice that even without the high heels, she's at least three inches taller than I am.

"That's what weekends are for," Laura says brightly. "Like you say on your blog, weekends are family time."

"Absolutely." Becca smiles as if she had an audience of thousands to dazzle. "This weekend, my son and I are harvesting lettuce and spinach for the first time. He's excited to make his own salad."

"That's so cute!" Laura exclaims. It's clear that she's overwhelmed by simply being so close to someone slightly famous.

"He's a great little helper." Becca smiles with the grandeur of a princess. "The best thing we can do when raising a young man is to teach them that domestic duties are for everyone."

My chin is already nodding. "Absolutely."

Before I can ask her anything else about her son, an older man in a gray suit comes over and murmurs something in her ear. Becca leans forward to whisper conspiratorially. "Sorry, ladies. There's a potential donor here that I must speak to immediately." She sashays away, swinging her stilettos slightly one in front of the other like a model.

Laura grabs my shoulder and squeezes. "Don't you just want to *be* her?"

I have to answer honestly. "She really is something."

"Becca has the perfect life." Laura steps a bit closer, keeping her voice low. "Except for her unusual arrangement with her husband. That part might not be for everyone."

My stomach tightens. "Arrangement?"

"Yes. While she's busy being a social media influencer, her husband pays for a part-time cook, a twice-weekly housekeeper, and a wonderful full-time nanny."

"Wow. Sounds expensive."

Laura shrugs. "Apparently, he makes a fortune – some high-tech bigwig. But that means he's traveling all over the place, so he's only home Friday through Sunday."

That weird spot in my guts begins to twist much harder.

"He's only home three days a week?"

"Yes. But I guess that's the price you have to pay to make that much money." Laura's deep brown eyes sparkle as she grins. "He spoils Becca to bits – new jewelry, accounts with different stores for her clothing and accessories, and... Well, if you've seen her channel, you've seen their house. It's stunning."

The edges of my vision begin to swim as I reach out to grab my water and take a sip.

How many women have three-day-per-week husbands?

The answer is staring me in the face, no matter how much I don't want to believe it.

The theory that Craig could have two families just went from insane to absolutely probable.

Which causes my throat to feel like it's glowing bright red as a signal that I am utterly humiliated.

9

CRAIG

The view from my windshield is the way I've seen most of the world lately. That's fine. Driving is one of the very few things I truly love.

It clears my mind and helps me think in straight lines instead of the endless snarls and tangles. They tend to go dark. Too dark. Sometimes so dark it becomes... unproductive.

That's why I never listen to music, just the hum of my own thoughts and the traffic around me. It gives me time to breathe and ponder tiny details.

They say the devil is in the details. Maybe there's something divine as well.

Details are incredibly important to my projects. There are a great many things I need to check with my own eyes at the actual location before making concrete decisions.

My wife has mentioned, humorously, I hope, that men are always sloppy. I need to prove I'm the exception to the rule. Make her proud of me. Let her know that I really am in control of things.

Sometimes I'm terrified she's going to leave me, and I honestly don't know what I'd do without the structure of my schedule and home life to hold me together.

Lifting my foot off the gas, I allow a truck to merge, not wanting them to have to slam on the brakes. Safety first. Which is something that worries me about the next project. I always arrange things so that they're as predictable as possible.

Yet a few have gone wrong lately. There's nothing worse than watching helplessly as a project goes off the rails.

Not this time. This one is definitely going to be perfect.

I check my speed, then nod to myself as the sign for the turnoff appears. One of my projects went very wrong not too long ago. I had to switch things around at the last minute, which was exhausting and put me behind on the next one.

That's always the way – you plan something down to the letter, then when you need to rely on other people doing their jobs and playing their roles, they let you down.

Of course, I had a few contingency plans. It turned out adequately instead of great.

Not this time. I've found an asset that is predictable and stable. Everything is going to go flawlessly, and she will be proud. I hope.

She'll be angry with me if I don't get this particular project taken care of on Monday. She's beautiful but fussy. A hardass with me and in her business, yet gentle to our son Asher.

It's wild how much I miss him when I'm away too long. The way his mind ponders things, then makes connections. His endless questions. His creative side and the way he always wants to try new things.

I didn't know what it was to be a man until I had a son. I'd love to have a dozen of them.

I'll make her proud of me by getting the next few projects done right, and making extra money. She's been pouring her heart and soul into her business, and I want to be able to help her even more than I already do.

I flick my finger, and the blinker makes its familiar click as I glide into the right lane. I do love the puzzle-solving and brainstorming parts of my job, but all of this tranquil driving is a close second.

10

AMY

This is not happening.

Yes, it is. And I'm going to deal with it.

Somehow.

I set my water down quickly so that nobody sees how shaky my hands are. My left eye is twitching, and my stomach is trying to digest itself. My palm presses to the base of my throat – my skin is on fire. Of course, I'm completely flushed.

Forcing myself to take a slow breath, I find it impossible to pick apart this rush of emotions. Obviously, I feel utterly humiliated for having the wool pulled over my eyes for so long. That feeling is being forced to take a backseat to make room for the absolute rage that spears my soul like an M240 machine gun through a paper target.

Luckily, Laura is called away to speak with an old friend, and I'm left alone in the crowd for a few moments to collect myself. I watch with morbid fascination as Becca chats grandly to what looks like the principals of three or four schools. As two of them laugh, she tucks her hair behind her ear and drops her shoulder as if posing toward a camera.

Wow, she certainly knows her best angles. Geez – is this a school function or a media appearance?

How can she be swanning around like she's queen of the world when I'm standing here absolutely shattered? I feel hollow. Yet my legs are concrete. I honestly don't know if I can walk.

It's too much of a coincidence for me to even consider brushing it off. A husband who's only with Becca from Friday to Sunday, and my husband is only with me from Tuesday to Thursday? There's no way Laura could have been talking about anyone other than my Craig. My back teeth grind together. I suppose, if he has two wives, he could be considered "our" Craig.

The thought fills me with absolute revulsion. How could he be with another woman?

I could almost... not quite, but *almost*... understand if he cheated on me with some business associate while on a trip somewhere. Or a random hot waitress while traveling. A one-time quickie. I mean, by all accounts, men are animals. Even though Craig is the most clean-cut, civilized man I know. He went to Harvard, for goodness' sake. That's a fact that instantly pegged him as a good guy when we began dating.

But another family? Another wife, another son, another home?

How much of the rest of his life is also a lie? Does he really travel as much as he says he does, or is he just with Becca and the other boy the entire time he's away from us?

My heart clenches tight in my chest. *Oh no...* her child

seems a bit older. That likely means he was with her first. Am I the other woman?

Unless... if they were together before Craig and I met, maybe she's his ex and she simply doesn't mention it online for fear of the stigma of being divorced? Yeah, the odds of that are miniscule. My mind is grasping for straws. Panic adrenaline is a heck of a drug.

The chattering hum of the event swirls around me, droning in my ears like a distant radio. I can't be here anymore, and I can't leave. My feet are blocks of stone while my knees quiver.

Craig always called me his little pixie. A cute, sweet fairy. He said that I was exactly his type and that I was the most beautiful woman in the world. How on earth do I compare to someone like Becca? She's a glamazon – stylish and polished and immaculate. She's the kind of woman we'd all aspire to be if we had the time and money.

Money. Ugh. My stomach flips over again. Here I've been scrimping and saving, feeling spoiled whenever Craig takes us all shopping for winter coats and boots, or bringing home takeout that I consider expensive. Meanwhile, he's been showering Becca with jewels and a freaking full-time nanny?

I don't know if I've ever truly felt jealous of anyone before. Now it's hitting me from all angles.

My natural instinct is to run away. To leave immediately, go home, and try to figure this out. Or to burrow into my bed and ignore everything for a while until I can breathe steadily again.

Breathe. In. Out.

This is one of those situations where I need to jump in and dig for answers while I have the chance. Demand the truth before I can chicken out. No matter how desperately I would prefer to apply wine and ice cream to this problem.

Straightening my shoulders, I see my opportunity as Becca excuses herself from the others and walks over to a quiet back corner of the gym. As her thumbs fly across the screen of her phone, I pull out my own, opening one of the rare photos I have of Craig.

There's a crackle in the back of my mind as details begin snapping together. No wonder he never wanted his photo taken. I had to beg to get a photo of him this past Christmas. He wouldn't want photos of himself on social media if he were juggling two families. It also explains why Becca's husband isn't in any of her perfect family photos.

"Becca," I announce my presence once I'm practically nose to nose with her. Holding up the photo, I stare into her eyes as she looks at it. "Do you know this man?" My voice is quavering, but it's clear enough.

Becca pauses, staring between me and the photo for an awkwardly long time. The murmuring of voices echoing around the room seems to dim. Her expression is unreadable. I feel like she should be curious. At least put on edge. Yet she seems oddly reserved.

"I guess you know I do," she says quietly. Her voice no longer has the tone of someone who is putting on a show. She almost sounds... Certainly not meek. But softer.

She flips to a calendar app and scrolls for a moment. "I have a window of time tomorrow between two and three. Shall we have coffee?"

What the... How the heck can she be so businesslike at a moment like this? While my hands are clearly shaking? It's either admirable or obnoxious. Or both.

Although a tiny part of me needs to grab her by the

throat and shake her, demanding to know everything immediately, it's definitely not worth making a scene. "Sure."

"Let's say the main restaurant of the Hilton at two.
Eduardo always seats me by the front windows."

"Fine."

Before I can ask her anything else, Becca flounces
directly into the center of the crowd. She's already tapped
back into her "*look at me!*" energy simply by tossing her
lustrous hair. Several women begin competing for her focus,
gushing about her recent video on the vital importance of
grade-one education and non-plastic toys.

I have a choice to make. I can be the kind of woman who
turns tail and runs. Or I can be the kind of mother who does
what's best for her child. Even though my head is spinning
with a million questions, I raise my chin and take a deep,
slow breath.

From the corner of my eye, I see that Becca looks
surprised when I rejoin the group, walking straight to Principal Cutler of St. Mary's. He seems to welcome the attention as I ramble about his wonderful school, going on at
length about how excited I would be to meet with him to
discuss if there's room this fall for one more student whose
address lands on the borderline of the two districts.

Somehow, I manage to restrain my inner turmoil to
appear businesslike. As if I'm cosplaying a perfectly
composed person.

Principal Cutler waffles, not wanting to make a commit-
ment one way or the other, until I casually suggest my
husband and I could possibly make a donation to their
library. Suddenly, I have an appointment for a week from
now to discuss things in depth.

That might be a bit of a lie. I have no idea what kind of

donation we could wrangle right now, but at least I'll have a proper shot to plead my case.

While I mingle and chat with several of the faculty, Becca's gaze burns into the back of my head. Although I refuse to look directly at her again, she's clearly watching me. I detest the feeling of being tracked with every step I take.

Fine. Let her be confused. If she thinks I'm going to be timid and let her take control of whatever this situation is, she is seriously mistaken. If she wanted to play nice, she would have stepped outside and had a conversation with me immediately. That was the only civilized response.

What kind of woman finds out her husband is two-timing her, and makes an appointment to talk about it tomorrow?

A woman who already knows precisely what is going on.

11

BECCA

It's always something.

I gave Craig crystal-clear instructions to keep that woman away from me. Told him I never want to see her in person. *Ever.* I even made him say it out loud three times, which is how intentions become reality.

My nails tap on the steering wheel throughout the drive home. Could my instructions possibly have been more clear? Perhaps I should have written them in crayon.

Men. They never pay attention to the details. Always sloppy. Always thinking they can just wing it. Even when they have a plan, or a list, or a brainstorming board.

This is why women like me are so helpful in the online community. We help everyone become more organized. Even when *certain people* apparently drop the ball anyway.

Amy's earnest pixie face ruined my night. I'd been dazzling the local moms before she got there, and had been on the verge of recruiting a handful of new paid subscribers. Plus... I have to admit that the fact she's prettier in person just burrowed right under my skin.

Now the only way to keep Amy in line is to chat with her in person? *Ick.*

I roll my shoulders down and back. It takes effort to relax my features.

At least this gives me an excuse to shoot fresh content at the Hilton. Since I can't afford to go places like that as often as I should, I always take a ton of photos. Once they're stylized and grouped correctly, it can imply that I've been there several times over the past month. Even women who are pretending to be loaded need to be frugal from time to time.

Although with the way things are going, that won't be for long. Within a month or two, I should be following my own mantras and living the life I truly deserve.

As long as I can keep that crazy woman from sticking her nose into our business and ruining everything.

12

AMY

FRIDAY

After a fitful sleep, I eventually give up and shuffle to the kitchen to make coffee while snuggled in my robe. Without work to go to on a Friday morning, I'm lost. I need the comfort of a hug, but I have nobody to turn to.

I've always turned to Craig. Even when he's away, he would cheer me up with a text, a silly photo, a sweet voice-mail. Or we'd schedule one of our twenty-minute "super-chats", where we alternate five minutes of talking as fast as we can, going through everything that happened that day.

Of course, in Craig's case, he's always super-vague about work. He mainly talks about the travel logistics of trying to find a decent coffee in certain cities, or how different the food is. Usually, without telling me which city he's in.

He's tried to explain what tiny bits of his job he can – computer security and top-level surveillance systems. Not spyware, exactly, but something corporations need to use for their most secure systems. I swear he's explained parts of it to me ten times, and I just don't understand it. He always gets excited and starts speeding up, cutting me off with technical jargon before I can ask any more basic questions.

There's no online footprint of this company. What are his coworkers like? No idea. But he's apparently one of the top guys in the country, which is why they need him to go in personally to a different place every week. All I know is that he occasionally brings home notepads and pens from a huge variety of low-key tech companies that are named with indecipherable initials. Plus, he loves his work and has a decent salary.

Which might not be true as well. If he really has two families, one of them with a wife who prefers high-end, highly trendy luxuries, he must be making a fortune.

My hands aren't shaking around my mug. I'm past upset. Past freaking out. I'm... *curious*. The need to know the truth is eating me alive.

It's not surprising that Craig didn't leave me another voicemail, since I didn't respond to his last one. I have no idea what to say to him right now. What if I'm blowing things out of proportion and this is just a weird misunderstanding? What if I'm being thrown off kilter by the water main break, and my anxiety is taking over?

Yeah, I'm not that stupid. Something seriously strange is going on. But it's early, and I need to hang onto the faintest possibility that everything is going to be okay. At least until I'm caffeinated.

Once I have a steaming mug in one hand, the other scrolls through my phone. Fiona has sent a slew of texts about a new true crime documentary on one of her favorite topics – rich bitches getting what they deserve. She always wants my input, since I deal with these so-called rich bitches every day.

Honestly, only maybe twenty percent of my clients are genuine bitches. Those are almost always the ones whose parents have wild, extreme lifestyles. So it's not entirely their fault they turned out a bit feral.

I try not to share any details of their lives that aren't already online. Okay, once in a while, when it's hilarious or they're particularly mean and I need to vent to Fiona or Craig. Otherwise, I keep up the wall of client-vendor confidentiality, if that's even a thing.

I bring my coffee and laptop over to the couch, next to Asher's basket of toys. I'd give anything to have him here with me now for a few minutes. To cuddle him, answer his endless questions about everything from dinosaurs to deep-sea fish who live where there's no light, to why my eyes look puffy.

I certainly can't have him around while I'm in this sort of mood. He understands when Mommy is tired from working long hours. There's no way he could understand this.

Flipping open my laptop, I have a pen and paper handy, sipping my coffee too fast. Research mode. Time to figure out what the heck is going on before I meet with this bizarre woman.

Is it completely twisted that I instinctively want to ask for Craig's help with this? He's the puzzle expert. He's the one who managed to get twice the shelving into our bedroom closet, with room on the floor for suitcases. The one who is always figuring out what Asher is talking about while he explains precisely how his toys should be displayed on shelves in his room.

Craig always knows what's wrong with my car simply by listening to it, and remembers every single detail of my stories about customers at work. Even their assistants' names, and how often they come into the shop. The colors of their purses, which are occasionally super-tacky. The customers who are kind or cruel, or just drive me nuts with impossible requests.

At the time, I thought that he was showing a huge interest in my customers and my work as some sort of over-compensation, because I can't ask him about what he does. When he explains his work, it almost sounds like he is deliberately trying to talk in circles. Something about using a variety of different tech at different levels to attempt to breach various systems in order to improve their security.

But he needs to travel to the company, and can't do it remotely due to the... Blast, I can't remember what he said. Now I have to wonder... was he intentionally being vague with me? Is there a reason he doesn't want me to know about his business?

I've never been a computer person, beyond a basic laptop. I work with my hands. Leather and tools. Things you can see with the naked eye. I wish I were working at the shop now, instead of waffling between how angry I am at my husband and how confused and hurt I feel.

The knock at the door nearly sends my laptop careening across the room. At least I know who it is from the volume and urgency. There's no point trying to pretend I'm not home, since Fiona can see that the lights are on. *Please, please don't let her know about the Barrett Street fiasco.*

Pasting a sleepy look on my face, I answer the door. "Hey. What's up?"

Fiona's eyes narrow, darting around the front hall and living room like a detective searching for clues. She slowly rotates her lucky silver key necklace around her index finger, which she always does when she's being extra nosy. "You don't look sick. Why aren't you at work yet? I saw your car still here while I was starting my morning walk."

That's how Fiona is able to drink wine and eat junk food like it's her career and never gain a pound. Constant long walks. She says it's for her health, but I suspect she's keeping an eye on the entire neighborhood in her perpetual search for drama.

Given that her job is doing the bookkeeping and payroll for her father's athletic sock manufacturing plant, it's understandable that she needs some excitement. She only works four days a week, Tuesday through Friday, and relatively short hours. Which means she's always around.

It's extremely handy when I need an extra set of hands to move a table or dig out a shrub. Not when I'm trying to make sense of how I might be sharing a husband with a tall, gorgeous supermom.

"I'm working." Does my smile seem genuine? "Thought I'd do some of my paperwork from home today since I don't have any early pickups. Treat myself to an extra hour in my PJs."

Since she works from home in her rainbow array of track suits and yoga outfits, she nods immediately. "Comfort first. Good for you. Tight clothing restricts your lymphatic system, which is why so many women—"

Before she can launch into a tirade, my head jerks up and I glance back toward my phone as if it pinged. "Sorry, I have a bunch of reminders set today. Have to get back to it."

Her left eyebrow rises slightly, yet thankfully, she nods and steps back. "Work first. I get it."

I reach into the closet and pull out a canvas shopping bag that's been hanging on the back of the door. "I forgot last time I saw you, but here is the belt you needed repaired, and the thriller you wanted to borrow." It's a great book, which will hopefully keep her distracted for a few days.

Her face lights up. "Thanks so much – have a good one!"

I wave with a cheery smile and shut the door. Then lock it.

Maybe I need to start mentioning new friends, once I find some. Go on at length about mom groups. I don't want to end our friendship, just turn it down by at least half. The feeling of being constantly analyzed by my so-called best friend is not helpful.

Especially since I cannot even begin to explain what's going on in my life.

I have no idea myself.

Yet the heaviness in the bottom of my stomach says I'm about to find out.

13

AMY

I attempt to fall into research mode as if I were examining accessories trends for work. Opening a new tab with my upcoming coffee date's website, I read, "Becca Roberts – Mom, Dreamer, Inspiration Conduit." What the heck is that even supposed to mean?

She has an extremely curated online presence as the stereotypical "perfect wife, perfect life." Her vibe seems to be promoting herself as a well-balanced woman who puts her child and home first, but never neglects her own health and well-being.

Sure – that's pretty sweet if you don't have a day job. Okay, to be fair, creating all of this social media stuff is her job now. But still... Posting photos of herself washing grapes for a "powerful antioxidant snack" doesn't look like hard labor.

Some of her posts and video clips involve sponsors and partnerships. There are generic things like a state-of-the-art toaster. Specialized things like educational toys, including some that Craig brought home for our son. It turns my stomach thinking of him buying two sets of things, one for each kid.

My hands are clenched so hard on the edge of the laptop, it's a wonder it doesn't snap. That would be tricky to explain to the insurance people.

There are a whole bunch of beauty product deals. Wow. From the look of her "daily routine" with all of these serums and potions and botanical mists, it's a wonder her skin can even breathe.

That strange writhing feeling of jealousy roils up as I zoom in on some of the photos of her home. It's absolutely incredible. It's not just decorated straight out of a generic home and garden magazine. Every single item is designer and expensive, with a few unique twists that make it noteworthy.

I don't really follow home style trends, but I do know the brand names of those appliances mean they cost a fortune. They're the kind that play sparkling jazz riffs when they're done self-cleaning.

In the photos she's posted this morning, Becca's perfect nails are a pale sage green. Likely to complement her gardening this weekend. They're long enough to be elegant, and short enough to be realistic for a mother. Is there anything imperfect about this woman?

Ugh. Now my fact-finding mission is degrading into nitpicking. I want to find something messy. Something flawed or faulty. I mean, she's over the top, which I suppose is kind of sketchy, but that's a reach.

My heart sinks as I see the espresso maker in the kitchen. Craig insisted on getting that one for our house. He said it would keep him from wanting to run out and get a proper coffee in the morning, so that we could spend more time together.

My fingers drum frantically on the side of the laptop. When Craig was here with me Tuesday, Wednesday, and Thursday every week, he said that it was when he did his best brainstorming work. Just him and his notebook or laptop right here on the couch. Since Asher was in junior kindergarten for the mornings, and I was at work, he had the house to himself.

Our security footage only goes back two weeks at a time, and I hate myself for calling it up. What kind of wife checks up on her husband? Well, this one. I've had it with defaulting to politeness all the time.

The video from last Wednesday shows me leaving from the front door, with Asher in tow, as I drive him to school. Then nothing for hours. Just before eleven a.m., the mail arrives. Then nothing until Craig leaves to pick up Asher at noon.

I almost move to check the next day, yet my finger hovers for a second. With a click, I open the footage from the back door camera. We haven't checked that one in so long that we never even think about it. This is a completely safe neighborhood.

The video is... *smeared.* Blurry and dusty.

I rush out to the back door and see a big smudge of dirt across the tiny lens. Something either dropped from the roof or someone smeared mud on it on purpose. Maybe it's been the dry weather over the past few weeks, but the dirt has flaked off on one side, leaving some clear patches. My breath fogs up the lens, then I wipe the dirt off.

Back inside, I wash my hands, then return to the laptop. Although the footage is foggy, a shadow leaves the house and goes to the garage at nine-seventeen, and doesn't return until eleven-forty-five.

Craig has never done woodworking or anything requiring tools. There are no crafts or projects out there in the garage, other than the puzzles he does with Asher. What would he be doing out there for so long?

Quickly skimming the next day's footage, and the next, I see a definite pattern. Every morning that Craig is here, he spends just over two hours out in the garage.

Even though the video isn't clear, it doesn't look like he takes his laptop. On one day, he's carrying a book in his hand. Possibly his notebook, but I can't be sure.

I notice what time it is and jump up to find something to eat before it's time to get ready. I certainly can't eat in front of Becca, since my stomach will be in knots. And even though there's no way I can compete with her seemingly effortless glamor, I can't look like a frazzled mess either.

All I can manage is a sandwich, since anything heavier is bound to come right back up. I chase it with peppermint tea in an effort to calm down.

While I shower and style my hair, one thing keeps rolling around in the back of my mind. If Craig has two families, why wouldn't he want to keep them in different states, or something? If Becca lives in the St. Mary's district, she's only about a forty-minute drive away, at most.

Of course, that's just enough distance that I would probably never meet her if I weren't so determined to get Asher into that school. The Westfield moms usually stick to this side of town.

I yank the hairbrush with a bit too much force. I suppose

in a twisted way... if you're going to have two wives, you might as well have them as different as possible. Men apparently love variety. So have one wife be a supermodel, and the other be a quirky, mellow craft person.

Just before I dash out the door, I check to see if Becca has posted anything this morning so that I can see what she's wearing. Yes, I'm angry with myself for being so curious about her. She's a new fixation, and I need to uncover every single detail.

There are three new photos. A closeup of a teacup holding some chunky mix that looks like compost: "Cleansing tea for a cleansed me!" Another closeup of her fancy phone with her fingers creating an X across it: "Media cleanse long weekend – not ingesting any outside information".

Then there's a photo of her son hugging her leg that must have been taken by someone else: "Moms need to go out for coffee with a girlfriend now and then! Luckily, Asher just loves his nanny as well."

Asher?

Asher.

The entire world grows hollow.

My shoulders collapse as I fall back against the chair. Craig was so insistent on that name, and seemed so relieved that I loved it too.

He has an incredible memory, but is sometimes scatterbrained if he doesn't have a pen and paper in front of him to focus.

In his phone message, Craig slipped up and referred to Asher's baseball game. But my Asher plays soccer.

He gave his sons the same name so that he wouldn't make a mistake and mix them up.

A flash of heat washes through me. This isn't the flush I get from anxiety.

This is pure military-grade rage.

I swear that if Craig were here right now, I might wrap my hands around his throat and squeeze.

14

BECCA

My knuckles tighten on my faux-fur steering wheel, preventing me from fully absorbing the lovely sage green of my nails that was supposed to make me calm. Color theory isn't going to work today when I've been blown off course like this.

What the hell was that pasty little bitch Amy doing at St. Mary's? And how the hell did she find out about Craig's other life?

Lifting my chin, I try to relax my shoulders so that my decolletage doesn't wrinkle. No matter how furious I am, I cannot hold stress in my body.

Everything depends on Amy liking me and thinking that we're in this together. I just have to figure out a way to manage her. Find out her ultimate goals, and give her what she wants. Within reason.

Craig hadn't been sure at first about what I refer to as his "second job". I think it's a perfect way to manage this situation. It's the best thing for both of our lives, strange as they might be.

Even before Asher was born, I knew that Craig was certainly not the love of my life. Frankly, he started to annoy me even more than usual. He needs a lot of attention and a lot of mental stimulation to keep him calm. Yet those gorgeous hazel eyes, quick wit and charm were so engaging that I knew he could provide great genetic material for a beautiful child.

Turning a corner, I chuckle to myself as I pass a restaurant he loves. My Craig is so basic. He's a homebody who desperately loves family life. But his version of entertainment is pizza on the couch with an old movie. Puttering in the garage and playing with his stupid-ass brainteasers.

I have a social media empire to build. I don't have room in my world for things that aren't aspirational.

Since Craig secured his second wife, his duties and attention are split, which gets him out of my hair. He was so desperate to have a second son immediately that it was easier to just give him what he craved – just not from me.

Now I have the illusion of a perfect family life with minimal effort wasted on my dull but useful half-husband.

Luckily, Craig just loves puzzles. Figuring out the details of a fake ID, a fake wedding certificate, and how to keep his lives separate kept him fascinated for the first two years of this arrangement. The logistics of juggling two lives keeps him in check. That's why his extra job is working out so well for us.

Yet now that Amy is finally figuring out a few things, I'm going to actually have to pay attention to this little homebody. *Ick.*

Nodding along with the latest hit song from WBLW, I try to remember the few details Craig has told me.

Obviously, Amy repairs handbags and has a specialized

wealthy clientele. Other than that, I haven't paid much attention. I'm just glad that she was super-quick to give Craig the second son he wanted. It got him off my back. Like I can risk having children too close together, without getting my body in tiptop shape first.

"*Thank you for listening to WBLW — your top hit songs and the news every fifteen minutes. Barrett Street is still a mess, with crews working round the clock to repair a broken water main. Derek will be sharing more news about another missing young woman. Police are speculating that some of the recent disappearances might be forming a pattern. But first, Dave needs to warn us about tomorrow's weather, where we'll be—*"

Son of a... It *cannot* rain tomorrow. I have a full day of gardening content planned, and Asher hates the rain. He hates anything cold or wet or loud... or basically anything that makes the child even slightly uncomfortable. At just six years old, he expects the world to revolve around him.

Maybe that's my fault for bribing him when I need to get better content from my darling son. Now the brat knows his worth. Sure, he might be spoiled rotten, yet the kid knows how to work his angles and create the perfect expression for whatever mood I need him to convey.

Since I trained Asher so well, maybe I can find a way to keep Amy in line. She's been playing her role like a champ – giving Craig another kid and the more "normal" home that he craves. Normal, as in, so boring I could cry. At least he keeps me in both antiques and high-end modern art.

After pulling up in front of the Hilton, I shoot a quick video clip of me handing the keys to the valet, and the side of my car driving away. Then I shoot the steps of the Hilton and up to the logo. Once I add some dreamy filters,

I'll tag it something like "Moms need a break to spoil themselves!"

Luckily, I arrive a few minutes early, and Amy isn't here yet. Eduardo escorts me to the table by the window. I always insist on it for the best light. Plus, it doesn't hurt to be seen by anyone passing by. This is the most elegant hotel in the city, so it has the most upscale clientele.

Everything is quietly classy, from the fine linens to the crystal chandeliers. The kind of environment where I belong. I should be coming to lunch here several days a week. Hopefully, once Craig earns us more money and I get more sponsors, I can start living more of the dreams from my latest vision board.

My usual order appears before me without even asking, which is super-classy. I take a few sips of coffee for the caffeine, then rinse my mouth out with the sparkling lemon water so my teeth don't stain, also ensuring I don't have coffee breath.

From the corner of my eye, I see Amy approaching. Her body language is timid. Does she have a sunburn on her neck, or is she breaking out in hives or something? She's definitely nervous. I can use this to my advantage.

For goodness' sake – if I'm an influencer, I should be able to influence one meek housewife who just happens to be having a relationship with my husband. Poor little Amy just doesn't know it's somewhat fake, that's all.

The second she reaches my table, I spin and jump to my feet, giving her a warm hug. "Amy. Thank you so much for coming."

As expected, she's thrown completely off guard. "Thank you for meeting with me."

My bottom lip wobbles slightly as she orders a plain

coffee. Then I reach across the table and grasp her hand. "I'm sorry I wasn't ready to speak about this last night. You shocked me so badly, I guess I froze up."

"So... What do you think is happening here?" she asks quietly.

She's either calmer than I expected or faking it. Her fingers tremble slightly. Good.

I sniffle delicately. "I assume that you're having some sort of relationship with my husband?" I squeeze her hand. "It's not your fault, of course. He's a handsome man, and has that... that..." I retract my hand and fan my face, looking up to the ceiling and blinking quickly as if holding back tears.

Her hands stop trembling, and that odd flush across her throat is fading quickly. "He's very charismatic, yes." Amy nods slowly. I'm surprised that she's not more emotional. It almost seems like she's studying me.

"You know," I lean forward to lower my voice to a murmur, "I've suspected that he's up to something for a while. Sure, he travels constantly for work, but his energy is just all over the place, you know what I mean?" My head shakes, fanning my hair out slightly. "A good husband and provider should be steady. And Craig just hasn't been steady lately."

"Was he in the beginning?" Amy sips her coffee. The cup shakes a tiny bit. Perfect.

My lips tilt up in an uneven smile. "In the beginning, we always see what we want to see, right? When we met seven years ago, he was so excited to have a child with me that we got married and I got pregnant almost immediately."

Amy nods slowly. "And your relationship has been... relatively normal?"

It's clear what she's getting at. She needs to compare her marriage with Craig to mine. *Ha.*

"Well, yes. For the most part. I guess there were a few little things... Like Craig never wanting to be on camera. And him taking over our garage to do puzzles with Asher so they have alone time without me."

Smiling sadly, I fuss with the edge of my coffee cup as if wiping lipstick off it. Please, like I would wear a cheap brand that transfers. "I guess he needed some space to himself, since I'm a bit fussy about keeping the house completely tidy." I shrug. "I mean, having a nice home is part of my job."

"You really do have a lovely home," Amy says slowly. "I took a peek online."

I pause, nodding. This is the part where everyone gushes about how beautiful my home is, how perfectly curated and how they wish they had a home just like mine. I've heard it so many times, yet I never tire of it. A home base truly is a woman's empire. Those particular quotes that I spew aren't bullshit.

The murmur of the other customers is a rustle, barely over the tasteful piano jazz as I lean in, ready for fresh compliments about how my stunning home is a dream mansion.

"It must be wildly expensive to heat," Amy says before sipping her coffee again, glancing casually out the window.

What? I study the line of her shoulders, the way she's sitting. I honestly can't tell if Amy is grief-stricken or kind of angry.

Women's intuition is something I babble about to my followers all the time. I've never bothered to think about mine. Those are just sayings that sell well for notebooks and mousepads.

Yet my long-dormant intuition might be kicking in right now. There's something in Amy's eyes. The analytical way she studies me. The way her emotions aren't quite authentic. Whatever she's feeling, she refuses to let me see it. The unnerving way she is examining every movement I make is creating a severely disturbing sensation in the pit of my stomach. Almost as if I'm prey and she's considering choosing her moment.

If she's that brilliant at hiding her feelings, what else is this supposedly timid woman hiding?

15

BECCA

"So, what kind of relationship do you have with Craig?" I ask, as if I didn't already know most of the details. Giving my hair a toss, I shake off that creepy feeling. I must be mistaken – this woman is a mousy little mom type. The kind who looks to people like me for inspiration.

Amy looks at me flatly. "The same as you, apparently. Three days with me, and four days traveling for work. Except I guess in reality, he spends three days with you, three days with me, and one day traveling for work."

My lips tighten as I stifle a laugh. She's absolutely right, just not in the way she thinks.

"You don't get lonely, living in a little house alone four days a week?" I ask.

Her lips tighten strangely. "Who said my house was small?"

I sigh. "Well, you made a crack about my big house being a pain to heat. So I just assumed."

"'The space isn't so bad." She half-shrugs, her eyes following the server for a moment as he walks by. "Our yard is a bit smaller after Craig built that huge garage a few years ago, but he was really excited about it."

He did what? It takes a moment for me to realize my fingernails are tapping noisily on the side of the mug. The bastard built a garage? How much of my money did he waste on that? Well, money that should have been mine.

Not to mention... I don't like him having puzzle time with his other son if I'm not around to keep an eye on things. Why wouldn't he have told me about that?

Amy smiles sweetly. "It seems like Craig is a family man through and through, isn't he?"

"Yes. He is."

She hesitates, smoothing the napkin in her lap. She's not acting as impressed as she's supposed to be.

"Whatever it is, Amy, you can tell me. Or ask me." I give her my best inspirational smile. "We women have to stick together, don't we?"

Damn, now I wish that I had studied Amy a lot more over the past few years. Some of her expressions are absolutely unreadable. "Heartbroken women are the glue that keeps this country together," I say softly. "That t-shirt is one of my best sellers."

Amy gives a wry smile. "I'm too numb to be heartbroken just yet. I'm simply surprised that he has such a decadent life with you, and such a modest life with me."

Dammit. I should've known. It always comes down to money. And jealousy. If I let her know how much of Craig's money is funneled into my lifestyle and business, she'll be seriously upset. I can't let her fly off the handle at a time like this.

Not when such a major project is on the horizon.

Looking around to make sure no one is within earshot, I

lean in and whisper. "A lot of what you see in my house comes from sponsorships and promotions. Some of them are announced, and some aren't. Companies send products for me to test, and if I like them, I'll put them in my home to be in the background. I'm also working on some very lucrative sponsorship deals that have been brewing behind the scenes for a while."

I've never had to make an expression of begging before, and hope that it looks natural. "Please don't say anything. It's tacky to talk about money with my viewers. Also, Craig is embarrassed by that much money."

Amy nods. "I've always been the frugal sort. I don't need much. That's why I was just surprised to see him living in such a palace."

At least she finally said something complimentary about my house. I was starting to worry. In a roundabout way, Amy's eye for taste and style is something Craig and I depend on.

My eye is drawn to the message notifications building up on my phone. Although it's on silent mode, I can't help watching as the numbers increase. Amy is unbelievably boring, as expected. I'm wasting perfectly good shooting time by sitting here commiserating with her.

"What do you think we should do?" I ask.

Amy's face falls. She's looking so sad that I almost feel sorry for her. Almost. "I guess we'll have to sit Craig down and have a chat," she says softly. "Whatever happens, I think it's in all of our best interests to be calm and open about this, right?"

"Absolutely." My shoulders unclench a bit. It's a huge relief that she's not going to become a drama queen and ruin everything.

"Craig is away at a conference until..." Crap, I nearly said Monday. "Tuesday or Wednesday, I think. He wasn't clear."

"Where is this conference?" Amy asks. "He forgot to tell me."

Staring into my coffee, I try to think. "You know, I don't remember. I feel like it was one of those big conference cities. Like New York or Chicago." I smile sheepishly. "He mentioned it while he was packing, and I was distracted by trying to keep our son out of his way."

"Yeah, kids can be a handful." Amy meets my eyes. "My Asher hates it when Daddy has to leave as well."

My mouth falls open in shock as my hand flutters up, eyes wide. Damn, I wish I had my camera out to shoot this performance. "You have a son named Asher too?"

Amy nods sadly before turning away. It takes everything I have to keep from laughing at her.

She has no idea that I am the person who chose the name of her son.

Since men are always sloppy, it was my only choice.

16

AMY

"You're listening to WBLW — news highlights all day long.
Police are gathering evidence about several recent robberies of
wealthy young women. The victims come from all around the
state, and although they don't have many details in common, a
pattern is gradually emerging. But first, Chad fills us in on
tomorrow's chance of rain, wind, and possibly hail. That's bad
news for the Barrett Street repair fiasco. Over to you, Chad."

I'm so angry and freaked out and fragile that it's taking all
of my focus to steer calmly. Even though Chad is usually
pretty hilarious, I turn him off to concentrate on driving.
Veering back and forth between anxiety and rage and total
numbness is sapping all of my energy. I'm going to end up
with brain whiplash.

Since I'm into handbags, I'm aware of fashion trends,
although I don't bother with them much myself. Yet I'm
fascinated with what people's clothing choices say about
them. Becca's bright fuchsia dress had screamed "Look at
me, I'm important!" to the entire restaurant. Heck, the
entire block, from her perch at the window. Her hair and

makeup were fancier than some brides'. It was embarrassing to be at the same table as that drama queen, except I realized there was no way anyone was paying a shred of attention to me.

Not to mention, Becca's voice is polished. Practiced. Intended to project when she wants to. As if she took vocal lessons simply for ordering coffee in the most precise way possible.

I've never met anyone that I kind of hate, and kind of want to be more like. I question her choices, yet she speaks her mind so clearly that I can't help but find bits of her persona admirable.

She's giving me mental tornado vibes, even though she's the most inauthentic person I've ever met.

Which makes Becca dangerous. She's hard to read. It's extra tricky to tell when she's telling the *actual* truth, since if she believes something, it's *her* version of the truth.

On my way home, I pick up enough takeout Chinese food to last me the weekend. I tend to stop eating when I'm upset, and I need to be as sharp as possible right now. I certainly don't want to cook, since I don't trust these shaky hands with knives right now.

Becca was lying about many things. I'm positive that she knows exactly where Craig is, and I don't think it's Las Vegas. She also already knew that I have a son named Asher as well.

It wasn't just the pause before answering, and the way she touched the side of her face every time she lied. It was too much direct eye contact. When she was pretending to think, she looked up and slightly to her left. She was processing, not recalling.

I thought that Dad was a bit nutty when he taught me

these details of how to read people. Now I'm incredibly grateful.

Even with all of that, though, I can't help but like Becca on some level. Maybe "like" is a strong word here. Curious. Or maybe, fascinated. She's dazzling, like a movie star. And she's inspirational. Well, maybe not to me, but definitely to many other women. Who doesn't dream of being a gorgeous woman in a stunning house with people hanging on their every word?

Yet there's so much more she's not sharing. Why should she reveal any of her secrets to a stranger, no matter what we have in common?

The scent of spicy chicken noodles fills the car as I turn toward my neighborhood with a strange sense of calm washing over me.

The back of Becca's jaw twitched when I mentioned the garage that Craig had built. Although I'm positive she already knew Craig had another wife and child, she definitely didn't know about the garage. So I'm going to start searching there as soon as I look up one more thing.

The second I get home, I load up on two spring rolls and a quarter of the chicken fried rice to get some carbs into my frazzled brain. That tiny sandwich feels like it was hours ago. The food at the Hilton had smelled incredible, yet there was no way I could eat in front of Becca. Partly because my stomach was busy clenching and twisting, and partly because I might use the wrong fork or something.

I already felt frumpy and awkward near her. Why does that bother me so much? I wish I could read her mind for just a few minutes. That polished princess definitely knows a lot more than she's sharing.

I put the coffee on and plug in my laptop at the dining

room table. It's horrible to even think about it, yet I need to prepare for the worst. If this all comes down to brass tacks, Craig was clearly with Becca first. It will be them against me.

Although... Do I even want him anymore? I honestly don't know. I don't think so. I'm so frazzled and irritated that it feels like there are wasps in my veins instead of blood.

I love Craig so much. *Loved*. Used to love. Might still love, but a lot less? In some ways he's plain and simple, and that works for me. He's an amazing husband – caring and tender and thoughtful. Not to mention, sexy when he wants to be. There's a certain sweet charm that he's able to turn on that I don't think any woman could resist.

The closeness we felt was real. Or so I thought. Now every memory is tainted... like a blood stain on a carpet. Even if you get most of it out, you'll always know it was there. It's imperfect. No longer pure.

Until recently, I had been positive Craig was devoted. An honest man whom I trusted completely. Now I have no idea what is true and what isn't.

Staring around the kitchen where we've shared so many meals, I feel my mind spinning. He said he bought that old-fashioned teddy bear cookie jar on one of his trips. For all I know, it could have been leftover swag from some promo of Becca's.

I reluctantly call up her website again and examine the photos closely. Then I do some quick searching on her so-called sponsors, and how the whole system usually works, with paid posts and promotional products.

An hour later, my notepad is covered in scribbles and I'm still confused. There's no way she's making that much money with her current number of followers. Although she acts like a superstar, Becca doesn't even have a quarter million followers on any site. Apparently, sponsors rarely speak with influencers with under a million unless it's something extremely specialized.

Becca certainly isn't specialized. She's as basic as they come. Her biggest quotes and mantras for "Moms and Dreamers" appear to be stolen from a variety of philosophers, books, and other influencers. She's not an inspiration. She's a cheap copy. Kind of a fraud, to be honest.

So how is she getting all of this money? Sure, it could be from Craig's salary, since I have no idea how much he makes. He must be subsidizing her income quite a bit.

I know in my guts that Becca already knew about me and my Asher. Why would she let him contribute to another house and other family? Wouldn't she see that as wasting money? Or... is that why she hates me – because I'm a wasteful expense?

It was so strange that when Becca was talking about herself, it didn't appear that she was lying. But when she spoke of Craig, I observed a faint tension in her eyes. The pitch of her voice rose by a note and a half.

If Craig is not at a conference, where the heck is he? And why isn't he with her either?

My eyes close as I push the notebook away and take a deep breath. I can't imagine ever speaking to him again. The thought itself feels like acid in my blood. As if I've been breathing in a chemical warfare agent.

If the idea of talking to Craig again makes me think of deadly poisons, I am going to avoid it at all cost.

Yet it might be unavoidable. If I do, I'm going to have to be deadly cool. Most of all, I'm going to have to look into absolutely every detail. Turn over each piece of information.

My mother certainly didn't, and I don't even know the extent of the damage it caused her.

I've always known that my father kept secrets. Yet I have no idea what the secrets were. Only that they were probably the reason he disappeared when I was thirteen.

It seemed like my mother only knew about half of his life, and remained blissfully ignorant of the rest. How sick that I'm repeating Mom's mistakes, and didn't even know it until now.

I'm going to have to fight. For information. To stay calm. Fight for the truth so that I can figure out what I must do to keep my family... Well, not together. Probably. But to keep things stable for Asher.

I'm going to have to keep the lines of communication open with Craig, even though I've never been angry with him before.

Just picturing those deep hazel eyes... I can't be lost in him anymore. Can't back down. I'm going to have to dig deep, grow a backbone, and do what's right.

Including examining the parts of his life that have nothing to do with Becca.

Which means searching his stupid garage like a freakin' detective.

17

AMY

I finish my coffee, wash my hands, then grab my phone in case I need to take any photos. If Becca was stunned about the existence of a new garage, there's a good chance there's a clue somewhere.

I pause to read a text from Mom.

> Hey, honey. Just wanted to report that Asher is becoming a master at spooning muffin mix. Pretty soon we'll have him cooking for us!

There's a photo of my son's adorable grinning face, with just a few smudges of batter on his nose and cheek. A deep wave of love for my sweet boy rolls through me. I miss him already.

> So cute – Give him a hug for me!

Asher is the reason I'm going to hold it together and make it through this. No matter what is going on with his father, I will take care of it, and keep this stress far away from my son.

Out the back door, I look around at the space between the house and the driveway. It's pretty wide and sheltered by our house and the garage next door, so Craig and I usually park side-by-side without even using the garage.

I turn my key in the flimsy lock, and step inside. As far as I can tell, nothing has really changed in the past month or two. The last time I looked, it was pretty basic. The riding lawn mower, some gardening supplies, the winter tires, and the scrub brushes for washing the cars.

Huge storage racks take up the entire east wall. Craig wanted to get a bunch of my leather scraps and old tools out of the basement, saying that he didn't want our toddler getting into them and we needed to put in a playroom. Now that we have this space for dozens of large plastic bins and a few toolboxes, our basement feels huge.

A lawnmower starts up next door, making me jump for a second. Once it levels out, it creates a background hum that makes me feel more sheltered. Like white noise drowning out the pounding of my heart in my ears.

At the back of the garage are several hanging lights and a long workbench-style table. A shelf on the side wall holds two stacks of jigsaw puzzles. There are also some metal brain-teaser puzzles, wood blocks, and a whole bunch of notebooks and pens. Flipping through them, I can see the books are empty. There's a basket with craft supplies, and a few of Asher's markers that I thought had gone missing.

There are two high stools, a regular chair and a bench. I can picture Asher climbing all over and around the table as he does puzzles with his daddy.

So what has Craig been doing out here by himself?

Feeling like a snoop, I check the garbage. Just a few paper towels with a faint orange tint – likely used for mopping up juice spills. Plus some shavings from colored pencils. Nothing seems ominous or out of place. If anything, it's too clean in here for a garage.

I stare at the back wall for a minute, and a flutter passes through me. Something doesn't feel right. The distance from the wall to the window is... wrong?

I go back outside and count off how many steps it is from the side door to the back wall. Inside, there are fewer steps. The inside wall is around three feet short.

That inner gut prickle is buzzing like a chainsaw.

The wall looks completely normal. Just drywall painted a dull blue-gray, plus three hooks with extra extension cables coiled neatly. Once my nose is nearly to the wall, I see a faint vertical line down the side. As if one drywall panel wasn't plastered to its neighbor.

This is weird. And weird is precisely what I'm looking for.

Nothing seems different when I peer up at the ceiling. Or the middle of the floor. In the far corner, almost under the table, is a large steel box. I try to move it, nearly straining my wrists from the incredible weight. It takes a few minutes, as I brace myself against the wall, then I manage to slide it forward, out of the corner.

What the actual hell?

The box was covering a latch on the floor. One of those metal sliding puzzles like the kind Craig gives to Asher all the time. Which always irritates me, since he's far too young for those and just gets frustrated.

Thankfully, it's based on a puzzle I've watched them solve together every few months. Craig said that repetition helps young minds make the connections, so he repeats some of the puzzles at various intervals.

It takes me four tries, but once I arrange the metal slats just so, there's a deep clicking sound. Something between the floor and the wall shifts, and a tiny handle swings out of the bottom corner of the wall.

Another wave of confusion, rage, and curiosity floods my nervous system. It's one thing that Craig insisted on building a garage back here that we don't even use. But a hidden panel? How could he hide something like this from me?

A sharp knock at the garage door has me leaping to my feet, spinning to face our next-door neighbor, Mr. Rueckert, as he walks in. His hands fly up, covered in neon green gardening gloves. "Sorry! I'm so sorry. I expected to see Craig out here."

I need to clutch my heart, but don't want the elderly man to feel worse. Shifting so my leg blocks the strange handle on the wall, I force a smile. "It's fine. I'm always jumpy."

His head shakes, giving me a warm smile. "Wait until you're older, dear. My Margaret jumps in the night if a butterfly sneezes five blocks away."

"Great." My eyes roll dramatically. "Something to look forward to."

He smiles, looking around the concrete and metal space. "I've never seen you back here. And Craig seems to run out the door if I'm ever around." Leaning against the door frame, he chuckles, dark eyes sparkling. "You're not hiding one of those hipster mini stills back here, are you?"

My laugh is too loud, yet honestly feels refreshing. "No. I wish."

"You sure? I swear I won't say a word as long as you give

me a bottle at Christmas. My uncle used to make apple pie moonshine."

"That sounds amazing." Looking around the space, I nod with a smile. "It's a fun idea though. Maybe someday."

He scrubs the back of his glove across his forehead. "I was just about to trim the row of hedges across the back. Should I do your side while I'm at it? Once I get going, it only takes another few minutes. Just don't want you to think I'm a prowler back there."

I sigh with relief. "That would be wonderful, thank you."

He smiles again. "You need more fresh air and sunshine. You work too hard."

"Mom tells me the same thing."

I want to ask him precisely how much time Craig spends out here, and how much they chat, yet that would sound awkward. Possibly suspicious.

He gives me a half-salute with a flash of neon green before shuffling away, calling back, "Always listen to your mother."

I press my back against the wall for a moment, catching my breath until I hear the electric clippers running. Shutting the door, I lock it, then hunch back down to the weird handle in the wall. I shove it to the left, revealing a pocket door that slides open nearly halfway across the space.

As I stand up, my hands and fingers turn to ice. My heart races like an overcaffeinated rabbit.

Why would Craig have a three-foot hidden space built into the back of the garage unless he had something serious to hide?

18

AMY

This feels sinister. Forbidden.

More villainous than a man simply having two families, as horrifying as that is.

I want nothing more than to slam the door to this garage and never come in here again. Drown myself in takeout and old movies until this creepy feeling dissolves out of my system. But that's not me, I hope. If it comes down to brass tacks, I want to be a fighter, not a doormat. Fighter or not, my hands are still twitching from the nerves and rage that keep surging through me. I'm so curious that I slide the door open all the way to reveal the entire hidden space.

It's... quite businesslike. There are narrow filing cabinets directly in front of me. Several slim open shelves containing what looks like tools and electronics. Some cables, and a plastic bin filled with USB keys. Nothing is dusty, and the air doesn't smell stale. This isn't an abandoned space. Craig has definitely been out here recently.

Wedged into the far end of the space is a four-by-eight-foot whiteboard covered in photos, writing, pinned notes, and lines connecting things. The largest photos are of a pretty brunette in her early twenties.

A shimmer of revulsion zaps through me. Shuffling back, I bump into the edge of the table hard enough to smack my elbow and ulnar nerve so hard I could scream. I don't want to be near this... whatever it is.

Craig absolutely adores these "discovery and brainstorming boards". Three years ago, I had a huge board set up with paint and curtain swatches when I was redecorating my shop. I called it a "vision board." He jokingly referred to it as my "murder board" like they use on cop shows. On TV, it gives the detectives something to stare at while they're pondering the crime. It helps them see connections and process the case when they can see all of the details at once.

Why would my sweet, loving husband have a brainstorming board hidden in the garage of our charming home?

Swallowing hard, I stare down at my feet while I take several slow, deep breaths. This is seriously creepy. *Come on, Amy. Hold it together.*

I can't even pretend that it's not Craig's. That's his handwriting – abnormally tidy printing, like an architect's. He's the person who spends the most time out here. The husband I thought I knew would never hide things from me. Wouldn't have a massive home project without telling me about it. Geez – he sent me a photo from the hardware store last month, asking me which of the two blue plant pots I wanted for the dining room because he wanted my input.

He's always been so attentive and loving. The perfect husband in every way except for his odd schedule, and the fact that I couldn't know the details of his job. Yet that made sense at the time, since he works in high-tech security.

Does... doesn't he?

My hands land on my head as I smooth back my hair, trying to stop my shoulders from locking up.

Now it's extremely clear that I don't know my husband at all. Every single thing he's ever said may have been a lie. Every encounter, every discussion of our dreams... all lies. Or potential lies. I've been sleeping with a total stranger three nights a week and had no idea.

Oh my... What if he's dangerous? He's spent so much time with Asher that I can't even...

No. Craig adores Asher. That's clear. No matter what bizarre things he's up to, I know that he'd never harm our son. That's pretty much the only thing I know for sure.

But a brainstorming board about a strange young woman... There cannot be a single wholesome reason for that. My mind instantly floods with idiotic ideas, wanting that to be true. As if he would be recruiting contestants for a game show or something harmless in a hidden mini-room in our garage.

This is something ominous. Something wrong.

Once the room stops spinning, I grip the table to hold myself steady and examine the board. The beautiful young woman looks familiar. Yet she's so fashionably generic and overlit it's hard to tell.

Along one side is a compilation of notes in a list, with locations and addresses. There's a schedule on the other side. A photo of a slick, silver car. A photo of the woman coming out of a nail salon. A photo of her walking into a gorgeous French bistro.

Her name isn't written anywhere, but it comes to me in a flash. Mia Harrington.

Holy mother of... Staggering forward, I grip the edge of the board, staring at the largest photo. She's on the patio of a café, holding a glass of wine. There is a handbag sitting on the chair close beside her – a limited edition bright pink Von Rubis I worked on several months ago. It was brought in by a nervous assistant who was terrified to even hold a bag that expensive.

My hand is numb as it slides into my pocket to pull out my phone. Using my camera as a magnifying glass, I zoom in on the photo. There it is – the slightly thicker handle stitching.

That is my work.

Although my store database is super-slow on my phone, it eventually loads, so I can skim this year's Von Rubis repairs to confirm it. An assistant named Grace Zhang has been bringing in Mia Harrington's things every few months since the shop opened. I remember Grace – super-efficient, and eager to do a good job, no matter how demanding Mia was.

That was right when my reputation for being able to fix anything spread like wildfire through some new social circles. Conveniently, it was also when a couple of nearby malls brought in designer outlet stores that made my shop worth the drive. That's where many of the assistants pick up classic clothing at a fraction of the price, so they can look appropriate for work.

Staring at the notes all around the board, I wonder where Craig got some of this information about Mia. Parts are written in codes and abbreviations. There is mention of Mia's impossibly rich family and connections, including some friends and distant relatives.

To the side is a list titled, "Assets." Her watch, jewelry, the lavish handbags she uses most often – the woman has an admirable collection from Lola Q's of London. Bank account totals, with dates – presumably when they were last checked? The make and model of her car, phone, laptop.

There's also a list of her favorite restaurants, with her dining habits. Her favorite stores, with her shopping behavior. Since everyone is obsessed with displaying their lifestyles on social media these days, it can't be that hard to find someone's routines. It says here that she goes to the gym on Monday, Wednesday, and Friday mornings. On Monday afternoons she pampers herself with a mani-pedi, facial, and the works at her favorite salon. She has a standing lunch date with her university girlfriends on Thursdays.

A dark cloud presses down on the back of my spine. This feels like criminal activity. This is more than a puzzle. This is a tracker. My husband is tracking one of my customers like prey.

A hot young girl.

My fingernails dig into the edge of the table as I realize this might actually be a real planning board.

No, that's insane. Craig is clearly a liar and a cheater, but what would he have to do with Mia? Why would he even pay attention to her? She's a flighty socialite.

Quite frankly, she wouldn't be interested in a family man. Although he really is charming as hell. If he set his sights on a woman, he'd make some headway, for sure.

Oh, crap.

My gaze darts around the room. If Craig has been doing secretive things in here, would he have any spy cameras? Could he be watching me right now? It's freakish that he must have smeared dirt on the back door security camera on the house. Since he's the one who took care of the construction of this garage, he could have anything out here and I wouldn't know about it.

At the time, he seemed so delighted to invest in this property. After he paid to replace some of the doors and windows when he first moved in, he'd been itching to find another project to upgrade our living space.

I bought the house a few years before I met him, when I was still running my repair business out of the basement. Luckily, Mom was able to help with the down payment. Technically, it was a loan. Although I've been making small monthly payments to her, I don't think she cares if she ever gets the money back.

She just wanted me to have a nice place to live where I wasn't also renting out a workshop. Apartments don't really like tenants having customers coming and going, and the smell of leather conditioners hovering in the air.

It was shortly after I opened my own shop – with the help of a much smaller loan from Mom – that Craig happened to wander in one day. He wondered if it was worth it to repair an old leather belt. It wasn't expensive, he just hated the thought of wasting something because there was a small weak spot.

I was instantly dazzled by his striking eyes, his charming smile. The way he held my gaze as we spoke. Plus, it was kind of sweet how he didn't want to be wasteful.

I fixed the belt almost invisibly, and he left the store. For a full minute, it had felt like my heart was a stone, sinking into my shoes.

Then Craig returned, handing me a hastily sketched bouquet of flowers on a piece of notepaper and asking if he could take me out to dinner. We clicked in every possible way, and before I knew it, we were married and I was pregnant immediately.

We were so happy. So in tune with each other.

Or at least... that's what I believed until yesterday morning.

The air in the garage feels dry and clammy at the same time. I hurry back into the house to chug a glass of water, and sit down at my laptop again.

Just as I'm typing "Mia Harrington" into the search bar, something tweaks in the back of my mind. I've heard her name this week somewhere. It's on the edge of my mind. Like maybe I heard it while I was doing something else, like on the news...

My mouth falls open as I grip the laptop with both hands, jaw dropping at the headline: *Rich party girl heiress Mia Harrington was found dead on Tuesday after a freak car accident.*

It was just a few days ago. An accident, not a murder. *Maybe.*

19

AMY

Staring over the laptop at the blank wall, I don't know what to think. Craig's planning board... did... did it come true? He couldn't have been responsible for a car accident?

I quickly skim the tiny news blurb. It looks like Mia was driving too fast on slick roads and went off an embankment five weeks ago.

That poor woman. How horrible.

And yet, am I horrible for being kind of glad it was an accident, not a murder?

It sounds a bit woo-woo, but even having her photos on a board that looked like he was plotting something against her... could that have put negative energy into the universe until something happened? Of course, that's ridiculous, but right now, anything could be a possibility.

My phone rings and I startle, my knee hitting the laptop as I spring backward from the phone. Ow – it feels like I've bruised the top of the patella. That's going to hurt tomorrow. I've never been this jumpy, but no wonder. It feels like my entire life is imploding, and I can't make sense of any of it.

Craig's number is on the screen.

Normally, I leap to answer his calls whenever he's away. This time, I don't make a single move. Soon, the red dot appears, to indicate I have a voicemail, and I reluctantly play it.

"*Hey, sweetheart. Hope that your day wasn't too busy.*" He chuckles. "*I mean, I hope you have lots of clients, but I don't want you wearing yourself out. You know what I mean.*"

There's a pause, and I can just picture his beautiful hazel eyes staring blankly at the nearest available wall as he usually does during phone calls.

"*I've been absorbing so much new tech information that it feels like my brain is about to explode. There are wall-to-wall presentations all weekend long, so I might not have the energy to call or text much. Just know that I'm thinking about you, and I can't wait to see you next week. Bye – love you, gorgeous.*"

A day and a half ago, it made my heart leap whenever he called me that. Now his deep, resonant voice doesn't even sound like my husband's anymore. Is he still my husband? Or just the man I'm becoming increasingly terrified of?

There were no clues in the background noise, wherever he was. It didn't sound like a hotel, or a conference center, with voices in the background. It was absolutely silent.

My phone drops to the table, and my face falls into my hands as I curl up in a ball. What am I supposed to do? When I got home from coffee with Becca, I immediately wanted another conversation with her about what to do about Craig. You know... once she had some more time in her busy, overly scheduled and curated life.

Partly to discover more bits about this other side of Craig. Mostly to find out more about this woman he's been spending a huge portion of his life with. Yet I'll probably unearth more information on my own, since Becca is pretty good at guarding her expressions and every single word she utters.

Now, my apparent sham of a marriage is on the back burner, since my so-called husband has a planning board in the garage featuring a girl who recently died. Naturally, I want to uncover everything about Craig and Becca, but a sudden death takes precedence.

Sitting up straight, I roll my shoulders back and take a few deep breaths. It was a car accident. Craig had nothing to do with her death. Why else was he studying her?

Well, he is in some secret, high-tech security. Maybe Mia's father wanted someone to spy on her, for some crazy reason? Maybe she was getting too close to his rival's son. Or he wanted to know if she was spilling family secrets. No, that sounds like a cheesy soap opera.

Maybe Craig was doing espionage on the Harrington family to try and find a way into her father's business? He could have been working for the rival. That sounds like an even cheesier soap opera.

My breath is still unsteady.

With the list of "assets" clearly labelled, robbery is the most likely reason he was studying her. Mia was loaded. Just an hour with her credit card could change someone's life.

I need to talk to somebody, but there's nobody available. My friends Katie and Drea were close, but after high school they've drifted away, focused on their families. Katie just got pregnant, and she's on her baby moon in Spain, I think. I certainly can't disturb her with something upsetting. Drea has a toddler and just got promoted. Our group messages consist mostly of birthday wishes and random restaurant recommendations.

Fiona is too highly strung for me to even consider telling her about this. The one time I told her about a client cursing me out for taking too long on a job, Fiona demanded to know the woman's address so she could go kick her ass.

Seriously, I was about to change the password on my laptop and phone for fear that Fiona might try to get her address. I've never seen her so livid. I think she's been grasping at straws to try to get close to me again. Of course, I feel bad that I've been spending less time with her, but she must understand that my work and family come first.

I can't tell Mom anything. She has the world's worst poker face. The kind of person who reacts first and thinks later. No wonder Dad left – she's not the kind of person who can handle any kind of... *intensity*.

And if there's anything I've learned from Dad is that total control in a crisis is the most important life skill. Ever.

This level of stress certainly cannot come anywhere near Asher. He's already an empathetic boy.

Maybe it's strange, but I've gotten relatively close to our nanny Penny over the past year. We've been bonding over childcare psychology articles and nutrition news. Yet I'm certainly not going to bother her when she's sick. She's kind of young and fragile. I wouldn't want her to be disturbed by something so dark.

How could I even put this into words, anyway? *"Hey, how are you? Hope you're having a good start to the weekend. By the way, do you think there's any chance my husband Craig, who I just found out has an entire other family, is a murderer?"*

I've never been brilliant at social etiquette, yet I'm pretty sure that wouldn't be well received by anyone.

Jumping to my feet, I make myself a cup of peppermint tea and manage to swallow a few huge spoonfuls of cold noodles.

I honestly wish I could speak to Becca as if she were a normal person. If I could get her to drop her façade for a moment and speak to her woman-to-woman, maybe we could figure this out together.

Naturally, I'm livid that she's Craig's first wife. But if there's any chance Craig is... *Ugh.* What is he? At best a spy or a thief, at worst a murderer. Whatever he's up to, she should know so that she can protect her son.

Even though I have the distinct impression that she knows a lot more about what's going on than I do, she couldn't possibly know about this. Becca is all sweetness and light and appearances. Serious crimes don't really fit into her "aspirational lifestyle" brand.

Well, it doesn't fit in my life either, dammit. I grab the notepad, pencil, and my phone, and march back out to the garage. My gardening shoes stomp through the backyard as if I'm trying to tell myself I'm a woman on a mission.

Although I don't want Craig to be involved in anything sinister, my need to know the truth is much stronger than any connection I feel toward that man right now.

Whoops – I left the secret panel open. Not that anyone could see the brainstorming board from the street or next door. Should I even be concerned about keeping Craig's secrets at this point?

A shiver runs through me as I think of all the times Craig saw one of these boards on a detective show and leaned in, fascinated. I thought it was simply his brainstorming puzzle mind at work. I thought that he needed to study productivity and creative thought processes because of his job.

I would never have dreamed that he was a stalker on the side. It just doesn't feel like him.

Which points out once again that I don't know that man at all.

The photos of Mia break my heart. She was so young. Like so many of my clients, these women come from rich parents. Their fathers hold the keys to all sorts of top-level business deals. These are the kind of girls who get kidnapped and held for ransom to pry both money and information from their daddies.

Clearly I've been watching too many movies and true crime shows.

I take hold of the frame and pull the board out of the hidden panel and angle it so that nobody could see in the window.

Staring at the photos and notes, I try to blank my mind and let the information wash through me. It's clear that it's Craig's handwriting. It's clear that he was studying Mia. Stalking her – either in person or virtually, I don't know.

The lists of all of her activities could have been gathered from social media, I think. Her Instagram is noted on one of the panels, so I check it on my phone. Sure enough, she's one of those girls who makes a big deal of posting every time she leaves the house as if it's some grand adventure. Lunches with friends, hair appointments, shopping excursions. A big night out in the next city over for some glamorous charity function.

I check the date. That was almost six weeks ago. Her car accident was apparently five weeks ago. Mia didn't post anything for seven days? Why the huge gap?

The analytical part of my mind starts making excuses... Maybe she lost her phone and it took a while to replace it. That's definitely bull – she would have a new phone delivered to her within hours. Maybe she went on a bender and didn't document it. That could explain the crash. But her copious photos show her jogging, drinking smoothies, and going to yoga classes. Being strung out for a week isn't normally the habit of a health nut.

The best thing I can do is lock this back up, go inside, eat some more noodles, and try to get a full night's sleep. At the very least, I need to get away from this space that's becoming increasingly creepy as the sun drops.

As I start to push the rolling board back into the space, it moves, sending me pitching forward as I grab the edge of the board for support.

It starts to flip over. Slowly turning, the panel reveals another board on the reverse.

My hand claps over my mouth. With these photos, I recognize the woman immediately.

Olivia Rhodes.

Megan's boss. Another of my customers.

The date circled at the bottom is Monday – just three days away.

20

CRAIG

I deeply admire women. It's always been fascinating to study them. Their mannerisms, speech patterns, and the things they choose to focus on are incredibly different. They seem to keep busier. They're sometimes more delicate, except when they're suddenly much stronger.

Now that I'm regularly tracking women, I'm learning so much more.

Some women spend over a hundred dollars, plus nearly two hours of their time, to get their nails done every two weeks. Some spend double the money on a personal trainer just because it's a good-looking guy and they get a little thrill.

And the way they shop for shoes? Military commanders should take note of the way they plan their route to hit six different stores, in the order of how likely they are to find precisely what they're looking for.

It's like I've been immersed in an alien society, absorbing the lingo, the patterns, and an entirely new culture.

It's utterly captivating.

I've always loved problem-solving. It hits something deep

in my soul, even more than fine wine or the perfect steak. An indulgence of sorts. Having the time to set everything aside except the puzzle in front of me.

But in order to solve the puzzle, I need to research all of the information. Dig down until I understand everything I can uncover about the... *target*? I really do need a term for my subjects. *Victim* sounds cruel. As if I hate them. I don't. I'm fascinated by them. Plus, they are an extremely convenient means to an end.

Subjects will have to do for now. That's relatively neutral.

My subjects fascinate me until I'm dreaming about their schedules, their friends, and the elegant places where they consume expensive wine and perhaps three bites of food.

In a way, it's like admiring the peacocks in a zoo. They're so beautiful that it's easy to forget they are filthy, loud, obnoxious creatures who have no purpose beyond decoration.

They're only worth the price of their feathers.

21

AMY

The photo staring back at me is definitely Olivia Rhodes. Even without the initials OR marked on the board, she's impossible to forget.

She's come into my shop many times – the first time with her mother, Felicity Rhodes, who has been one of my fairly steady customers from the second I opened my repair business. Felicity found me when I was still working out of my home.

Olivia was warm and sweet when she first came to my shop with her mother. The next visit, she was solo, and we had a great conversation about how to keep leather looking new and what brands were worth investing in. The following time she came in with Megan, and was quite bossy. Almost like she was asserting her dominance over her new assistant.

I didn't love the way she also started treating me like her personal assistant. One time, Olivia called me herself to demand that a purse repair be finished immediately because she had an exclusive event to attend. She was downright vicious, with language that was utterly shocking. It was one of the few times I vented openly to Craig, Fiona, and even Mom about a client's behavior. Then I saw on her socials that her father had humiliated her mother in a horrible scandal. Yes, it's childish that she was lashing out. Yet without proper parenting, this young woman is kind of still a child herself.

Backing slowly away from the board, I can't stop staring. It's sinister. Nobody should be this focused on a stranger's life. Even if the woman is begging for attention at every opportunity.

I've seen plenty of super-rich girls act like that. If they were on a psychiatrist's couch, it would likely come out that they're trying to find themselves in their early twenties. Sneaking out from under their parents' thumbs and establishing their own homes and lifestyles.

I'm extremely sympathetic to the fact that nobody wants to turn out exactly like their parents.

Most of these rich girls use their assistants as personal ego boosters. "My assistant will take care of that" is practically a mantra.

Speaking of mantras... a dark part of me wonders why Becca doesn't have an assistant, beyond the nanny she occasionally mentions, and her part-time chef. Maybe an assistant would clash with her "I do everything myself because I'm a superwoman" façade.

Olivia certainly has a superiority complex. Megan was telling me a few months ago that her tech mogul father had just become a billionaire.

We had a good laugh about it, as I always try to boost the spirits of stressed-out assistants when they need a laugh. Megan confided in me, opening up about some of Olivia's cattier moments. The way she has the salon repaint her nails if the color doesn't show up correctly in her photos. How she blames the valet whenever she dings her Porsche. How her friends even think she's crossed the line into Full Bitchdom, but since Olivia is invited to the best parties, they keep quiet to tag along.

Then I remember how polite Felicity was with me. Yet the second they were out the door, Felicity was already tearing into poor Olivia. Treating her like a burden. An idiot for not asking me more direct questions. She clearly didn't realize the window was open, and I was treated to a first-hand glimpse of how sheltered Olivia must have been over the years, while being shaped into the princess she's become.

I take a photo of the entire board, then flip it back to Mia's side, slide it back into the hidden space and lock it. Glancing around the garage, I wonder if Craig has cameras out here. That creepy thought sends icy tendrils down my spine. Could my husband be dangerous?

I lock the garage, then go into the house and make sure every door and window is locked. My hands shake as I change the house alarm's security code. If Craig comes in, I need to be wide awake immediately. It's impossible to determine if I fear him at this point.

Staring out the kitchen window at the darkening backyard while I heat up some food, I begin to pace. I'm too jumpy to sit, so I eat standing at the counter. Three bites into my noodles, the fork falls out of my hand.

Craig always asks me about my customers. Since he can't talk about his work, we chat about my job quite a bit. His eyes always light up when I share stories of who has acted spoiled, or been a bitch to their assistants.

Does Craig have some sort of fetish for vicious women? I mean, he's apparently with Becca, and she's obviously two-faced. Well, possibly three- or four-faced, if there is such a thing.

Some of the photos on that board were pretty sexy. To be fair, young women in their early twenties with personal trainers and no day jobs lounge around looking sexy twenty-four seven.

I was talking about Olivia with Craig just a few weeks ago. Did I mention the part about her father becoming a billionaire? If that's the case, he's likely just after her money. Sick as it is, that's a relief. You can rob someone without hurting them. Maybe.

Reaching for my phone, I look up Olivia's social media pages. Thank goodness – she posted something just a few hours ago. She's going out with friends tonight, so at least she won't be alone.

By the time I finish my dinner, it feels like I've eaten rocks. Once my face is washed and teeth brushed, I throw on baggy old yoga pants and a cozy sweatshirt.

Yet I can't bring myself to get into that bed, where just last week Craig was so passionate that I would never have believed he could so much as look at another woman.

No matter what I do, I won't sleep well tonight. I've tried sleeping pills on other stressful occasions, but they don't really work on me. It's like my system is impervious to tranquilizers – I pop back awake in no time. Which has made some dental procedures extremely uncomfortable.

I grab my pillow and a couple of blankets, then go down to make a fort on the couch. Turning off all of the lights but one, I get as comfortable as possible. Maybe that's the problem. Maybe both of Craig's lives became too comfortable, and he decided to rob easy targets for a little thrill.

Sitting up straight, I reach back to massage across my

trapezius muscles, which are threatening to lock up. Dad's constant anatomy lessons sure come in handy when my body is stressed.

Craig is about to turn forty in a few months. Maybe it's a midlife crisis and he's trying to date younger women to prove he's still young and virile?

Women like Olivia and Mia and the rest would never date a guy like him. Although, I've seen him charm the heck out of restaurant hostesses, always getting us the best table. What if he used that knack for other reasons?

Most men ogle models, and I don't entirely blame them. When I would occasionally watch runway shows, Craig seemed interested in learning a few designer names, and which were the trendiest and most expensive. At the time, I found it adorable.

It's pathetic that I miss the faint leather and wood scent of his soap.

I roll onto my side, my hand flopping out from under the blanket to drag on the carpet. Forcing my eyes to close, I try to do some deep breathing.

Twenty minutes later, my eyes snap open. Should I warn Olivia? If someone had a brainstorming board about me, I would want to know that something was up. Monday is coming fast.

If Mia's board sent bad energy out into the universe, and she ended up dead, the same could happen with Olivia. Or, Craig could've been planning some heist, or whatever was going to happen in several months, and Mia accidentally died before that could come to fruition.

Or... *oh my*... could Craig have messed with her car? Could that have been his fault?

Flipping onto my side, I set my phone to play a sleep track. My mind is ping-ponging all over, and it's exhausting.

I need to talk to Craig.

Dad taught me to trust my gut. I need to see Craig face-to-face. I'll know if he's lying if I accuse him directly.

Even though my head, my heart, and my guts are at war, I'm not in love with him anymore. How could I possibly be in love with a man when so much of him is apparently a total stranger?

Now that I'm fully mentally detached, and know that our relationship is over, I can really get to work.

THREE WEEKS AGO

The alley between the nightclubs is narrow and filthy. Music pumps out into the crisp night air every time the back door is opened as tipsy people emerge from the VIP lounge to sprawl on the hidden private patio.

It's not especially exclusive. Just an astroturfed zone next to the employee parking area. But with fancy patio lights and cushy furniture, they don't look out at the concrete past the decorative green fence.

Nobody sees me in the dark. The VIPs only have eyes for each other.

When the music swells again, she strolls out, draping herself across a chaise lounge. She doesn't smoke, but two men sitting across from her do. She's had her eye on them for a few weeks. Yet she's so aloof, they might never have the courage to make a move.

Nobody notices as I take photos and notes of everyone she speaks with. What they speak about.

It's so easy to read a woman who is an open book.

22

AMY

SATURDAY

A piercing whine yanks me from the best ten minutes of sleep I've gotten all night. Scrambling for my phone, I fumble to turn off the screeching noise. My heart is in my throat as I try to focus, blinking stupidly at the screen until my vision clears.

It's the store alarm.

Somebody is trying to break into the back door of my shop.

I'm on my feet so fast my head spins.

Luckily, the alarm at the shop must have been even louder than my phone. As I examine the video, a shadow figure slowly pokes around at the lock, tries the door, then runs like crazy when the alarm sounds. The footage on my phone is grainy and dark. It's hard to see any details of the person at all.

Which means I'll have to go in and download the higher resolution video from the shop. Rolling off the couch, I stretch quickly, my entire body aching from tension and lack of sleep. My muscles are retaining the aftershocks of terrible dreams.

I put the coffee on, and it's ready by the time I finish my lightning-quick shower. I brush my hair into a high ponytail and smudge on a bit of eyeliner and mascara. It's unhinged that I don't want to look completely unpolished in case I run into Becca today.

I fill a traveler mug and pull on a sweater since it's starting to rain. By the time I get to Barrett Street, it's absolutely pouring. There are workmen milling around everywhere, looking downright pissed off due to the water in their eyes, but they're trudging along beside their huge metal machines.

At the end of the street, a workman waves his hands for me to stop. I crack the window as he shakes his head. "You can't be anywhere near here, miss. Everything's ripped up."

"I just have to get in the back door of Pristine Purses. Somebody tried to break into my shop."

"The drilling could've set off the alarm," he says with a shrug. "Like a car alarm if it gets shaken."

"I saw the video. It was a person." I hope he can sense the pleading behind my eyes. "Please – I just have to check quickly."

My lungs nearly seize as I hold my breath. *Please, please, please.*

He hesitates, scratching his two-day-old beard. The poor man looks as disheveled as I feel. "If you park over there at the mall," he points, "you could run down the back alley. But we're turning off the power to the whole street because of the rain and the area we have to open up next. You only have maybe twenty minutes before we're going to be blacked out for a couple of hours."

"Thanks."

I park at the mall and take off down the back alley at a quick jog. Thank goodness I wore sneakers instead of rain boots. My feet are soaked, but at least I have a good grip on the weathered asphalt.

Slowing down, I creep to the building side of the alley while looking around. If anybody is lurking around the back door, I'm going to need my breath.

It's not just the chill and the rain making me miserable. It's as if the rug of my comfortable, predictable life has been pulled out from under me, leaving me in a drenched, stinking alley with wet shoes, damp hair, and seventeen minutes to grab the footage to see who was trying to break into my shop.

Holy crap. Am I racing into serious danger? I'm running in as if I could do anything to protect myself. My only physical prowess is doing an amazing standing bow pose on the rare occasions I make it to a yoga class. Well, and my exceptionally strong hands from the leatherwork.

Breathing slowly, I stand perfectly still for ten seconds. Feeling every part of my feet against the ground, I remember how to calm my heart rate. Then I skulk down the narrow space like a burglar. There's nobody around when I reach the back door of my shop. The rain lets up a bit, yet it's still so dark and dingy I feel chilled straight through.

The back door is almost never used. Once I unlock it, I have to use both hands and lean back with a hard jerk to get it to open. I rush in, disable the security system, then listen. Other than the construction commotion out front, the store seems quiet.

Although nobody got in, I wonder for a split second whether I should call the police just in case.

What if this wasn't an attempted robbery, but someone was looking for me? I shake my head. That's ridiculous. The stress is obviously stirring up my anxiety like a blender.

Which is proved by my heart leaping into my throat when a jackhammer kicks in for several seconds, vibrating the front window so badly I honestly don't know if it's going to survive.

I grab a USB key from my drawer and download the footage from this morning that shows movement at the back door. I'll analyze it properly at home, away from this racket.

A loud bang on the front door makes me almost knock the laptop clear off my desk. Pulse thrumming in my throat, I look out to see a petite blonde girl tapping on the window.

My shoes slosh across the tile floor, dripping mud as I hurry to open it. There's a loud cry from a workman outside, "Yo, c'mon, lady, they're closed!"

"I'm so sorry!" The girl dashes inside out of the rain. "I was just about to leave when I saw someone moving around in here. I know you're closed, but please... Claire will kill me if I can't pick up this bag for a charity event tonight. Her whole outfit depends on it."

I don't recognize her until she shakes her hair out. Dana. Claire Morgan's assistant. Pasting a polite smile on my face instead of my instinctive eye roll, I nod.

"We have to be fast. I don't have time to boot up the system." I take her ticket, then punch in the code to the storage room. I make her sign the receipt by hand, and do a half-assed job of wrapping the purse in a shopping bag.

"Hurry – we're losing power in a few minutes, and I have to set the alarm."

Dana's eyes are tight as she forces a smile. "Thank you, Amy. I swear you've just saved my job. Really, thank you."

I flash her a huge smile as I practically shove her out the door, locking it behind her. Then I make sure the storeroom is locked, and check to see if the security footage has all transferred to the thumb drive.

I take an extra few seconds to make a backup of all of my customer contact files onto the drive as well, just in case anything happens to the shop itself. This information feels too private to keep in the cloud anywhere.

Standing up to leave, I sink back into the chair again, hoping that I have one more minute.

I open the security footage, zooming in to show as much detail as possible. The figure lurking around the back door is wearing a huge coat and a big floppy hat. It's a clumsy, awkward disguise, but it works. I can't get a good look at any features. From the way they move, I'm fairly certain it's a woman. They're also wearing gloves, so there won't be fingerprints anywhere.

Just as I move the mouse to turn the video off, I stop.

The shadowy figure tucks their hair back over their ear, then drops their left shoulder.

I've seen that exact move before.

23

AMY

My husband's other wife tried to break into my shop?

My common sense is being choked by a nasty tangle of dark thoughts.

It was definitely Becca. Although part of me can't believe she'd be caught dead in a dirty back alley in the rain. Her hair tuck and shoulder drop are subtle maneuvers models use to make their collarbones look elegant. It's one of her signature moves on her website, to the point where I'm sure it's automatic.

I check the time on my phone. Crap. I'm cutting it right down to the wire.

Grabbing my things, I dash out the back door and set the alarm with trembling hands. I've barely backed three feet away from the building when the light at the end of the alley goes out.

A deep sigh rattles my flushed, overly warm chest as I trudge through the rain back to my car. Getting out of there in the nick of time was the first bit of good luck I've had all weekend.

It's a challenge to drive home calmly, since I don't actually want to get there. Every time I find out something new, it makes everything worse.

There's a dark undercurrent surging deep inside me. *Ugh.* I need to get home and check some things online before I freak all the way out. Even though I'd rather burrow under the covers with a glass of wine and a romance book until the outside world disappears.

I switch on the radio out of habit, hoping to hear the weather. The news can't make anything worse at the moment.

"You're listening to WBLW — your top hit songs and the news every fifteen minutes. Police are currently analyzing the tragic car accident of heiress Mia Harrington. No official details have been released yet, but it might be more than a simple accident. Apparently she was recently robbed, and there have been several robberies of similar young women in the tri-state area. Stay tuned for more. But first, Dave fills us in on today's wild weather – from rain to sunshine to possible thunder-hail this evening. Is that even possible, Dave?"

Thank goodness I'm already pulling into the driveway, since my hands lock up around the wheel. I snap the radio off, take three slow breaths, and force myself to get into the house so that I can read the news. Somehow that feels more manageable than listening, since I can go at my own pace.

I'm so flustered in the front hallway that I forget I just changed the security code. It takes three tries, then I manage to hit enter a split second before the alarm sounds.

Stress and exhaustion wrap around me like a blanket as I lock the door behind me and stagger to the kitchen. Water. Multivitamin. Put the coffee on. It feels like I'm on autopilot. Or like I have the flu.

Forcing myself to eat a bagel and peanut butter, I sit down with my coffee at the kitchen table with my laptop.

Flipping to a new page on my notepad, I search Mia Harrington and slowly scour the latest headlines. Since her body was found at the scene of a car accident, the earliest reports assumed that was what killed her. Once the coroner examined her, it was determined that she had been killed approximately a week prior to the crash. They aren't releasing the actual cause of death. But they are saying that the car crash was a cover-up, and that it's now a murder investigation.

Murder.

The murder of a young woman whose face is all over a murder board locked up in a secret compartment in my garage.

Daggers spike into my stomach. I've met Mia, and joked about her with her assistant.

She was probably killed intentionally. There could be some evidence about her murder on my property. That was created by someone I... used to love. Used to trust. Used to know, or so I thought.

What would a normal, sane person do in this situation? Well, I'm not normal, and my sanity is certainly in question at the moment.

I flip to a fresh page in the notebook and start a web search on Craig Taylor. Assuming I'll need to go to the police about this, it will look better if I have some verifiable information on the man.

He told me that his parents were long dead and that he didn't have any siblings. Is there anything else I could possibly use to search for him? He has such a common name – not helpful.

A football star, a police officer, a chef, a brain injury test subject, an award-winning glass blower, a ton of office workers and corporate types, a top-level computer coder, and a few semi-famous musicians. Nothing about him or his tech career. He's always said the company was top secret, but he's not even on any business networking sites.

Oh no... My fingers fly over the keyboard. I'm not even sure at first how to search the university site. Craig was very proud about going to Harvard. The only Craig Taylor with a connection to Harvard graduated in the sixties, so that's not him.

My back teeth start to grind on the left side.

I search Craig Roberts, with no meaningful results either. Of course, Becca could have kept her maiden name. Why wouldn't she? It's likely part of her spiritual identity. Her name aligns with her personal brand and intentions, or whatever.

I search for the name Craig through the five years of photos when he could have been there. None of those Craigs could be him.

My feet shuffle to the kitchen. I pick up Craig's university mug and stare at the Veritas shield that dates back to the 1600s.

Veritas. Latin for *Truth*.

He lied about going to Harvard. That detail was part of his entire identity.

That detail is also the final straw.

White porcelain smashes against the wall of the back hallway.

24

BECCA

Well, dammit. It took me nearly an hour to straighten my hair after being out in the rain. What kind of paranoid woman has such a wild security system in her tiny, stupid, out-of-the-way shop, even though she has a massive safe of a storage room inside?

Timid little Amy, I suppose.

I swear that woman must be afraid of her own shadow. To be fair, watching her schmooze the principals at that school event was impressive. They probably didn't notice her flushed throat and fluttering fingers like I did. If I were on camera, I'd say, "Oh, the poor little dear," and flash my most sympathetic smile.

Yet when it was just her and me having coffee, Amy seemed quite restrained. Focused.

Fluffing my hair at the makeup station in the lavish closet I had made out of a spare bedroom, I'm nearly ready to shoot more content. It'll be posted so quickly there's no way Amy could think I've been anywhere else today.

How could I not have seen the camera until I was leaving? It was intended to be a quick lockpick job. According to the online videos I've been studying, it was supposed to be a piece of cake. All I wanted was her client list. It should have been simple.

But once again, Amy complicates things.

It makes my skin crawl when people make me feel stupid.

One of these days, Craig will come to realize that he should be planning how to earn us more money. Use those three days a week productively rather than wasting his energy on some annoying leatherworker. We don't need her anymore.

I've sent him a wish list of the new camera and lighting equipment I need to elevate my kitchen shoots. Except in this case, it's not really a wish list. He knows that if he doesn't keep me in the gifts that I demand, he doesn't get to see our son.

Fair is fair. He needs to know that he's only good for one thing.

Adding lavish comfort to my life.

25

AMY

Pouring a fresh coffee into my mug covered with kittens wearing bow ties, I sit back at the laptop. This is like studying for an exam. I was always good at that.

Planning, preparation, looking for anything that could be improved. That's how my mind works when it has the space.

I choke back a laugh – the only person I could call who would be excellent at solving this puzzle would be Craig. Sipping my coffee, I think back to when Craig and I first met. I had just started my shop and was relatively settled in my life. Of course, I hoped to find a husband and have children someday, but it wasn't my main mission.

When Craig appeared, he seemed to fit absolutely everything I needed. He had his own life, which means I didn't have to change to suit him. He loved my house exactly the way it was, just wanting to add the garage for storage to clear out the basement, which seemed completely reasonable.

When I suggested that he contribute and make the space his own, he added a few tiny things that complemented each room perfectly. His main goal was to have a child as soon as possible. He was hoping for a son.

When I look at the situation with fresh eyes, I should have been more suspicious. Everything was far too perfect. He sidestepped right into my life and was exactly what I needed in every possible way.

Maybe it's my fault for not looking into the details. When you start dating someone, you don't think to check their driver's license to confirm their name.

Oh wow... The only time I've watched Craig sign his name was on our wedding registry. At the time, I thought the slight hesitation before he scrawled his last name was due to nerves. A shaky hand. Was it him reminding himself to sign Taylor, not something else?

I'm so accustomed to texting him whenever I have questions that my hand keeps jerking toward my phone. It's like I've been programmed.

Wait. Maybe there is someone I could text about one little detail.

> Hey – this is going to sound weird, but has Olivia been okay this weekend?

Since Megan, like all of the assistants, is practically glued to her phone, it's no surprise she responds within three minutes.

> Okay? Girl has gone off the deep end.

> What do you mean?

LOL! She lost one of her purses last week, and gave me the lovely task of replacing her phone and keys and everything. Then after all that, some dude emails – he found it and will return it to her in a few days.

Who is this dude?

Sorry – gotta jet. Literally. Off to Cancun. Being glared at to turn off the phone. TTYL.

Well, great. I'm pretty sure her purse wasn't lost. It was stolen.

I jump when my phone rings in my hand, then I'm instantly relieved when I see Penny's name on the screen.

"Hello?"

"Hi, Amy. How are you?"

I certainly can't tell her the truth. "Fine. And you?"

She sighs. "Just wanted to confirm – you don't need me at all this weekend, right? Not until Wednesday?"

"Right."

She exhales loudly. "Thanks. Sorry to bother you. I've been completely out of it the past few days. This... stomach flu or whatever it is, is knocking me right out. I've been so dizzy I forgot to write it down."

"No problem at all. Is there anything I can do? Bring you food, maybe?" I've driven Penny home several times when the weather's been bad. She lives alone in a tiny apartment a few minutes south. It's not a great neighborhood, and I wish I had the money to hire her a bit more just to help out.

"Thanks, Amy. That's kind of you. But I'm fine – when I'm able to eat, I've got plenty of soup and crackers."

"Okay. Call me if you need anything at all."

She hesitates, creating a long, awkward pause. "Um, thanks. I really appreciate it."

The second she disconnects, I sigh with relief. She didn't sound sick, to be honest.

Looking down at my feet, I realize that I'm pacing around the kitchen. Penny has always been bright and perky, but she's sounded subdued for the past few weeks.

Penny had that odd hesitation in her voice, like the time I came home to discover Asher had skinned his knee from running on the stone patio. As if she felt guilty. Frantic. She probably just feels bad for being sick for so long. She's always been healthy as a horse, and the only person I know besides myself who can keep up with Asher's endless questions.

She's a lovely girl. Although I wasn't entirely sure about hiring her. Luckily, Craig was home to help with the interviews, and he asked all the right questions. The first nanny we spoke with had a lot more experience.

But when Penny arrived, she pulled out a keychain and said that Asher should help her choose a name for the ladybug. They clicked immediately.

He grabbed her hand and wanted her to play blocks with him on the dining room floor. She sat down on the rug with him, not caring about her nice interview dress or that it may have seemed awkward for her to answer our questions while making a block tower.

She was just so sweet, and Craig said that spending time with her would help ensure that Asher is a sweet boy. He made a crack about all successful men needing more sweetness in their lives.

Craig said kids have better internal radar for top-quality people. I didn't doubt him for a second. Now I have to question my own internal radar, since he has photos of so many young ladies hidden in the garage.

Maybe I should return his calls, just so that he doesn't think there's something strange going on. The awkward pressure on my sternum doesn't want me to talk to him. I don't want him to worry about me, and I also don't want him to think that there's anything wrong.

Not to mention, I'm becoming paranoid. I can't think of any reason why Becca would have tried to break into my shop. She has many gorgeous handbags, and simple robbery doesn't feel like her style. Could she have been searching for information about my life with Craig? Or what he's up to in the garage?

I check the house cameras again. There's nothing on the camera at the back of the house, so he hasn't been in the garage, thank goodness.

The front camera shows a teenager dropping off sales flyers. I've seen him once a week for as long as I can remember.

Then there's someone else.

A tall, well-built man with a coat over his head comes up the driveway, looking around furtively. It looks like he's about to walk toward either the back door or the garage when he sees the cameras and runs off. I check the time to see that he arrived just five minutes after I left this morning.

It's not Craig, since I know the way he walks. This man is taller and thicker through the shoulders. Younger, maybe.

This person is definitely a stranger.

26

AMY

My dining room table has become a research station. I've printed out the clearest images from the stranger at my house, and of Becca at the back door of my shop, and stuck them on the wall in front of me with painter's tape.

Notes are beginning to cover the entire left side of the table, and my laptop, coffee mug and water glass are on the right.

I snort, realizing I might as well wheel in Craig's discovery board and use that. Although this is no laughing matter. Olivia might actually be in danger.

The doorbell rings, making me nearly jump out of my skin. I snap the laptop shut and grab the cardigan from the back of my chair to toss across my notes. Then I flip the curtains in front of the photos.

Peeking through the window, I feel my tense body sag as I see it's just Mom. I fling the door open, already expecting bad news. "Hey. What's up?"

"I didn't think you'd be home." She looks at me strangely. "I was going to just use my key."

"It's a good thing you didn't. I just changed the alarm code."

"Why? I thought you did that at the start of every year." Her brows are high, pupils are wide, as she looks me over carefully. Checking to see if something is seriously wrong is one of her constant habits. Mom has usually been able to see right through me, but now is not the time.

I shrug casually with a smile that I know always mellows her out. "The other day, I read one of those home safety articles. You know how jumpy I can get."

Her eyes roll theatrically. "Do I ever."

She always understands my need to put work first. Lying to her turns my stomach, but I don't have the energy to explain what's going on. "Everything is fine, but I'm in the middle of some important research for work. What is it that you needed?"

"Asher is asleep in the backseat. He was upset last night that he didn't have his green blanket."

"Sure. Hold on." I dash to Asher's bedroom, grab the blanket and one of his squishy fish stuffies.

By the time I get back downstairs, Mom is approaching the dining room table. "Sweetheart, it looks like you're as busy as when you were in school. What's all this?"

I wrap the fish in the blanket and hand it to her. "New trend report," I lie as smoothly as possible. "Lots of stuff going on that I have to get ahead of, because I think it's going to be pretty busy in a couple of weeks."

Mom smiles sympathetically. "Don't overwork yourself." A faraway look drifts through her eyes. Then her gaze meets mine. "Your father used to fixate on work projects. Don't go overboard." She looks at me pleadingly, her bottom lip pulling slightly to the side.

My blank stare and head toss imply I have no idea what she's talking about. But I remember. That's where I learned my focus. And plenty of important life lessons.

She hesitates. "Sometimes I worry that you're too much like your father."

I know that's a worry she's had for a long time. Nothing I can say will truly ease her concern. Usually, she says it more like a compliment, yet for some reason, this time it feels more like a warning.

"It's fine, Mom. I just focus when I have to during busy spells." Squeezing her arm lightly, I smile. "Thank you so much for taking Asher this weekend. I didn't realize it completely, but every now and then..."

She laughs. "I know. Trust me, I know. We love our children to bits, but sometimes we need a breather without the pitter-patter of tiny deafening feet."

"Exactly. Especially when I'm trying to focus."

Mom grins. "I'll get out of your hair before he wakes up and wants to see you."

"'Thank you."

As soon as she leaves, I lock the door and watch to make sure she drives all the way down the street.

I've always been a worrier. But Mom? Ten times as bad. Possibly more. She used to joke about having to worry about me enough for two now that Dad left.

I was only thirteen, so I didn't correct her. I'm pretty sure Dad wasn't afraid of anything. My anxiety began shortly after he left.

The dining room chair skids as I plop back down at the table. Then I get up and turn the house alarm on. I never do that when I'm home. Yet I can't help the prickling feeling of being watched.

I shouldn't feel so disturbed by a quick visit from my own mother. Dad was the suspicious, over-prepping type. Mom worries like a regular person. Well, a regular mother. I shouldn't feel offended that she's constantly concerned with her only child.

I flick the curtains open to stare at the photos again. Holy crap. Here I am with a discovery table to practically mirror Craig's discovery boards. Maybe we really do become like our spouses, like it or not.

Now that I realize the woman in the floppy hat is definitely Becca, I can make out a few more details. At least, I think I do. She looks irritated.

But the man? The video shows his casual gait as he strolls up to the house as if he were heading to the back door. Or... was he going straight to the garage?

I check the time of that snippet of video. It was taken just after I left the house this morning. Which was earlier than if I had left for work normally. Could Becca have sent him after the alarm went off, since she was the only person who knew I'd be rushing to work to check it out?

At this point, I wouldn't put anything past her. The woman is vicious.

Leaning in, I study the body language of the man in the video. He was completely relaxed.

Squinting at every possible detail, I find nothing noteworthy about him. I have to admit he has a great body, from what I can see in those nicely fitted jeans and the wide shoulders as he turns away with the coat over his head.

What's that?

I squint at the photo, zooming in as much as possible. His hand and wrist are visible as he holds the coat over his head. The guy is wearing one of those bright blue and red woven string friendship bracelets that you tie on and never take off again. The hippie boho trend that people buy at festivals. Not exactly what I would expect a burglar to be wearing, but what do I know?

That's it. I need more answers.

And those live in the place that now creeps me out the most.

Yet I'll have to go back.

27

AMY

I pull the charging cable from my phone, grab my notebook, and march back out to the garage. I don't care if Craig finds out I've been snooping. This is my property. My *home*. Whatever he has built on my land is now my business.

I shove the table and heavy box out of the way, then fit the puzzle pieces in place to pop open the door latch. Sliding the door open, I still can't believe that I'm staring at what can only be described as a murder board, especially now that I know Mia has been killed.

It takes a bit of finagling to slide the filing cabinet out of the hidden space. I try the drawer, which of course, is locked. Luckily, it's not high-quality metal. More like your average office filing system that's only designed to keep a few nosy coworkers out.

Before I have to decide whether to pick the lock or pry it open with a crowbar, I see the tiny gold key hanging on a high nail on the hidden wall. The drawer unlocks smoothly. My hands are fluttering as I pull out several thick folders. Using the long worktable, I begin to spread out the contents.

My blood turns to ice.

Each folder contains the contents of a previous discovery board, with a Polaroid neatly paper-clipped to the inside showing how that board had been arranged. I didn't even know Craig owned a Polaroid camera. But there it is, in the bottom drawer.

Clever of him to take all of these notes without leaving any digital trail. If it weren't about robbing wealthy young women, I'd almost be impressed.

So many photos of young girls in their early to mid-twenties, with that same classy look. Pampered. Fashionable. They all know how to pose just right for the camera. These pictures must have been printed from their social media pages.

My stomach lurches from the realization that the high-res color printer in our basement was obviously not a gift from one of Craig's clients, but a tool for his... whatever this is.

Each folder has initials written on the bottom of the Polaroid in Craig's tidy printing. But I know who each set of letters stands for. Echo Radcliffe. Leah Kline. Casey Lowell. Claire Morgan. Alexandra Coldwell. Piper Jones.

I know *all* of these women. They're my clients. Every single one.

And they all live within a three-hour drive of my shop.

I spin away, staring out the window at a nearby tree to try to ground myself with a hand clapped over my mouth so I don't retch.

Collapsing into a chair, I stare down at my feet to stop the dizzy spell. I especially remember the name Piper Jones. She's a new client who came in on Olivia Rhodes' recommendation just six months ago. Although Olivia was often unpredictable mood-wise, she really did send a ton of business my way.

As soon as I mentioned Piper to Craig, his eyes lit up. He said he would love the name Piper if we decided to go through with our plan to try for a girl next year.

That dream is definitely gone. Yet I still can't believe that he would have gone through with it. Juggling two families is hard enough. He wanted to add another baby into the mix?

It's absolute insanity. But then... so is making detailed planning boards that feature the lifestyle and habits of young women nearly half his age.

My phone lifts in my quivering hand. I should document the way I found them. Just as I hit the button to take a photo of the array of pictures and notes, a call comes in, and my shaky hand taps the button to answer it.

It's Craig.

Oh no. Are there cameras out here? Did I trigger something that notified him when I changed the house security codes?

What can I say to this.... *lunatic?*

"Hi."

"Hi, honey. How are you?" Craig sounds perfectly normal.

"Good. Yeah, pretty good. How's the tech hootenanny?" I've always teased him about his high-tech hoedowns. His rich laughter calms me down slightly.

"This one is only a shindig, actually. No banjos."

My laugh is forced, and I'm not sure if he notices.

"I was just thinking about you," he continues. "And how's my boy?"

That comment sends a wave of tension through my back. If it comes down to it, Asher is *mine*. There is no way that this man is holding any claim over my son. Even if he is technically the father.

"He's great." I smile hard, hoping that it comes through in my voice. "He's with Mom today. She's been teaching him to bake muffins."

He chuckles. "I bet he's very helpful, when he's not making a mess." His voice grows slightly quieter. "Is Penny still sick?"

"Yes. She'll hopefully be better for next week."

"Good." A pause. "Poor thing."

"Yeah. Well, I should keep working. Busy day."

Absolute silence.

I can hear Mr. Rueckert next door slide his patio door open to let the cat out.

"Really?" Craig continues. "I heard on the news that Barrett Street was shut down."

Dammit.

My reaction of instant sparkling laughter is designed to make him think nothing in the world is wrong. "Yes! Oh my goodness, I can't believe I forgot to mention it! I'm working at home, doing my seasonal research and cleaning out the database."

"Really? You normally don't do that from home..." He trails off. "Well, that's great that you're still productive without your sewing machines."

"Don't worry, I'm ahead of things, so it'll be fine. Have to keep Tuesdays free for our date day." My perky tone sounds a pinch unnatural, yet hopefully convincing.

Thank goodness he seems to buy it. "Okay then."

"Hey – if you're walking by one of those quarter slot machines, drop one in on my behalf, okay?"

There's just enough of a hesitation that makes me even

more certain he's not in Las Vegas. "Great idea. Sure. Talk to you soon, baby."

The second we're disconnected, my breath falls out in a huge whoosh. Note to self: Put my phone in airplane mode while creeping around a pile of potential murder boards.

It's getting late, and with the sun down, the garage is becoming chilly. I scoop up the folders, plus the ones from the bottom drawer. I don't want to touch the boards that are hung up in the secret space, so I just take photos on my phone. First one large photo of the entire thing, then close-ups so that the text can be zoomed in.

Just as I'm finishing with the second one, I lean in to take a couple of close-up shots of what looks like receipts in the corner.

Thwack.

I scream, leaping away from the noise at the side window. It's the black cat from next door, perched on the window ledge as he peers in at me.

The clatter in front of me happens in slow motion as the board bends from where my hand smacked it and crumples to the floor.

Oh no.

Not only have I messed with what could potentially be evidence, there's no fixing this. The paper is crumpled, and several photos are torn away. No matter what I do, Craig is going to know that I found his concealed stash.

The back of my jaw tightens. Fine. When I hand him over to the police, he'll definitely know that I know. Even though I'm not entirely sure what I know.

The question starting to tease at the edge of my brain is... is Craig dangerous? When he finds out that I know more than intended, is there any chance that he might come after me? He was clearly not planning for me to discover any of this. And he's obviously capable of... dark things.

It's out of my hands now. He's going to know, and I'm going to have to deal with it.

I leave the secret room wide open, although I point the board away from the small window a bit. I lock the garage before going inside and dumping everything on the end of the dining room table.

After I devour the last of the chicken fried rice, I go back to Becca's social media to see if she has any connections to any of these girls. Maybe they go to the same salon, or have friends in common or something.

An hour later, my brain feels like soup. This "momfluencer" crap is so strange. Becca's messages bounce back and forth, with no coherence.

"Good morning, friends! Want to be an earthy mama like me? Natural wooden toys are much better than plastic for so many reasons..."

"When it's cold and flu season, be sure to gather up all of your child's plastic toys for a bleach rinse..."

Everything contradicts something else she's said in the past month. And she's clearly not aware she's doing it.

Yet it's the bits of her life with Craig that hit me the hardest. There's a shot from just a few weeks ago where Becca is showing off the design she made on her husband's fancy latte. It's an organic leaf pattern that Craig taught me how to make just a few days later.

A photo from Becca's kitchen as she's stirring something, with a male hand reaching into the frame at the side. Wearing Craig's watch. That I helped him pick out.

My heart breaks over and over as I stare helplessly at the fragments of his life with another woman. His new Italian shoes in her foyer. His favorite pens in the mug in Becca's office.

I keep scrolling, making myself feel dirtier and creepier in the process. Just after New Year's, there are several photos of Becca's new vision boards.

My stomach tightens to the point where it's crowding my spine.

Right in the center of a hot pink bubble, three words are written in purple ink.

Baby Girl Piper

28

AMY

Something inside me snaps.

The last few shreds of hope that Craig isn't a monster are slashed away.

It's one thing to be stalking and robbing women. It's another to potentially be connected to a murder. It's another altogether to be planning to have two more daughters named Piper, with two wives.

Yes – it's insane that I'm more offended for myself than for others. Whatever. My brain is rattling.

No more pacing around this house, casually drinking coffee, and trying desperately to pretend I'm going to somehow magically make this all better. As if there is an answer to be found in all of this data.

Sitting back at the dining room table that has become my command center, I need to gather enough evidence to go to the police before I lose it entirely. This is what my life has come to. Turning in my own husband for suspicions of crimes. But also for being a two-timing piece of garbage that has lied to me for the past six years.

Part of my brain is still refusing to believe this is real. Craig couldn't be a stalker. He couldn't be stealing from these girls. But he could. He lied about Harvard, for goodness' sake.

I feel like such an idiot. I had no reason to double-check anything that he told me. Why would I? Everything seemed so reasonable. Whenever he talked about technical things and computers, he certainly sounded like he knew everything. He brought back trinkets from his trips.

Of course, now that I think about it, very few of them had a city or location name on them. I never saw a single receipt from any of these endless trips.

Just that one school photo sheet. All this time, and this was his first mistake, apparently.

My fingers tighten around the edge of the table. I was positive that Craig loves me. Nobody could fake the kind of love that we have. But he did. He's a liar. A conniving, plotting son of a bitch.

Stretching my hands like I always do before a workday at the sewing machines, I unlock my laptop and begin by searching online for the girls in the top round of folders. Two are reported missing. Two are assumed to be on an extended vacation in Europe. A few of the others aren't on social media consistently, so it's hard to tell.

Have the police connected these missing girls? I avoid most of the news that doesn't directly affect this city, so I might be out of the loop. These particular young women seem to be flitting around the world all the time. They disappear for a weekend dance party in Ibiza. Or hit the latest fashion shows in Paris. Most of them post every detail of their lives on social media, yet sometimes it's not until weeks or months later.

One of the girls is assumed to have taken off with her boyfriend to who knows where, so it doesn't look like they searched very hard. Another disappeared just a few weeks ago and is assumed to be traveling. Her parents have been posting notices for people to get in touch if they've heard from her because they're starting to get worried.

No contact from your daughter in a month? Geez, I'd be more than worried. Yet these young people cavort all over the globe at a moment's notice. If the families aren't super-close, is it normal to go weeks or months without being in touch?

Two of the girls have been gone for over two months, and their families have been hitting the media outlets hard for the past few weeks with an array of photos and promises of huge rewards for any information on their daughters.

My fingers tap nervously on the keyboard. At least two or three of these girls in these files are... *gone*.

I can't even think about whether they're... *worse than robbed*.

A jolt runs through me as I stare at the photo on the wall of Becca in her floppy hat. She seemed shocked when I mentioned that Craig had a garage built here. He also spends time at her house. What if he has another garage? Other files? Even more...

Even more girls that he's stalking. Or maybe worse.

Please, please, please don't let it be worse.

My breathing nearly stops as I open an incognito window on my browser and start a search for the traits and habits of serial killers.

Several minutes later, my eyes are dry from not blinking enough. At first glance, Craig fits the most basic profile. Male, Caucasian, twenty-five to forty-five. Check.

The deeper I go, the more I start to feel unhinged. Superficial charm? Absolutely – Craig lights up a room, and is everyone's favorite customer or appointment. When he occasionally comes with me to drop off Asher at junior kindergarten, the other moms and teachers all crowd around him. He manages to get perks and discounts wherever we shop just because the staff want him to like them.

Intelligent? He's the only person I know who does crossword puzzles in ink, and does them row by row without having to jump around to the topics he knows best. There is no game or mental challenge that can stump him, as far as I've ever seen.

Lack of empathy, especially regarding the weak, such as small animals? Staring into space for a moment, I try to think of any fitting examples.

When our neighbor told us that her dog passed away, Craig made all the correct expressions of sympathy and patted her shoulder, telling her to let us know if there's anything at all we could do. Then we turned back toward our house, and his face cleared completely. It was as if he flipped a switch from empathetic to neutral. The second we were out of earshot, he muttered, "Glad we won't have to listen to that barking anymore in the middle of the night."

At the time, I chalked it up to him claiming to be underslept for several weeks.

These websites say that serial killers are manipulators. I hate to admit that it's clearly true. Craig always got what he wanted. Like talking me into building that garage when I wasn't sure. And convincing me that a destination wedding with just us would be more charming than a huge wedding here.

He was right. Hawaii was absolutely magical. Yet now I

realize it was so that our wedding couldn't be talked about by anyone in the community who could possibly know about him and Becca.

I don't have any evidence of Craig being cruel to animals, being antisocial, or asserting his power... Likely because he was always preoccupied with playing the role of being the perfect sweet husband for me.

Wait. Carefully thinking back to a few times when I was not clear-headed, a few details surface.

Two days after our wedding in Hawaii, I got incredibly tipsy over afternoon fruity drinks. Craig had left me at the table with water and a plate of fresh fruit, and I partially overheard as he berated the bartender for over-serving me and demanded some free sports drinks and espresso immediately to help me sober up.

At the time, I'd had way too much sun and excitement for the weekend, and thought it was sweet that my husband was overprotective. Looking back, was he actually a cruel jerk to the poor bartender?

A few other incidents surface. Craig being demanding with a server when he thought I couldn't hear. Assuming that we'd get special perks whenever we stayed in a hotel. Expecting special treatment, when I couldn't imagine why he thought we were special.

When Fiona and I are devouring true crime shows, there is always a collection of something. Craig's puzzle collection likely doesn't qualify.

I flip to a new website detailing the habits of serial killers. They go on about how they usually keep a token of every kill. A trophy. Some personal connection to the deceased that they can treasure forever.

I certainly haven't seen a row of shoes, or body parts,

especially hair clippings. Or heads. *Ugh.* That's one of the most popular. Driver's licenses. Class rings. Underwear.

A loud squeak fills the room as I shove my chair away from the table. It feels like a band is tightening around my forehead, like an oncoming air pressure headache.

Every folder in front of me is a collection of notes and photos. It's a bunch of objects that he's spent time with while he... I can barely think it.

Are these really murder boards? And are they trophies of the murders of innocent young women?

Is my husband truly a serial killer?

29

BECCA

There is something definitely wrong with Craig.

I'm lying on my yoga mat with a dozen other Lycra-clad ladies. We're supposed to breathe deeply and ground ourselves. Yeah, I've never been able to do that, no matter what the sayings in my online shop say.

This is the time when I try to clear my head of any tangled thoughts and think of solutions. Like why I'm worried that my husband might become disobedient.

I've noticed that over the past two months, he's been acting extra-sketchy. Even for him. Since he's definitely a weirdo, it's sometimes a bit of a gray area. Yet I feel that something is off.

He's been cagey lately, and extra-careful to lock his phone when he's around me. As if I care one whit about his little love texts with his other wife. Honestly, I'm simply grateful that she fulfills his need for a semi-normal relationship.

He couldn't be up to something, could he? Craig is supposed to be busy earning us money in the careful, methodical way we agreed to. Other than that, he is supposed to keep himself busy and quiet, with his reading, his research, and his puzzles.

Maybe I need to buy him more crossword books. In another language, to really challenge him.

My limbs slowly relax as I finally settle into a slow, rhythmic breathing pattern. I need a good class today so that I can shake off the nasty vibes that Amy has brought into my life.

That mousy woman has served her purpose, more or less. I'll have to find some way to start preventing Craig from seeing her as often. Make his business trips run longer. Or relocate him. Anything to force a wedge between them.

Admittedly, it's not very zen of me to be plotting the unravelling of a relationship while in the midst of a yoga class. But where better to contemplate ways to increase my level of calm?

And that Amy woman definitely disturbs my calm.

30

AMY

My foot pushes the gas pedal a bit too hard. I've never gone over the limit in my life, but I'm in a ferocious hurry.

After a twenty-minute nap to reset my brain, I refreshed all of Becca's social pages. She just posted ten minutes ago that it's time for her weekly yoga class. This is my chance to check out her house.

More importantly, her garage. If I'm extremely lucky.

Since I happen to know the precise St. Mary's school borders, that narrowed my search. It was just a matter of collecting all of her outdoor photos and finding some land-marks. The church spire a few blocks from her backyard got me to the right street. Google Maps Street View did the rest.

My so-called husband isn't the only one who can solve a puzzle when it's down to the wire.

I continually ignore the soft beep that tells me he's sent another text. Reading them might make me emotional, and I do not have the time or the mental bandwidth for that. I'm already pretty fragile. Plus, I've zoned out at the computer a few times in an awkward position, and now my stiff neck is aching.

Knowing that I might finally get some real information makes my right foot press harder. I flip on the radio out of habit as I drive.

"You're listening to Lakeville WBLW — news highlights all day long. Police are wary of sharing any further news about the string of robberies of young wealthy women in the tri-state area. There is some speculation that the attacks have been in a cloverleaf pattern, within several hours' drive of each other, yet they will not yet reveal the epicenter of this disturbing pattern. Barrett Street, a main shopping artery, will continue to be completely out of commission for several more days as crews repair a nasty broken water main. But first, Chad fills us in on tomorrow's chance of early rain, wind, and possibly hail before a gorgeous evening. That's bad news for the poor workmen at the Barrett Street repair fiasco. Over to you, Chad."

My shaking hand snaps it off. Screw the weather. Knowing that the robberies probably involve the women spread across my dining room table is like a punch to the gut. There's a constant chant in the back of my mind... *Please let me find out what Craig is really doing, and stop him. Please let me find Olivia in time to stop her from being hurt. And all of the girls that it's not too late for.*

I knew from the photos that Becca's house would be impressive, but... that's not completely correct. It's nice enough, and fairly large. Very classic. Yet it's wedged in between a group of row houses and a mini-mall. Somehow, she manages to make it seem like she lives on a grand country estate.

Sure, it's kind of misleading. I already know she's a sneak

and a liar. But I have to admit the woman knows how to work the lighting and angles at all times.

I park in the driveway behind a battered old Jeep that's right in front of the garage. It's not even a surprise that the building is the same size, and same pale gray-blue siding as the garage Craig had built at my house. Once he finds something he likes, he sticks with it.

Except for wives, apparently.

I take a few steps toward the front door, then hear voices in the backyard. My shoulders roll back. My spine lengthens. Even though I wore flat boots, I roll forward on the balls of my feet slightly as if I were in heels. Since I don't know what I'm walking into, I need to be prepared to play any character at all.

"It's okay, Asher. Your hands can get as dirty as you like in the sandbox, remember?"

The backyard is filled with overflowing rose bushes around Becca's "meditation bench" that faces the dawn. Yes, I've been studying her profiles a bit too much.

Her son is playing in a sandbox, digging deep trenches with a variety of spoons and spatulas. My throat almost locks up. My son does the exact same thing. The similarity between the two boys is uncanny. He even holds the spoon the same way, like he's attacking the sand.

Beside him is a man in his mid- to late-twenties, who stands up and flashes me a warm smile. "Hey, how are ya?"

Wow. He is seriously attractive. Large, warm brown eyes lock on mine until I'm forced to break the hold. My gaze traces his height, his wide frame with impressive shoulders, then locks on the red and blue woven string bracelet around his wrist.

The hippie boho kind that you never take off.

It's him.

Hold it together, girl. "Awesome, thanks. How are you?"

He nods. "Enjoying the day. What can I do for you?"

My voice automatically rises in pitch. "Is Ms. Roberts in? I'm from Avenue PR."

His face falls slightly. "She just left for yoga. Did she know you have an appointment?"

I check my phone, then my fingers flutter over my mouth. "Oh, my goodness! I have the wrong date!" I stare up at him with wide eyes. "Please don't tell Ms. Roberts – she'll think I'm totally unprofessional."

He comes closer to shake my hand. "I'm Jackson. The nanny."

I'll bet he is.

"Catherine York." The lie spills out so fast, likely due to my surging adrenaline. "I'm sorry to disturb you. I was so focused on getting here at the right time that I didn't triple-check the date. You won't tell her, will you? I know that she's big on perfection."

His gorgeous brown eyes flip toward the huge back window of the house. "Yes, she is."

I lean in to murmur, "That's why she's a one-woman show – she's insistent on doing absolutely everything herself, right?"

Jackson breaks into a beautiful laugh while nodding, but doesn't say anything.

I pretend to scratch the side of my face to hide my mouth while whispering, "Cameras?"

He smiles and murmurs while barely moving his lips, "It's all about the content."

I stifle a snicker, simply smiling politely. "Gotcha."

I can see why Becca chose this guy to be her son's nanny.

He's the size of a bodyguard. He's also the kind of guy who would photograph really well for social media. Why doesn't she have him on her channels? He'd definitely be a selling point.

Even though he's a creep who was skulking around my house. Although to be fair, Becca could have told him any number of lies, and he'd likely do her bidding.

Before I can make up an excuse to look around, his phone rings. He holds up a finger and gives me a wink. "Hi, Becca." He freezes, his tanned face paling slightly. "Of course. I took it out of the basement freezer an hour ago." There's a pause. "Yeah, absolutely."

He hangs up and looks at me in desperation. "I'm so sorry to ask, but can you just stand here and make sure Asher doesn't run off for like five minutes?"

"Absolutely."

He tears off into the house, leaving me with my son's doppelganger.

And less than five minutes to unearth the evidence I need.

31

AMY

I guess since I'm supposedly a PR person, and there are cameras everywhere out here, I'm no threat. Especially since Asher is completely engrossed in his tunnels. The poor kid is likely used to all sorts of strangers and photo shoots and who knows what in this place. It seems like more of a showpiece and set than a real home.

He smiles up at me once as if to acknowledge my presence, then goes back to his work, digging into the sand to deepen every line. I stroll straight to the garage as if admiring the garden.

I don't see any cameras around this corner, and thanks to Dad's paranoid "life lessons", it takes me barely fifteen seconds to pick the lock with the long, industrial safety pin I keep in my purse. Now that I know the puzzle, since of course Craig used the same one at my house, it only takes seconds to release the hidden door.

There's no time to examine anything, so I just take photos. The whiteboard. The other side of the whiteboard.

Another gold key is hanging over the filing cabinet, so I open the top drawer.

Glancing outside, I can see Asher is still digging.

It's been about two minutes. I take photos of as much as I can, trying to keep the phone steady as I flip as quickly as possible. I don't have time to get it all. There's no excuse that could justify me being in the garage at all, much less inside a secret compartment.

For some odd reason, I don't want Jackson or Becca to know about this place if they don't already. That's not out of some loyalty to Craig. It's more like I don't want them in my way.

Could they both be in on whatever he's doing? Becca had a strange reaction when I mentioned that Craig built a garage at my house. She definitely has the temperament for intense reactions. Somehow I feel that Jackson wouldn't, yet I don't know if I can trust my gut on reading people anymore since I've obviously been so terribly wrong about Craig.

Flipping and clicking, I barely see what's on the pages, just that there's a ton of information, and many different colors of ink and glued-on paper on each discovery board.

I force myself to stop when it's been three and a half minutes since Jackson left. I put everything back in place and get the heck out of there. I'm out of breath, and a hand at the base of my throat confirms that I'm slightly flushed. By the time he comes strolling back, I'm crouched by the sand tunnel system, pointing at the far corner.

"What's this?" I ask Asher.

"The waterfall goes there when Jackson gets the hose."

"I see. Are there boats for the canals?"

He grins, nodding as he proudly lifts some paper sculptures. "We made them already."

"Cool. You're a great worker."

His smile fills me with mixed emotions. Such a bright, interesting boy. Yet he's being raised by a woman who can easily be identified as a narcissist with control issues.

"Thanks," Jackson says, nervously running a hand through his thick, floppy brown hair while looking like a movie star. "I forgot to take the chicken out to thaw. It's soaking now, so I think dinner is saved."

"No worries. Thanks for keeping my secret." I stand and hold up my hands. "I wasn't here. I'll quadruple-check next time."

"Hey, I think she's mostly free tomorrow if you want to try for then. Just email her in a few hours."

"Thanks, I appreciate it."

With a wave to them both, I head back to my car. The last person I want to see right now is Becca, but it's sweet that Jackson wants to help out a stranger. There's something genuinely good-hearted about him. I'd bet he's a great nanny.

I can't help but want the best for the other Asher, since he's so much like my own son.

I'm nearly home when it hits me that not everything was identical in the other garage. The hidden door, the whiteboard, the filing system, the key – everything was the same. But not the boards themselves.

The ones at my house were all in black ink. Craig's printing. There were some pale yellow sticky notes, and a few things torn from a cream legal pad that he always has handy.

The ones from Becca's garage had much more color, but I didn't have time to really look.

As soon as I pull into my driveway, I grab my phone and zoom in on the photo of the hidden whiteboard. There are notes in a handwriting that is definitely not Craig's. Very feminine handwriting, in purple ink.

Like all of Becca's vision boards.

32

AMY

The second I get back inside my house, I put on fresh coffee, then return to the "inspiration nook" on Becca's main website. She goes on at length about purple being the color of mystery and magic, so it's the best ink to use for affirmations and intentions.

I transfer the photos to my laptop to open them on a full-sized screen. The new boards have a lot more of Becca's handwriting than Craig's. Which means that she was fully involved with a lot of the planning. Each one features another beautiful girl in her early twenties who apparently comes from family money.

Becca has helpfully pointed out the restaurants and salons that the women post about on their social media. A list of their assets, especially fashionable things that have been clearly displayed recently on their social media. Things that would be easily resold.

Which means that Becca is helping to stalk them and...

A shiver runs through me. I hate not knowing what actually happens to them. I'll definitely hate it when I find out for certain.

It seems like they are either being robbed or about to be robbed. Yet why wouldn't the women be reporting this?

All of the names are familiar. Every single one.

Running the names through my database, I find they're all clients who have been coming to my shop for a year or much longer. Many of them were referred by their mothers. It makes sense, since older women tend to be interested in repairing nice things instead of just replacing them immediately.

Families who originally came over on the Mayflower are less interested in fast fashion. They place more importance on timeless elegance. Including the top-of-the-line leather handbags that get passed down from generation to generation. Handbags usually filled with expensive phones, car keys, and credit cards attached to Daddy's money.

Some of the women on these new "Becca Boards" have stopped posting on social media over the past weeks, or even several months. Two are reported missing, but again, it sounds more like they could have taken off traveling. A few of them have gaps in their posting. As if they went on a holiday and came back quieter and more subdued. Definitely not bragging about all of their designer things as much.

Becca's notes include more personal details, such as who might be feeling vulnerable after their best friend had a huge success. Or who recently broke up with a boyfriend and will be an easy target.

Damn, Becca is cold-blooded. And wily. Conniving. *"Her best friend just won a bikini contest at their club, so she'll be going to the gym three times as much over the next month!"*

I'm pretty sure that my gut knew before my exhausted brain caught up. Of course Becca has something to do with these disappearing girls, not just Craig.

The tiny fragment of my mind that is still desperately in love with Craig wants to blame her completely. There's no way that's the truth. Craig has lied and snuck around far too much to be guilt-free.

I mean, once a man is busted with two wives and nearly identical sons, I know I need to chuck all hope for him out the window.

And yet...Why aren't the women reporting him? I listen to enough of the news that if there were a series of robberies, I'd hear about it.

Craig would be hard to describe to the police. He looks like... well, he has the bright eyes and engaging charm of a newscaster, but he's slightly more attractive. As if a top Hollywood actor were playing an anchorman. He has no distinguishing features beyond tall, dark and handsome. Which makes him sound bland on paper. When he's standing in front of you, it's much different.

I can't explain that to the police. I'll have to stick to the facts. Which are, what, exactly? A bunch of women are being targeted... for something. Probably robbery. Possibly worse, yet I just don't know.

My thoughts are tangling in circles. My brain needs to recalibrate.

I need fresh air. And a task that isn't this pile of information.

Moments later, I'm on my knees in the front garden, pulling weeds with a viciousness that these little green trespassers really don't deserve. Some people hit a punching bag or run around the block to burn off steam. I calm down by tearing the crap out of ugly plants that invade my territory.

"Amy!"

I startle, looking up to the chirpy voice above me. "Hey, Fiona."

"What are you doing?" She stares at the pile of weeds beside me. "It's been raining off and on all weekend. You must be chilled right through."

The rain stopped an hour ago. Thick, dark clouds lurk on the horizon, ready to pick their moment. I'm reminded of the time years ago when Fiona and I considered going camping, checked the weather, then spent the long weekend holed up in a hotel watching movies and drinking cheap wine instead of being soaked in a dank tent. Suddenly, I feel like a bad friend. My instinct should be to ask for help, not push her away right now. Yet I still feel secretive about everything until I've formed my own opinions.

"I just needed some air after I got home from work. Breathing in the dampness really clears your head, right?"

Fiona smooths down her emerald green tracksuit. Today she's wearing dangling silver earrings to go with her lucky necklace, and her hair is up in a huge floral clip that is rather garish, to be honest. "I guess." She looks at the shrub in front of me and laughs.

"What is it?"

"I'll have to send you the link. I was listening to a podcast yesterday about a guy who killed his boss so that he could take over the company. His wife was completely redoing their backyard, so he pitched the dude under the bushes just before the area was backfilled."

"And he was caught?"

"Of course! His wife found the dude's wedding ring... still attached to what was left of the finger."

A shiver runs through me from the disturbing image. Fiona has always found gore to be amusing, while I flinch away. "Charming." I brush off my soggy knees while standing up. "Did he stop at one guy or did he become a serial killer?"

She seems delighted, grinning ear to ear. "Just the one! Which is weird. Since it went so easily, I expected them to go on about all of the other killings." Her eyes narrow. "Sounds like the boss truly deserved it though. You know that makes it okay."

Fiona and I have always had very different opinions on whether murder was acceptable. She's always argued that if someone was truly evil, that was... well, not socially acceptable. But morally understandable. The few times we've discussed it, she's been very clear on her stance.

I, of course, refuse to answer one way or the other. It's not the kind of thing I've ever wanted to delve into. Quite frankly, it's icky to think about.

"There was another one about a really weird serial killer," she continues, following me as I gather the weeds and toss them into the composter at the side of the house. "His trophies were business cards."

Brushing my gloves off on each other, I turn to stare. "He kept the business cards of his victims? Didn't that make it ridiculously easy to catch him?"

She laughs. "No, the opposite! He had an old-school..." Her hand waves in a tight circle. "You know, one of those spinning desk things that holds all of the business cards. One section was real contacts, and the other was over twenty victims. Right there in the open!"

Fiona looks around at the state of the garden. "If you have an extra pair of gloves, I could help for a bit."

Once again, I feel guilty for brushing her off so much. Honestly, I miss the days when we had all the time in the world and I would drop by her house now and then. Even though my life is now completely different, a movie marathon for old time's sake might be a good idea on any other weekend.

An alarm goes off on her phone, and she frowns at the screen. "Sorry. Rain check. My delivery is coming early. I have twenty minutes to get home so that nobody steals the parcel from my porch. Wish me luck."

"Good luck!" I call out as she walks away at full speed, creating an emerald blur up the street.

I go into the house, locking the door carefully. Then I scrub my hands and look around.

Well. This is just lovely.

Of all the things I thought I might be doing this weekend, I would never have picked "search my home and garage for my husband's serial killer trophies".

33

AMY

I've given up staring at the laptop and started pacing instead. How has my life become so deranged? I just wanted to work and rest all weekend.

Even though I didn't have very much time to search the secret room in Becca's garage, it was just files and the boards. No bags of hair, severed pinky fingers, or whatever serial killers keep as trophies. I'm still caught up wondering whether the boards themselves could even count as trophies.

If they are, I need to go to the police. If not, I'll look like a psycho. Since there is so much potential evidence on my property, I need to know what I'm walking into before that happens.

It's time to do an official gut check. I need to know if these files and boards are actually murder trophies. My gut says to consult with some sort of expert.

If this all turns out to be a giant mistake, as unlikely as that is at this point, I don't want to be found out. *Hi, honey. Sorry about taking all of this evidence to the police, but at least I checked everything out thoroughly, right?*

Not that Craig will ever be my honey again.

There's only one thing I can think of. Officially falling into internet search quicksand.

An hour later, I feel absolutely numb. I'm now one of the weirdos with conspiracy theory-level suspicions about my husband. Fabulous. I drain my water glass, then click on the last link on my list.

"The Truest of True Crimes" is a long-running video podcast where experts discuss both solved and unsolved mysteries, and take viewer questions. The show is highly respected – the host, Brad Gilbert, has published two books and is used as an expert on news programs.

Fiona is the only person I know who is also into true crime, and she *hates* this podcast. She says Brad looks too much like her ex. I had to listen to her go on about it for an hour the one time I mentioned something from an old episode. Meanwhile, I'd been trying to get to the grocery store before it closed. Her little unexpected drop-in has ruined my entire night.

Apparently, I married someone who is into true crime from the other side. Maybe. I can't think about that right now.

I find Brad's video on serial killer trophies, and skim past the flashy intro and dramatic music. He thanks his special guest, forensics expert Dr. Fred Barrera, for answering questions.

"Let's jump right into it," Brad says, with the cheery atti- ·
tude of a game show host. "Mary has a question about serial killer trophies."

Dr. Fred nods, leaning in eagerly. I check his credentials – he's actually well known in his field as well. He's probably just doing this podcast as a lark. "What's the question?"

Brad holds up his tablet to read. "Most serial killers keep a personal trophy from their victims. I'm wondering if it counts as a trophy if they keep something that's not actually taken from the victims themselves."

"Does she have anything specific in mind?" Fred asks.

Brad skims further down the message. "You know those discovery boards they use on police shows with all the photos and notes connecting everything? To help them brainstorm?" He laughs. "I think she means murder boards."

Dr. Fred laughs with him. "Would a serial killer keep the board, and the planning tools and photos, as their trophy?"

Brad laughs louder. "Maybe if they were stupid."

Fred nods toward the camera as if he's concentrating, his head tipping from side to side, then steeples his fingers, leaning in. "That's an excellent question, Mary. If the brainstorming board and photos were the focus of their planning, that could be extremely personal to the killer."

"Really?" Brad asks. "Even though the victim has never seen or touched the board?"

"Absolutely." Fred's eyes light up as if he's fascinated by the thought. "The murderer has spent hours with that board. Possibly weeks or months. Some serial killers get high from the planning. The stalking is part of their fetish as much as the murder itself. Who knows how long they spent with the actual victim? A few hours? Maybe days? So the board itself truly could be their trophy."

Brad nods. "Huh. Yeah, I guess I could see that."

Fred smiles warmly. "I appreciate the question. Everything on that board was taken from the victim by the killer – photos and surveillance details, all recorded in secret. For what it's worth, yes, I definitely think that the murder planning board could be a trophy as much as a lock of hair or the murder weapon itself."

"Cool." Brad nods along. "Thanks for your question, Mary. Up next we have Jason, who wants to know if his cousin's best friend's collection of antique dolls..."

I turn off the video and roll my shoulders back. Now I have to face everything in a new light. I sigh, standing up as I trudge upstairs toward the shower. I have more than enough information to take to the police first thing in the morning.

First I have to sleep on it. Not just to make my final decision, but to make sure I'm clear-headed when I tell a total stranger in a crisp uniform that my husband not only has two wives and a son who is a doppelgänger to mine, but he's stalking, robbing and-slash-or possibly killing a string of wealthy young women. And I'm not sure whether he's doing this alone or with the help of his other wife.

I know that I'm just delaying the inevitable. I'm also taking care of myself and getting all of my mental ducks in a row so that I can attempt to stay calm in a freakishly creepy situation.

Prickles of awkward tension run along my shoulders. I'm trapped. There are no good choices to make. Only bad, and worse.

Yet the right decision is already made. It's the only one I've got.

And I need to hurry, since according to the unbelievably damning board discovered on my property, Olivia might be kidnapped sometime Monday.

Of course, I don't want her to be hurt.

More importantly, I don't want Craig to get away with it.

34

CRAIG

Diners are always the perfect place to be anonymous. I often end up at high-end restaurants while researching a project, yet the food is often not my style. The black and white linoleum floors, cream Formica tables, and blue-clad servers flitting by – it's the same in so many places.

Which means I can disappear and be myself for an hour or two.

Digging into a huge barbecue burger, I'm accustomed to a deep satisfaction rolling through me at moments like this. I don't often relax completely, but I've earned a little quiet time.

This time it doesn't work. I'm deeply upset. Which is not normal.

Other people have complained of feeling heavy when they're emotionally distraught. Is that why it feels like a metal weightlifting plate is balanced on my chest?

Amy hasn't replied to any more of my texts. That is not like her. I mean, she doesn't have a lot of friends or family, and I'm her only husband. We've been close since the beginning.

I worry about her all the time, but especially when I'm farther away than usual and can't keep a close eye on her. I've been driving so much that it's easy to zone out. Sometimes I get so lost in my thoughts that I barely hear the GPS telling me I'm about to miss an exit.

That's one of the reasons I adore Amy. She's self-sufficient and doesn't require a ton of attention beyond our three days a week.

One of the main things I cherish about her is that she gave me a second son. One child simply isn't enough, especially when I'm not sure how he's going to turn out. Redundancy is important in life. Important computer systems require backup power. Houses require a good roof, plus good insurance. There are brakes, and emergency brakes.

I've always known that I must have at least two children before I turned thirty-five. It was close, but I did it. Now I just need a few more to feel complete.

Especially since I'm not sure whether one of my sons will turn out very well. Having a camera shoved in your face at all times isn't really the way to raise an upstanding citizen. A future leader. Or successful... whatever he ends up being.

Reaching down, I sip my coffee. At both of my homes, I'm particular about my morning espresso, yet diner coffee is somewhat comforting no matter how good or bad it is.

"Top you up, sugar?" The cute waitress is smiling brightly, showing off her glossy pink lipstick as her long blonde ponytail swings behind her.

I nod. "Yes, thank you."

She leans in to pour my coffee, nearly giving me a peek straight down the front of her pale blue uniform dress. Her luscious bottom lip pushes out as my head turns to the window instead of ogling her.

It's not that I'm married. I don't want her to remember me.

I wait until she's sashayed several feet away before checking out her ass. Definitely early twenties with a perfectly tight peachy behind like that. There's just no sense wasting any energy on a woman who can't do anything important for me. Even if she does have sexy child-ready hips.

I hate to think that Asher Taylor might have a much better chance of developing into a quality human being than Asher Roberts. The whole nature vs. nurture debate – scientists should be studying the differences between my two boys.

I love watching Amy mothering my son. She's such a natural. So warm and loving. She's teaching our boy kindness and balance.

My fry stabs listlessly into a puddle of ketchup. I hate that Amy seems stressed. She's likely upset about her shop being closed because of the water main situation. I heard it on the news in the gas station, which was a total fluke. I never listen to anything while I'm driving, even though it's sometimes for a full day. My attention is already split between the road and problem-solving.

But why didn't she text me that the street is closed down? We always share news immediately, even if the other person can't respond right away.

I don't really get angry... I suppose I'm *irritated* that she didn't call me. I'm her man. The most important person in her life besides our Asher. She has always come to me first.

The thought of anything coming between us makes my

stomach turn. I'm barely halfway through the burger, yet my stomach feels too knotted up to handle much more. Chewing very slowly seems calming, though.

My sweet little forest pixie is probably rattled from worrying about her precious store. She's put her heart and soul into her business, and I have to admit, I'm incredibly proud of her.

I'll have to bring her something special from this trip. Where was I supposed to be this time? Oh, right, a conference in Las Vegas. I'll find her a glittery trinket supposedly from a tourist shop, then something nice like one of those floral silk scarves she sometimes ties on her purses.

Lilies are Amy's favorite. Becca detests them. Keeping all of their preferences straight is one of my fascinating mental challenges.

Becca always gets mad when I spend more than the bare minimum on Amy, but I can't help it. I genuinely love her, but I also really like her. She's so much more easygoing than Becca. Living with her is relaxing. I can almost be myself. Not that I'd know what that even means anymore.

Looking around the restaurant, I note nobody is looking into this slightly dimmed corner. Good. It's crucial that I never draw attention to myself.

I never speed, never break a traffic law. My mid-sized gray car is so boring that it nearly blends into the asphalt. It's almost like hiding in plain sight. Like everything I wear, how I have my hair cut, and the way I speak.

I'm medium in every way. Unnoticeable until I turn on my charm, light up my eyes, and talk women into... whatever I need them for. Well, most of them. Obviously not Becca.

Part of me is still offended that she only wanted me to give her one son. She was delighted that it only took two tries, and now she's done with me until the timing is perfect to try for a daughter.

It's crystal clear that Becca loves having me as her minion. Yet she's given me stability, so I owe her. Besides, it's good for me to have clear missions. Purpose.

I often wonder what things would be like if I'd met Amy first. My life would be incredibly different. A lot of lives would be different, actually. This is one of the things I'm not allowed to fixate on. It's what a string of therapists have all called "an unproductive use of mental resources".

After a few more halfhearted bites, I wave for the check. Once I'm back on the road, I should be able to shake off this melancholy, which is not productive.

I've always loved driving. It's one of my favorite parts of this enterprise. It clears the mind. Apparently, "ruminating" can lead one down negative thought spirals and makes us too susceptible to base urges, *blah blah blah*.

The only therapy I need now is having a problem to solve that serves a purpose. Forward motion and the fulfillment of goals. That's the key to happiness.

Even when I truly miss my sweet second wife.

Part of me wants to chuck the plan and come home early just to be with her.

Yet once I've put a plan into action, I can't stop. Not for anything.

35

AMY

SUNDAY

·

Staring into my closet, I'm at a total loss.

What on earth do I wear to march into a police station and dump a mountain of evidence on them, accusing my own husband? I don't think cops will be impressed or take me seriously just from the look of my antique Lola Q's of London handbag.

And how will I explain that this was happening right under my nose?

Hello, Officers. I'm still not positive, but could you look into this before Olivia Rhodes goes missing sometime soon? Oh, and yeah – I have a clear tie to Olivia, but my husband (the legality of that title being questionable since I'm his second concurrent wife) has no tie to her whatsoever. But he's probably the potential robber and possible kidnapper, not me. Thanks, and have a nice day.

This is not going to go well, no matter what I do. Slumping onto the bed, I don't know how I'm going to go through with this. Of course, I have to. It's the right thing to do, and I always pride myself on doing what's right.

No matter that it feels like betrayal to turn in my husband. The back of my mind is making up all sorts of logical explanations about how calling the police is always the last resort.

I need to do what's right. If Olivia is hurt, that will be on my shaking hands. Not to mention, all of the other girls from here on.

Curling up into a ball on the bed where I used to make love with the man I was crazy about, I finally let the tears take over. The sobs rock my shoulders, and my lungs compress until air feels like acid.

We wanted a baby girl. Asher would have been such an amazing big brother to little Piper. Or a wonderful big brother to another boy. They could make terrible messes in the backyard, and I couldn't be angry because I'd be laughing at the mud on their sweet smiling faces.

I've been excited about our future plans to visit Europe, and to plant a vegetable garden and put in a full wall of bookshelves across the living room.

This all seems completely trivial now. Tiny goals and minuscule dreams. But it was all I had. Work hard, have a nice family. It was enough. I've only ever wanted enough.

Now everything is gone, and I feel utterly wretched for crying about it because people's lives are at stake if I don't get this information to the police.

Sitting up, I take one deep breath, then go to the bathroom to splash cold water on my face. I need to hurry. Who knows how long it might take for them to make sure I'm not nuts, assign people to the case, get search warrants, and whatever other procedures have to line up before they find her?

Meanwhile, Craig might get to her first.

Dammit. That bothers me. No. It *angers* me. My entire body feels overheated as I pat my face dry and tie my hair up.

Rage gives me the momentum to get ready. Craig has been lying to me for years. He made a weird secret planning area at the end of our garage... the stupid building that takes up too much of the backyard anyway. Who does that?

He named our son after his first child to make things easier for himself. How dare he?

Grrr. Like hell I'm going to let him get away with this.

I pull on crisp black pants, a plain but businesslike navy shirt, and nice leather boots. Plus a long dove-gray trench coat, since the temperature dropped overnight. Comfortable and breathable, with full range of motion.

It feels like I'm preparing for a fight, not just dumping information on some poor unsuspecting officers. I guess it is kind of a fight, in a way. Letting that bastard Craig win is not an option.

While enjoying one last sip of coffee, I arrange the folders in order of who I think Craig is targeting next. I'll start with Olivia, with Mia next, to prove that he's involved in her disappearance and murder. Then the rest in the order it seems like he's planning, according to how much detail there is around their schedules.

Theoretically, the more detail means the more hours he has spent. Also, the more I study these, I notice that every woman's information seems to be focused on a different part of her life. With Olivia, it's her daily gym and grooming schedule. With Claire, it's her fundraiser attendance and club-going schedule. With Alexandra, it's her constant dates through a dating app.

As if I know what he's thinking. I feel like I should. I should have known about this all along. Should have known that this man I shared my life with was a psycho.

Placing my mug in the sink, I rinse it, then let the hot water pour over my chilly hands. There's no cleansing myself of this. Is total ignorance a valid argument when your spouse is doing something so horrible?

It likely depends on the evidence. Planning something is not quite the same as doing something. They'll need to find his fingerprints at the scene or whatever. Craig is extremely meticulous about some things. I hope that... Wait. I almost catch myself between hoping he did wear gloves and hoping he didn't.

That must be stopped. Today. My old life is over, and I will have no more life with Craig. Any one of these lies is a divorceable offense.

I want to cry again. "Divorceable" is now a word I've actually had to think about. Just a few days ago, I was positive that we were one of those forever couples.

Lugging everything out to the car, I check to make sure the house is tidy before setting the alarm and locking up. The thought of the police searching my house makes me cringe, but the thought of them seeing anything messy is nearly as bad.

It's occurring to me in waves that I'm starting to snap. Those priorities are totally backwards. Is there a correct way to behave in a situation like this? Hopefully, they'll understand why I'm a walking disaster.

I've been trained for many things, but reporting my husband to the cops for suspected murder was not on the list.

I glance at the route on my car's GPS, even though I

know where the police station is. This is certainly not the usual Sunday errand. I open the window a bit and turn on the radio, hoping for a distracting song.

"Thank you for listening to WBLW — we've got your favorite hit songs and breaking news all day long. We'll have an update soon on the Barrett Street water main repair, where crews have been working tirelessly day and night. We'll also have Lucy tell us about the slight damage north of the city after that bizarre thunder hail. But first, police have found the remains of another missing woman."

I usually turn off the news the second it gets dark. Now, I force myself to listen.

"Several well-known women in their early twenties have disappeared within several hours' drive of Lakeville. Some of their families initially assumed they were travelling, yet it's come to light that they are, in fact, missing. At first, authorities didn't see any connections, since the victims don't appear to know each other or travel in the same circles. However, investigators have determined that at least four of the missing women look quite similar, have similar lifestyle habits, and all disappeared on the same day of the week. Police are now searching for what they're calling 'The Monday Maniac'. They're warning all young women to be extra vigilant and keep safe. Over to you, Lucy."

Placing a hand over my heart, I'm pretty sure it's about to thump straight out of my chest. Pulling into the driveway of Delta's Diner, I park, then stare into the large front window.

Happy families are passing the ketchup and stealing each other's fries. A waitress in a pink and white apron pours coffee for a man, but shakes her finger sternly at the older man beside him as they all laugh.

The air in my lungs feels like glass shards.

I'm never going to have a sweet family lunch like that again.

My fingertips are blocks of ice against the steering wheel. Craig is with me Tuesday through Thursday. He's with Becca Friday through Sunday. Since he may or may not be traveling as much as he claims for work, he probably has one day off each week.

My husband is the Monday Maniac.

It's Sunday afternoon now. If he's planning on kidnapping Olivia, it's going to be tonight or tomorrow morning.

The pounding of my heart threatens to choke me. If I go to the police and speak with someone logical, they'll see all of this, take me seriously, and take over. That would be a huge relief.

But.

But...

If I end up stuck with a desk jockey who is one week from retirement and doesn't care anymore... They might have dozens of forms and procedures, and who knows what to dredge through before they even start looking for Craig. And that's only if they believe me.

No matter how tiny, there is a chance they could lock me up. I'm the one holding all of this evidence. I've never been one to depend on others. People are unpredictable.

What's holding me back?

Craig.

If he's been able to lie to me for years, he'll be able to lie to the police. And who would they believe? Probably him. Craig is the model upstanding citizen. I'll simply look like a jealous wife.

Any delay is going to slow down the process of discovering where Olivia is, if she's already been taken. I will not allow that man to get away with this again.

After three deep breaths, I turn through the parking lot, changing direction to drive uptown. My foot is too heavy on the pedal as I swerve semi-carefully around a truck.

I need to get to Becca's.

Now.

TWO WEEKS AGO

She comes out of the salon, turning her glossy mauve nails in the sunlight to check the color. She shrugs.

I think they look quite elegant. They'll go nicely with the dress she will probably wear to the fundraiser a few days from now.

Her expensive outfit is head-to-toe black today, with silver accessories. I've always thought that women look nicer in blues and purples rather than harsh black. It's softer. More feminine. Maybe that's an old-fashioned thought these days.

As always, her spine is straight, high heels propelling her straight to her Mercedes. She unlocks it with her remote, which has a row of silver charms dangling from it. Instead of getting in, she glances around once, then makes a few phone calls while half-leaning on the car.

Perhaps she's giving her nails an extra few minutes to dry before driving. Perhaps she doesn't like being out of touch for the ninety-five minutes she's in the salon.

It doesn't matter why. It only matters that she is consistent.

Her routine is like clockwork. I know it all.

36

AMY

After going over dozens of ideas on the drive here, I still have no idea what to say as I walk toward Becca's solid oak front door.

I'm supposed to be prepared before walking into any situation. Yet this is an unpredictable woman. If I accuse her of knowing anything, she'll get defensive. If I beg for help, she might become all power-trippy. So much of Becca's personality is artificial that I'm not positive how to play it. Plus, she is so focused on being gorgeous it's distracting.

Stepping onto the wide front porch, I take a proper look around. Geez, her house is so freaking charming, I'm tempted to take photos of the flowerbeds as inspiration. Wild roses are mixed with fancy old-fashioned Wollertons. Deep purple morning glory winds around the porch rail.

The doorbell plays a delicate chime. It's barely a minute before Becca flings the door open, her gently waved hair dancing in the breeze she's just created.

Holy crap, she looks like a bloody countess. Barefoot, in a flowing green and bronze floral dress, with lush emerald teardrop earrings. Her wide eyes are bright as her perfect berry lips turn up in a smile that does not feel genuine.

"Amy? How lovely of you to drop in!"

She surprises me by taking my arm and guiding me inside. I'm treated to a faint waft of her subtly exotic perfume, tempered by the fresh scent of more roses as we stroll past a huge bouquet in the foyer on our way to the kitchen.

As we pass a side hallway, I spot a long glass shelf displaying a few of her purses like trophies. A certain sage green baguette catches my eye.

The kitchen is enormous – all warm wood, marble counters, and exquisitely rustic terracotta tiles. Farmhouse chic to the absolute limit. I set my purse on a chair, then drape my coat over it.

"Shall I make us some tea?" Becca's bright eyes fix on me. She grows completely still, as if she's posing. Which I suppose she does a lot of. Her hand leans casually on the counter, the index finger twitching very subtly. It's a game of chicken, to see which of us is going to get to the point first.

"Hi!" Asher's face peeks around the door frame, then he waves to me. "The boats all floated! Next time you hafta stay and watch."

Becca's face seems to freeze as she turns to me, her jaw tight. "How do you know Asher?"

He walks over to her and chimes in before I can speak. "Yesterday she watched me in the sandbox and looked in the garage."

Uh oh.

"Yesterday?" Somehow, Becca manages to relax her fake smile, even when her eyes are hard. "How do you take your tea, Amy?"

At least she's willing to pretend to be civilized with her son nearby. I sit down at the table farthest from where she's standing, needing to keep some space between us. "Just a touch of milk, thank you."

Is Craig anywhere around? Even though I'm furious with him, curiosity is killing me. I need to see him with Becca. I need to see their connection with my own eyes. Sure, he's a liar and a robber, yet his attachment to this woman is the thing that is stabbing my mind the most. I should not indulge in feeling sentimental at a time like this, yet there's no way to stop it.

"There you are!" Jackson comes around the corner, laughing, as Asher starts to giggle, hiding behind his mother. "I step out to take a leak and you're gone again."

"I'm too fast!" Asher laughs.

Jackson scoops him up, then his free hand lands on Becca's hip. "Hey, babe. Did–"

Her eyes flick to me, and as his gaze follows, his mouth falls open and he snatches his hand back. It nearly chokes me to stifle a laugh.

"We have company," Becca announces, in a tone that clearly says *shut up.* "Why don't you take Asher upstairs to play until dinner?"

"You said pizza," Asher reminds her as Jackson carries him away at top speed.

Becca and Jackson are definitely together. Does Craig know? Are they just using him? My mind is swirling with so many questions I want answered immediately, yet I need to focus.

The electric kettle must have recently boiled, as it heats up quickly while Becca spoons loose tea into a strainer. My gaze trails around the antique copper pots at the top of her shelves, and the botanical watercolors of herbs and vegetables hanging over the huge farmhouse table. Peering carefully, I don't think those are prints. They look like signed originals.

"These are lovely," I say, surprised by my sincerity. "Honestly, Becca, you have such a good eye."

"Cut the crap," she snaps, sliding an elegant cream porcelain cup and saucer in front of me. "Speaking with my son when I wasn't here is unacceptable. It tells me what kind of game you might be playing." She sits with her hands artfully arranged to show off her still-perfect sage nails. "Why were you in my garage?"

I sip the tea carefully, acting like it's delicious. It's definitely some high-end brand. The fragrance is incredible, even if the floral flavor is overpowering. Some of the herbs are kind of bitter. Ugh, that one mouthful was more than enough.

"*Your* garage?" I ask smoothly. "Or did Craig have it made, with his special touches?"

Her jaw tightens. "How much do you know?"

I want to grab her by the throat and throw her against the lush ivy-drenched designer wallpaper. Instead, I pretend to sip my tea again, and take a slow breath. "I love how there's just a tick of clove mixed in," I murmur, setting the cup down gently. "Sometimes surprising flavors are so refreshing."

Becca simply glares, waiting.

"I know that you and Craig are into some very sketchy stuff." It's difficult to keep my voice calm, but maybe there's still a chance that I can work with her. "Becca, I'm sure you don't want nice young women to be hurt."

An immaculate green fingernail taps on the polished wood. "Nice? You think those spoiled brats are *nice*?" Her voice drops to a low snarl. "Those are the women clogging all of the social media channels with their bullshit shopping sprees and their endless vacations. Like they've actually worked hard enough to deserve a break. They have no idea what real work is."

Straightening up, Becca tosses her glossy hair back over her shoulder. "Some of us strive to be leaders. A light in the dark for women who want to elevate their lives all by themselves. Those of us who want a storybook life and are willing to put in the work to make that happen."

"Even if those women are spoiled, they don't deserve to be..." I pause when I see the way the corners of her eyes clench. "Harmed."

There's a round of laughter from upstairs as a cascade of heavy footsteps sound like Jackson is chasing Asher around a room. Becca's stern face melts into a partial smile as she glances toward the stairs.

"I know how much you love your son," I say softly, before taking another small sip of tea, using it to pause and slow the conversation. "Think about how much the parents of these young women are going to worry. How Olivia's parents will worry if she disappears."

Becca's head whips around to stare at me. "Who is Olivia?"

Before I can answer, a phone rings. She jumps up and grabs her purse from the dining room to get it.

It's a bright pink Von Rubis baguette. With extra thick stitching in a few spots that I recognize. It's clearer in person than it was in the photos. It has a new scratch on the underside of the handle, though. I've worked on that purse. That's Mia's bag. Does Becca even know that?

My stomach is starting to slowly churn as Becca's thumbs

fly over her screen, sending a quick text. Then she steps close to me, her voice barely a whisper. "Why don't we go to the downstairs playroom? We can talk more freely there."

I don't want little Asher to be upset, no matter what his parents are up to. Plus, I've seen photos of her entire home online. The basement certainly isn't some creepy dungeon.

"Sure."

I follow Becca down the plushily carpeted stairs to a huge rec room with baskets of toys in the corner. I want to admire the amazing plush floral couch in front of the massive flat screen, but there are suddenly too many things to think about at once.

Once again, questions are swirling in my mind until I'm dizzy.

Wait. No, I'm actually dizzy.

"This way." Becca grabs my arm hard, her nails denting my skin while shoving me roughly through a door to the side.

There's a deep hum of the furnace, and I realize we're in the mechanical room. She pulls a rickety wooden chair to the center of the space, near some tall metal shelves with clearly labeled cleaning products and house repair odds and ends. There are some tools lying around the big metal box of the furnace. Dingy cardboard boxes in the corner.

I'm staring at everything as if I've never seen... things... before.

My head is heavy. My hands are too big, and my fingers aren't... bendy. Sinking into the chair, I try to grip the arms and miss twice. "What..." My mouth is cottony.

Blinking stupidly at Becca's manic grin, I watch in fascination as shadows come in from the edges of my vision until there's nothing but darkness.

37

BECCA

Dammit. That was way too close. I almost didn't get Amy downstairs before that sedative kicked in.

Since it was my first time mixing a dose myself, I was nervous to use too much. I didn't stir it in, letting it coat the top of the tea so it hit her system immediately. Apparently, there's a floral flavor to mask the chemicals, which worked perfectly in the new MomFlowerPower energy tea I've been concocting.

Yet Amy is stronger than I thought; I have to give her that. She barely panicked.

I swear, from the moment this chick appeared at that school event, she's been intentionally trying to infuriate me.

Looking around the dingy room, I'm not even sure what's in here that I could use. I'm almost never in this room, and didn't plan ahead for something like this.

Prowling around the cheap metal shelves, I check the "things to repair" bin and am relieved to see an old leather belt. That should do it. It takes a few minutes to arrange

Amy's hands behind her back and tie her wrists through a bar on the back of the chair.

It's impossible to stop myself from automatically smoothing Amy's hair and arranging her shoulders so that she's sitting up straight. I truly live by the mantras I'm always spouting about women lifting each other up, even when there are no cameras.

Amy is not the type of person to ever have a grand life, yet she deserves to look tidy when she's passed out cold.

My hand twitches toward my pocket instinctively. I'm so accustomed to photographing anything new and different that the urge is automatic. Like I would ever show this plain Jane on my pages.

The phone in my pocket vibrates, and I step back toward the door for fear of waking her. It's him. "What?" I snap.

"Hey. How is Asher today?"

It's extremely annoying that my husband clearly cares much more for our son than for me. Of course, I pulled the old bait and switch as soon as we were married, not restricted by affection.

"Asher is fine. He's playing upstairs with Jackson."

Craig hesitates. "Sweetie, I know you focus all of your creative drive into your online channels, but I can't help wishing that you would spend more quality time with Asher. A child needs their mother."

Closing my eyes, I count to three, trying to allow my body to feel calm so that my mind will follow. That sentiment sells fairly well on my beautifully designed coffee mugs, but it doesn't work right now.

"I don't have time to play at the moment, Craig." I turn to face the woman in the chair, who has grown incredibly still. Is she still breathing? I can't hear over the hum of the furnace. "Amy is here. And she thinks she knows everything."

"What?" he sputters. "She doesn't know anything. How could she know everything? How could she have found anything out? She has no idea that—"

"Because you're sloppy, *sweetie*. Because men are always sloppy and don't pay enough attention to details."

"I did. I really did. There's no way she could know anything."

"Well, she does. And right now she's tied up in the furnace room after I had to knock her out with that sedative of yours. What do you think I should do about that?"

Through his phone, I hear the distant but aggressive honking of a car horn. "I'm on my way. I can fix this."

"I sincerely doubt it. She knows way too much already. But seeing you might make her realize that it's two against one, and she should really calm down."

"Oh." A long pause. "How upset was she?" I can almost picture the worried look in his hazel eyes, which, admittedly, are incredibly handsome.

I'm not jealous that he worries so much about Amy. I'm just concerned that he is a bit too affectionate with someone who has the potential to ruin our system just as we're getting started. Amy is a weak point. That makes our system vulnerable.

Footsteps on the stairs make me jump. "Hold on."

Sticking my head out, I see that Jackson is hesitating halfway down the basement stairs, looking around. Turning back toward Amy, I say, "Sure – take a look behind the wrapping paper. I'll be right back." Holding the phone low and pressed to my stomach, I murmur to Jackson, "What's up?"

"Asher keeps going on about having pizza tonight. He's

been really good all week, so I was thinking it could be a nice little project if we made it together."

Reaching out, I run my palm along his slightly stubbled cheek. Damn, this man is hot. The kind of toy I deserve. "You know I can't say no to you, gorgeous," I whisper, while leaning close to his ear. "Chef Timothy is already on his way. Can you keep Asher upstairs reading stories for a while longer? I just have a few things to take care of."

"Sure. We'll split one of those organic granola bars so that he doesn't get cranky."

"Good idea."

His eyes flick to the furnace room door, then he leans in for a lightning-fast kiss. "Can't wait for tonight, sexy."

Grinning back at him, I watch his beautifully sculpted ass as he walks up the stairs. Not the sharpest tool in the shed, but he's obedient and great in bed. *Oh!* That would be a great t-shirt for my shop.

Lifting the phone, I force my voice to remain steady. "She had some interesting details to share, your little Amy."

There's several seconds of silence, and I know it's not because he's concentrating on his driving. "We'll talk when I get there."

"You'd better hurry. I don't know how long she's going to stay out. And her attitude had better be improved when she wakes up."

"Attitude? Becca, you know that Amy is always a team player."

"Possibly, but she didn't know she was playing for our team now, did she?"

"She'll come around. I'll see to it. I promise." He sounds hesitant.

"Like you promised to take care of the latest–"

"I'm sorry," he barks. "I know a few of our... projects... have taken a bit longer than you expected. It's a matter of the pieces falling into place."

"Yeah. Whatever. Meanwhile, I'm still waiting to be able to lease a better car."

"Sweetheart," he drawls in the sugary tone that is supposed to placate me, "I'll take care of everything. I'm on my way. Just stay calm. Maybe try some of your breathing exercises."

"How dare you—"

"You're always telling women to practice what they preach. You're upset with your husband. So say a mantra or do your breathing. I should be there in fifteen minutes."

I disconnect the call, not wanting to say another angry word. Craig has started behaving even more strangely around me over the past two months. It's as if his attention is split even more than between his two wives. I don't know how much longer I can keep my metaphorical boot on his throat.

Unless it's time to make that real.

Even though it's annoying that Craig is right, I sit on the sofa and do some breathing exercises. I'll need to be sharp to figure this out. I open my phone to search for some meditative music, and accidentally get lost in skimming the comments on yesterday's videos for at least ten minutes. After a fresh round of admiration from my fans – even if it's not nearly as many as I should have by now – I feel properly invigorated.

Stepping back into the furnace room, I shut the door behind me, then jump as I see Amy sitting up straight, bright-eyed and with a clear expression.

"I'm glad to see there's one imperfect room in your

precious house," she smirks. "I guess that means you can't film in here. The lighting is terrible." Her left eyebrow quirks up. "People might realize your actual age, for goodness' sake."

How dare she. I will not accept criticism from a woman who clearly doesn't even use a skincare system.

At least it doesn't look like she's trying to break free, thank goodness.

"So you and Jackson really are together." Her polite smile is icy. "I assume that Craig knows? With all of the 'find your own truth' stuff you spout online, I couldn't imagine you keeping a secret like that from your beloved husband."

"Craig knows as much as he needs to know. We have an understanding."

"Oh, I'm sure you do. Like how he understands that another man is raising his son for him four days a week."

"That is none of your business." It takes some effort to lower my shoulders and my volume. I turn on my best charming smile. "After all, Amy, you should probably know–"

She snorts a laugh. "I should probably know a lot of things. You morons have been manipulating me from day one."

I hate sassy women who aren't me. They never quite get the details right. Yet I know one way to squash Amy's attitude.

I smile sweetly. This is going to be like twisting a knife in her guts. Shove a permanent wedge in her precious relationship with my breadwinner.

"Well, you're correct about that," I say slowly, savoring every syllable, "since I'm the one who chose you for Craig in the first place."

38

BECCA

Watching Amy's face practically melt is deeply satisfying. Her smug expression falls while her bottom lip trembles.

"Yes, mousy little girl. I've been the one in charge this entire time."

I am an enlightened person. I should not be enjoying the confusion and bitterness in Amy's eyes. Plus, the outright pain. But after all, I'm only human. And I've been dealing with this strange woman for far too long. She was supposed to make our lives easier, and had been doing her job perfectly up until last week.

I hate that I'm still annoyed that she's prettier than I originally thought. There is no way I'm going to allow myself to be jealous of this woman. Jealousy should be beneath me.

"Why did you come to that school event?" Somehow, I need to keep this conversation chatty and light. Maybe the sedative will kick back in. I don't know how those things work. Plus, if I'm being honest for once, I'm genuinely curious.

Amy's half-smile is slow and deliberate. "I want to get my

Asher into a better school. I found out there was another Asher who looked very similar to him. It was Laura, one of the Westfield moms, who accidentally confirmed that Craig is married to both of us."

I wish I were wearing shoes so there was more of a sound as I tap my feet. But studies have shown that being barefoot as much as possible truly is better for grounding oneself. Even in a dirty room like this.

"Evidently, you like the name Asher," Amy continues. "Which is why Craig was so insistent on that name for our son." Her eyebrow cocks up as she leans forward with a wink. "Obviously, that was so when Craig has one of his rare scatterbrained moments, he won't mix up the name of our kids, right?"

My smile feels brittle. "Of course."

She shrugs, leaning back. "We don't have to be enemies, Becca. We want the same thing, more or less."

"You think so?"

"Absolutely." Her bright eyes are tracking me. It's so unnerving that I stop pacing. "I mean, I'm pretty sure that I love Craig more than you do. You have your sexy nanny up there to keep you happy."

I find myself slipping into a genuine smile. What the hell, she already knows. "Yes, Jackson really is something. To be honest, he's a bit dim and never looks past the nose on his face. That works out well for me because he never pries into my business. Never asks too many questions. Plus, he's incredible with Asher."

She nods. "We both put our children first, no matter what. See? We have plenty in common besides Craig."

Looking down, my most recent pedicure looks quite lovely as I resume pacing across the gritty, cracked concrete.

The contrast of the high-gloss pink polish and the dull stone finish really pops. I should shoot a video of this later. Right – focus. Content will have to wait, for once.

"Don't you want to know why I chose you for our family man?" I ask.

Amy rolls her eyes. "Because I have a gigantic database of wealthy young women who come from old money?"

Dammit. She really is sharp.

"Why were you in my garage?" I ask.

Amy slowly sucks in a breath, as if considering her answer. "It's pretty much exactly like the garage Craig built at my house."

"I'm sure it's not exactly like it."

Her gaze burns into mine. "With the hidden closet space at the end? And the puzzle lock?"

Even though I'm steaming inside, I sigh with relief. "Oh, good. If yours has the same lock, that means you can't have looked in it."

"Of course I have," Amy snaps. "The puzzles aren't that difficult if you pay attention. That's how I know Olivia Rhodes is his next victim."

"Olivia who?"

Her head tilts as she stares at me as if I'm an idiot. "You have Mia's pink Von Rubis bag in your dining room. That sage green baguette in the hallway is Olivia's." Her eyebrow raises. "Don't you wonder where he got it?"

A cold wind blows down my spine. "But... Craig said that he bought that one. It was a special gift for me just a few days ago."

Amy's smiles are growing colder and colder. I don't like where this is going. I'm supposed to be the one in control.

"So he's letting you think he spent thousands of dollars,

and instead, he just stole it from his next target. Likely to get her phone and more information. Meanwhile, you have a second-hand purse from a woman who's going to be dead tomorrow if you don't snap out of it and help me."

"What makes you think she's the next victim? He hasn't planned anything. I would have remembered the name Olivia, for heaven's sake."

My feet stop in their tracks, then I spin toward her, slowly replaying what she just said. Craig couldn't have... he wouldn't...

"*Dead?*" I sputter.

Amy is looking at me as if I'm insane. Which I genuinely feel at the moment.

"Yes. I've seen the murder boards in my garage. They're just like yours, but without your handwriting. That means if anything else happens, you and I are both going down."

I take a step back. As if a few more feet between us will soften the meaning of her words.

Did my boring, predictable Craig actually have an original thought for the first time in his life? Did he put my life and my media career in danger?

For the first time in many years, I'm genuinely afraid of losing everything.

Why would he suddenly need to target more women than our usual careful schedule?

And why would he change the plan to transform from a cautious thief to a... I can barely wrap my mind around the word...

Murderer?

TODAY

I cannot wait for tomorrow.

39

AMY

It doesn't matter that I'm tied to a chair in a dingy, dusty furnace room. For the first time, I have the upper hand. Maybe. It gives me a shot of confidence to hold onto while I breathe deeply and clear the last cobwebs from my brain.

Even though the belt is digging into my wrists and this old wooden chair is extremely uncomfortable, I force myself to appear calm. What kind of psycho drugs somebody? Thank goodness sedatives never seem to work very well on me.

I knew that Becca was up to some shady stuff, but this is far beyond the scope of what she was capable of. Shame on me for underestimating her. Yet I have to keep her steady for now. She certainly seems to like having her ego fed. Maybe that will help if she sees us on the same team.

"Becca, you're the one with the power here," I begin slowly. "Surely you must see that we don't need to hurt anyone in order to get ahead. We could talk to Craig, and he'll listen to you."

"Oh, that he does," she smirks. "Such an obedient man. When I can get him focused, he's a great provider."

"Are you going to help me stop him hurting women?" It's taking some effort to make my voice sound gentle. "You clearly have plenty of money. It's not worth hurting someone, right? You sell a coffee mug that says, 'Women need more kindness from other women'."

Her laugh is a vicious snort. "That's crap I sell to idiots, of course. Half of the motivational experts online were selling that one six months ago."

My shoulders move very subtly as I stretch them out, planting my feet flat on the floor to shift my hips. I need to get ready. Pick my moment. "Being married to a kidnapper and killer is not great for your brand. Olivia will be the next victim of the Monday Maniac if we don't stop him."

Becca's hand flies over her mouth as she tries and fails to stop a giggle from bubbling out. "Monday Maniac! If we were marketing this, the alliteration would be perfect."

"Dammit." I shake my head, stunned. Is she not taking this seriously? "The news is already referring to the Monday Maniac. They've grouped some of his murders together."

Her face falls, possibly undoing the anti-aging effects of thousands of dollars' worth of potions. "What?"

I should be keeping a poker face, yet I feel my eyes growing huge. "You haven't been watching the news? You haven't been following along as the police are stringing together Craig's kidnappings and murders?"

Her bottom lip trembles, fingers fluttering as if trying not to clutch her dress. "N-no," she sputters. "I just started a media cleanse yesterday. Not taking in any information from outside sources for at least forty-eight hours. It's part of my Fresh Start weekend routine."

My eyes snap closed for a few seconds to keep me from rolling them at her. "They pieced together that the string of kidnappings in the area are related. And that everything happens on Mondays."

Watching Becca's expression, I believe that she genuinely had no idea. "Do they know anything specific?" Her voice is shaky.

Good. I should not be enjoying this. A nasty, dark part of me is bubbling out. It's thrilling to see the polished princess acting flustered. Watching her practiced smile drop. The way her confidence turns to nervousness so quickly. It makes me wonder how much is truth and how much of her persona is a total fabrication.

"They figured out that Mia's car accident was not the cause of her death, and that she was actually killed before that." My voice softens. "I didn't want to believe Craig actually killed her. I thought he was just kidnapping these women to steal their money."

"That was supposed to be the plan. But who the hell is Mia?"

My entire body sags. "Oh, right. Her murder board was in my garage, not yours."

Becca's luminous eyes are gigantic. "So he really murdered her?"

My gaze locks on hers like a laser beam. "I assume so, yes. When someone has a freaking murder board full of details about a woman and she ends up dead, that's probably what happened."

She wrings her hands, pacing in tight circles. Even in the midst of this, she stops to admire the way her pale bare feet look on the raw concrete floor. Although, honestly, that pink polish really is the most summer flower shade I've ever seen.

"'This is not good. I don't like that he was taking on..." She gives me a sideways glance. "Extra projects. Especially since they were planned at your house."

"I don't like that he was planning any of these projects at all." It's impossible to keep the anger from my voice. "So once again, I think we need to work together here. He was targeting them for the money, right? I think that's pretty obvious."

"Of course. This is a tricky lifestyle to maintain."

I bite my tongue thinking about her lavish lifestyle when I might have to sell some things for the donation money to get Asher into a better school. Another flash of jealousy heats up my core. I try to roll my shoulders back in this awkward position. Becca has absolutely everything, and still wants more.

I have enough. I always have. Yet it's still sickening to think that I could have had more – especially more of Craig's time and attention – if it weren't for her.

"Plus," Becca turns to me with one of her dazzling smiles, "you must know how much he loves puzzles. Tracking a woman, learning her schedule until he can predict her movements perfectly. It gives him purpose."

"Oh, yes, I know."

"Plus, it keeps his impulses for the perfect family life under control." Her head shakes slightly, sending chocolate waves of hair drifting casually around her narrow shoulders. "You should have seen him before I took control of his life. He was a mess."

"Really?" I'm torn between wanting to keep her talking about the kidnappings and learning more information about the side of Craig I don't know. "I know that he loves being the man who comes home from work to play with his son and have dinner with his wife. How was he a mess?"

She leans casually against the wall, as if automatically trying to lengthen her legs. "You know. Lost in research about this or that, without a clear direction. Not knowing what kind of home he wanted. He was one of my first life makeovers, actually."

"Okay. Yes, his job keeps him busy and focused. At least he's always had that going for him."

Her mouth falls open as her hand flutters up again. "Oh... wow, that's right. You don't know."

I half-shrug awkwardly. "You might as well tell me, right?"

Her eyes narrow as her soft giggle turns into a cackle. "Craig never had a job, you pathetic little girl."

My vision blurs, and this time it's not from weakly spiked tea.

Craig's tech career is one of the things I really loved about him. It was secret and fascinating and seemed to make him light up whenever he spoke of... whatever he was on about with new computer interfaces.

No job?

I don't know my husband at all.

Which means I truly don't know what these people are capable of.

That's fine.

Something deep inside me clicks *hard*.

They don't know what I'm capable of either.

40

AMY

I'm about to find a way to get under Becca's flawless porcelain skin.

Not because I'm sick of watching this bizarre woman ping-pong back and forth between a normal person and an overly polished, mantra-spewing, glossy-haired mannequin who seems irritated that she has to waste her precious time with the captive tied up in her furnace room.

She is extremely committed to her life being the way it is. If I destabilize it, she might become unstable as well.

I think I'm going to need that.

A deep, cloying wave of fear runs up and down my slightly stretched back shoulders. The wobbly wooden chair is beginning to creak as I restlessly shift my weight. It's slowly occurring to me that Becca could keep me here as long as she likes. Nobody but Jackson and Asher know I'm here, and they would certainly do anything Becca says.

All she would have to do is hide my car in the garage and pull the memory card from my cell phone. Then, boom. I disappear.

Is she capable of that? I have to assume so. If she's helping Craig with his string of robberies and kidnappings, she might be capable of anything. It's impossible to tell whether or not she would truly fight if she had to. If she would lash out and harm me. I need to be mentally prepared for the worst.

"You know, this is probably good for you," Becca says sweetly. "Craig says you're a workaholic. Always obsessed with growing your business and doing top-quality work for your clients. Right now, you have nothing to do but take a breath. Isn't that refreshing?" Taking a deep, slow breath, she smiles at me condescendingly. "Now, doesn't that feel better?"

"A little." Stretching my head gently by bringing my ear toward my shoulder, I pretend to be relaxing while my mind races. "I do need to stretch and breathe more often," I admit. "I only get out to a proper yoga class once or twice a month. I've been doing those five-minute yoga videos after work."

Becca makes a *tut-tut* noise. "Five minutes isn't nearly enough to sink into the breath and stretch properly." Her smile slides slightly to the left. "If we were actually friends, I would take you to see my yogi, Dahlia. She's an absolute genius."

"Well, you know that you have a spectacular figure. So she must be great."

She smooths her dress over her hips. "Why, thank you."

"I've been giving in to the carbs a bit too much when I'm super-busy." I half-shrug. "But it's good for endorphins. And my doctor says it's good for fertility," I lie.

Becca's eyes practically bug out like a cartoon. "*What?*"

I shrug again, then twist my wrists a bit so I don't lose

circulation. I am going to get out of here somehow. It's just a matter of picking my moment.

"Yeah. We started trying about six months ago. Since we're only together three days a week, obviously, Craig's time with me doesn't always line up perfectly with when I'm ovulating. But two weeks ago, it was probably the right time. I'm going to take a test next week."

Her mouth puckers as if she's just sucked on a lemon, toes tapping sharply on the floor. "You're lying."

"Why would I bother? We're obviously in this together at this point. Plus, Craig has already picked out the cutest name."

"*You will not name your baby Piper if you have her first!*" Becca screeches. Her fingers clench, eyes hard and glittering in the low light. "Craig and I have a system. We have a plan. I get the baby girl first. Don't you dare mess that up."

The way I'm pretending to stay relaxed, with a mellow half-smile, is clearly driving her crazy. "I was just trying to live my life. Mind my own business. You're the one with the systems and the schedules and everything."

Her mouth opens, then snaps shut as her phone rings like an old-fashioned doorbell. "Well. Craig actually got here quickly."

"That's your front door?"

"Yes."

"Why doesn't Craig have a key to your house?"

She's silent for what feels like an eternity. Then she steps forward, looming over me as her hair shadows her face. "He has his own place. He's here three evenings a week to be with Asher and for us to plan fun family projects for the camera. But I don't need to be tied to that man constantly." She steps back, pursing her perfect rose lips. "Unlike *some* people who apparently need a man to validate themselves."

Ugh, this woman is annoying. Becca is so difficult to read that I keep second-guessing myself. Still, forming a bond with her, letting her think that we are on a team, will be the most important thing for my safety. I need to stop ticking her off and find an actual common goal. I have to get out of here. Who knows how dangerous she is? Or Craig, or Jackson.

Somehow, I feel that painting Craig as the enemy might be the smartest thing to do.

Now that I have a clue about what's going on... at least I hope I do... I feel like I might be able to get through to Craig. Not that I want to talk to him. The thought of looking into those gorgeous hazel eyes makes me queasy.

Becca is the one with the power, at least for now.

"Not anymore." My chin lifts to look her dead in the eyes. "I don't need that conniving bastard ever again. Not that I ever needed him in the first place, of course. He was just nice to have around. But now, forget it."

"We'll see what Craig says about that."

"Don't you dare bring him down here!" I snap.

Her hand lands on her hip, and she's spreading her fingers as if she were posing on a red carpet. "I don't think you're in a position to give orders."

"Really? I've already told you about Craig's projects at my house. Told you the name of a previous target, and the girl he's targeting tomorrow. The date was written down and circled." Desperation rattles my voice. "I told you that he might actually be murdering these girls."

Becca's skirt flares as she turns away, then leans back over her shoulder. "Oh, honey. I hate it, but I assumed he killed some of them. It's the only way to get away with draining their accounts completely."

I notice the corners of her eyes. She's lying, I think. She didn't know about the killing part, just the kidnappings.

Becca's hand drags along the door frame as she smiles, showing way too many teeth. "Amy, darling, why on earth would I have that sedative on hand if not for Craig to use it?"

Just before she closes the door behind her, Becca murmurs, "Craig has always been a reliable breadwinner for *our* family."

As the door clicks shut, my heart snaps into a thousand pieces. Becca was speaking the truth. Her eyes were one hundred percent clear on that. I was his second choice. Second wife. Just there to keep him busy and give him another child. What kind of person am I if the love of my life has been keeping over half of his world secret from me?

Swallowing hard to stifle a whimper, I decide the truth tastes as bitter as that dreadful tea. I'm the kind of girl who ends up drugged and tied up in a furnace room.

Utterly helpless.

Except that I was raised better than that.

SECOND DRAFT OF O.R. NOTE:

Hello, Olivia. You were given a sedative to knock you out. Don't worry, you'll be fine. The water bottle beside you is safe and hasn't been opened. Drink that, then some juice or sports drinks as soon as possible. You'll find that your bank accounts are 90% empty.

I've left a small amount, in case any automatic payments go through. We all hate those extra banking fees when a payment bounces, right?

Some of your belongings are missing. Anything that looked like a family heirloom, like your tiny gold locket, was spared. I'm not a monster.

However, I am a person who knows all of your movements. Your family, your friends, your favorite restaurants, salons, and gym. I know that five weeks ago, you went to Madison's Art Gallery at 8:13 p.m. and were disappointed by the wine. You thought they *should have splurged for something nicer than, as you said, "a run-of-the-mill discount Sauvignon Blanc."*

I know that your grandmother's 73rd birthday party is happening in a few weeks at The Harbor Club. Your entire family will be there. If you want to ensure that everyone has a wonderful time, you will follow my instructions to the letter.

First, drink that water and go find some juice. There's a twenty-dollar bill in your pocket.

Next, you'll find your way home while making up some plausible excuse as to why you've been gone for the past half a day. Perhaps you went to a different spa in a shady part of town, and you were mugged on the way to your car. Or, perhaps you went on a bender, got wildly drunk, and don't know where any of your things went.

Make it realistic. Also, make it slightly embarrassing. People are more likely to believe a lie if it's something shameful. Why would you make something up that paints you in a bad light? Remember every detail, because you need to make this story stick.

If you contact the police, I will know. If you tell anyone the truth about this incident, I will know.

Right now, you've simply been robbed and inconvenienced. Let's not see what happens if I have to punish you for disobeying.

*Thank you for your cooperation, and have a pleasant
rest of your day.*

I'll need to proofread this again before printing it.

It doesn't really matter since this note is just in case
something goes terribly wrong. It's always faster and easier if
I don't have to worry as much about hiding my face. Sometimes I have to revert to the system I use with others.

But nobody knows about this one.

The last several projects I've taken care of myself have
been smooth as silk.

Which means spoiled little Olivia won't be waking up to
read the note at all.

41

BECCA

Craig may have actually killed one of those girls? Or more? I'm shaking as I race upstairs.

How dare he.

Naturally, I'm creeped out that this man has the capacity for murder. Yet I'm just as overwhelmed by the fact that he has disobeyed me. Taken things into his own hands.

Put myself and my fledgling empire – the only thing I've ever truly dreamed of – at risk.

My index finger greets my husband at the door by poking him in the chest. He steps back as I snap, "Extra projects? Another secret room in another garage? What in the bloody hell is wrong with you?"

His boy-next-door smile is almost disarming before it drops, and I watch his gorgeous eyes turn from warm to cold. "Can I at least come inside before you start berating me about the way I run our business?"

"*Our* business? This was supposed to be *my* business with you assisting." He pushes past me, then kicks off his shoes before I can remind him. It annoys me to no end that he heads straight to the kitchen to drop his phone on the charger as if he lives here.

"We started this endeavor together."

"Yes. To get more money for *my* business. My career."

His brows furrow. "And to give me something to do between the times your highness allows me to see my son."

"Don't start. We have a much bigger problem."

Tugging his arm, I drag him toward the door that leads downstairs. "Do you know anything about a woman named Mia?"

Staring deeply into his eyes, I know I'm extremely fortunate that Craig has never had a good poker face when confronted head-on. His expression attempts to remain blank, yet his eyes narrow and lips tighten. "Why?"

"Because she turned up dead, you idiot."

His entire frame stiffens and he takes a step back, straight into the wall. "What do you know about her?"

My hand tightens into a fist, the urge to crack him straight in the jaw almost overwhelming. *Breathe.* That's not who I am. I'm supposed to be someone who stays calm in any sort of crisis. I'm the woman who practices what she preaches. Well, most of the time.

Even though, at the very least, I'd love to slap him just to watch the hand print set in. Yet even with the door to the basement closed, I don't want Amy hearing any of this.

"You planned a job focused on Mia Harrington, didn't you?"

An icy sensation seeps through me at the look in his eyes. This is the man who has told me every detail about every afternoon kidnapping. Every theft. Every plan. Or so I thought. Now he's unable to meet my gaze straight on?

Something is terribly wrong. If I can't control him properly, I have no idea what's going to happen to us. To my perfect life. To our son.

This is not the first time I've questioned whether Craig is truly a quality father. His incredible eyes likely factored higher into my decision-making process than they should have. But he was also obedient. Willing to put my dreams first. He had his own money, or so I thought, and didn't take up a lot of my time or attention.

I dreamed of a part-time husband who wouldn't cramp my style and vision. Now I realize I should have kept a closer eye on the details. He's not the sort of man who should be allowed to make his own decisions without supervision.

Men are always sloppy. That's a lesson I've learned over and over again.

"Answer me, Craig. Now. What have you done with Mia?"

His lips press into a straight line for a moment. "You set me up with another wife. Another life. Another son. Did you really think I'd have a completely different set of hobbies while I was there?"

"Dammit, you're such an idiot." I check the time on the phone in my pocket. I need to get Asher fed soon. If he comes down here and sees Craig, he'll be excited and want to play. Plus, he'll want his dad to stay for dinner. Which would interfere with my shooting schedule.

"Did you rob Mia or did you kill her?" I hiss, leaning forward to lock my gaze with his.

This is the moment of truth. Even though I might not want to know the answer.

Craig is still as a stone, and just as silent.

Oh no.

He did.

42

BECCA

No amount of fancy breathing or mantra chanting is going to change the fact that I'm absolutely freaking out.

This moron half-husband of mine was supposed to rob easy targets. It was supposed to be an interesting mental mystery for him to untangle, to keep him busy and make us rich.

But murder? That is ten steps over the line.

I suspected Craig might have a dark side, yet I honestly didn't think he had the guts to take it this far. Now I'm semi-involved with a felony.

There is absolutely no way I am going to any sort of prison and wear orange, for crying out loud. The mere thought of it makes my blood boil.

How dare he? The urge to shove him down the stairs and be done with him is stronger than I'd like.

"Tell me what is going on." I give his chest an open-handed push. "I need to know so I can fix the situation."

"What situation?"

"Your other wife is tied up in the basement, you asshole."

His eyes grow huge as he straightens up. "You haven't hurt her, have you?"

Another pang of jealousy. He really does care about that weird, frumpy woman. "Yes. She came here nosing around, and I knocked her out for a few minutes with your... whatever that potion is."

Craig shakes his head sadly. "Sedatives don't work on Amy. The poor thing can't even depend on sleeping pills when she's anxious."

"Thanks a lot, jackass. I figured that out when I barely got her tied up tight enough before she came to."

He lunges toward the door, but I block it. "Let me check on her. If you've hurt her, I'll—"

"What?" I snap. "Be her shining white knight and save the day? Don't be so stupid." I bring my lips toward his ear. "You need to fix this problem. I can read you clear as a bell, dear husband. I know you killed Mia."

He blanks again.

"The news said that she died in a car crash. Then they figured out that she'd been killed before that. It was around the same time you came to me with some brand new gifts, didn't you?"

The idiot has the nerve to actually pout. "It wasn't my fault. I was trying to do something nice for you."

He's clearly lying. From the spark in his eyes, I know he enjoyed every minute of it.

"You brought me presents. What did you do with all of her money, Craig?" His eyes snap shut as his lips form a tight line again. Dammit. He really is up to something. "Whatever you suddenly need a whack of extra money for can wait. Right now, I need you to fix this problem."

"What problem? I'll just go down and talk to Amy, make up something that she'll believe, and take her home."

"The hell you will."

I can hear Jackson and Asher chattering in the hallway upstairs, as if they're about to come down. "You need to take her out," I whisper, glaring at him so hard I'm surprised the top of his head doesn't begin to smoke. "It's the only way we know she'll be quiet, and you've just proven that you're completely capable of it."

"N-no!" he sputters. "She's... No. I won't."

"Why not? You promised me that you would take care of us as long as I gave you a son. You clearly had no chance of finding a normal woman in the twitchy nutcase state I found you in."

"She's the mother of my son," he murmurs. "That's sacred."

"It's the only way. You're going to take care of it right now." I give him my best and brightest smile. "If you don't do it immediately, I'll have to do it myself. And I won't have the patience to be delicate and knock her out with a sedative first. Even if she needs a triple dose."

His handsome face crumples. He looks so much like Asher when he wants to confess he's done something wrong but doesn't want to hear me yell at him.

"Get downstairs right now, and take her out. That is your only option. Your only move."

He shakes his head, so I grab his face, grinding the back of his skull into the wall. "I'm going upstairs to check on Jackson and Asher. The chef is already setting up out back. So you'd better be quiet. Do not use this doorway until we're outside by the pizza oven. And you'd better clean up your own mess. Got it?"

His shoulders drop. "Okay."

"Turn off the furnace room light so I know it's finished."

"Alright."

"Get to it."

Smoothing my hair, I try to shake the tension from my face and posture as I stroll upstairs. One look at the gigantic building block fortress that's taking up half of the playroom makes me grin. "You boys have been so busy!"

They both grin, and Jackson tussles Asher's hair. "He wanted to see how many blocks he could get into place before dinner."

"Well, you must have worked up quite an appetite." When Asher looks away for a moment, I trail my fingers along the back of Jackson's neck, waiting for his knowing smile. "Is now a good time to tell you that Timothy is in the backyard, preparing pizza in the wood oven?"

"Yay – pizza!" Asher squeals, throwing his hands up in the air and wiggling his fingers.

I usher them through the kitchen and out to the cobble-stone deck, where my personal chef Timothy is kneading the dough.

Gazing out across my immaculate backyard, I have to smile to myself. I have a beautiful home, a cleaning lady, an occasional personal chef, a masseuse, and a sexy nanny. I have a charming and brilliant son. I have a husband whom I've transformed from a bizarre nerd who could barely speak to women to an obedient provider.

It's official. I've become one of those women who has it all. Almost. That is, as long as Craig remains compliant.

I pop back into the kitchen to fetch some lemonade and crack the door to the basement. It's absolutely silent. Perhaps Craig is lost in the moment, zoned out as he does his work.

That often happens when he's set on a project. The only time he's ever disobeyed me is with this Mia incident, so I'm going to have to allow him to take his time.

He's about to kill his second wife. I should have the courtesy to let him do things his way.

43

AMY

I knew that Becca was a freaking idiot. She tied me up with an old, weak leather belt. Me, who has been working with leather since I was a child.

The only reason I sat still was so that she would relax and start babbling. Good grief, that woman is high on herself. She's accomplished a few interesting things, I'll give her that. Yet she's one of those people who thinks she's a ten when she's actually a seven.

She's also one of those people who underestimates me.

It's simple to snap the weakest point of the belt beside the buckle with quick pressure and a twist against the square edge on the back of the chair. Standing up slowly, I roll up the surprisingly long belt and tuck it into my pocket, then rub my sore wrists. Then I move silently toward the stairs, listening carefully to the male voice talking to Becca.

Craig is here.

A queasy, heavy sensation floods the pit of my stomach as I realize I don't want to see Craig and Becca together. Even after everything I've just discovered, the thought of my husband with another woman still sickens me to the core. Jealousy never makes any logical sense, yet I feel it flooding my body like poison from a snake bite.

Shoving the influx of emotions aside, I tiptoe up a few stairs so that I can hear clearly as Becca demands to know about Mia, and Craig doesn't say a word.

As they talk, I'm struck by the tone of his voice. I've never heard him like this before. With me, Craig is an equal. We are partners in life, around our home, and in marriage.

An icicle slithers down my spine. *Were.* Not *are.*

With Becca, Craig sounds like a young boy who got into trouble and is ashamed he's been caught. He sounds desperate to please her, as if he's nervous about what might happen if he lets her down.

What kind of relationship do they have? Does she always boss him around that way? Of course, I'm furious, but this entire situation also has me wildly curious.

Becca is speaking more quickly, and it's hard to hear, but it's something about Asher and pizza. "Got it?"

"Okay." Craig sounds sulky.

"Get to it," she snaps.

Rushing silently back down the stairs, I know what I have to do. Even though the thought of it feels desperately wrong. I must take control of the situation. Taking command is not really who I am. Until now.

Disappearing into the shadows behind the furnace room door, I force my body to calm down. Box breathing: inhale for four counts, hold for four, exhale for four, hold for four. My shoulders begin to lower as I feel the soles of my socked feet grounding down.

I was a bit brave when I went to the St. Mary's event and spoke to a bunch of strangers. I was kind of brave when I made it through the rain and construction to check the security footage at my shop. Now I'm going to have to be brave and corner my husband, and somehow shake the truth out of him.

Footsteps jog down the stairs, then I hear quiet shuffling noises as Craig looks around the rec room, the laundry room, then he sticks his head into the furnace room.

I left the chair in the far corner. Since this mechanical room only has one bare lightbulb, it's shadowy enough that he has to step all the way inside before he can see that the chair is empty. I slip a few steps to the right, closing the door with me in front of it.

Craig whirls around, facing me with shocked, wide eyes. "Amy!" I watch as he arranges his features into a warm smile. "So good to see you, honey."

This is totally bizarre. This man is so damn attractive to me that it used to be startling every time he came home. His scent turned me on. Those gorgeous hazel eyes were captivating.

Now he's standing right in front of me, and I just feel... numb. Just a few days ago, I would have run into his arms, needing comfort. Needing warmth. Needing my husband to help me make this horrible situation go away.

But now this man is a stranger.

Have I ever really known him? Or even witnessed glimpses of his true self?

I might never know. And that is going to absolutely eat away at me.

He's wearing a long-sleeved, slightly wrinkled dark gray t-shirt. I've never seen him leave the house in anything but a crisp button-down shirt. For some reason, this is the detail that causes me to genuinely fear for my sanity.

If I don't truly know him, I have no idea what he's capable of. Or how he'll react to me. I've never seen the real version of Craig. Well, he hasn't seen all of my sides either.

It takes a great deal of effort to stop my hands from shaking, so I nod toward the chair. I refuse to seem weak.

Anxiety can bite my ass this time.

"Pull the chair to the center of the room, and sit down with your hands on your knees."

He blinks sharply at the ice in my voice. "Amy..." He raises his hands slowly, taking a step toward me. "I can–"

My left hand lashes out, grabbing the steel crowbar leaning in front of the furnace. I lunge toward him, and the metal bar slashes through the air, stopping barely an inch from his nose.

"Do as you're told."

His mouth falls open as he freezes for a solid ten seconds. Then he nods once, grabbing the chair and sitting down directly under the lightbulb. I hate that this looks like a cheesy spy movie. I hate that I have so many questions for him and no time. I hate that it breaks my heart to see him staring at me with anything but love.

"Tell me if Olivia is still alive."

Craig's eyes almost bug out cartoon style. The urge to laugh hits me straight in the solar plexus. "How do you know about her?" he rasps, his shoulders pitching forward, fingers clenching his knees.

"I found your murder board in our garage."

He draws in a slow, shaky breath, staring down at my knees. "Does Becca know?"

Watching him like this makes my heart ache. To see him so *changed*... squashed under Becca's stylish designer boot... It's demented, and I'm having trouble processing everything.

It's like the square peg that won't go into the round hole of Asher's preschool toys.

"Yes. More importantly, why are you kidnapping and robbing these women?" He stares down at his shoes for a moment, until I roughly tap the bottom of his chin with the crowbar. "Look at me, and answer honestly."

He obeys, thank goodness. I honestly don't know what I'm going to do if he becomes unreasonable.

No. I *do* know what I'm going to do. It's just so revolting I can't think about it.

"Becca needs to reach the next level. Which means advertising, marketing, and getting better designers for her merch."

"She doesn't have enough subscribers to warrant having extravagant merchandise," I practically spit. Then I shake my head. "Stay on point. Why are you the one who has to fund her social media schlock?"

He smiles sweetly, his head tilting to the side. "She's the first one who's really seen me. It's fun to watch her build her own empire. Plus, she's really clever at things she's interested in. Like her content and channels. It's kind of her own puzzle. Working out exactly what sort of content to make in order to grow quickly. Finding her audience in interesting corners online."

His eyes light up when he speaks of her. Has he ever been that proud of me?

"Why do you have to steal the money? I thought you made..." My free hand lands against my forehead. "Right. You don't have a tech job. What did you do before Becca?"

A sudden flash of pure madness in his eyes makes my hands tighten around the heavy steel. "I bounced around.

Did all kinds of things. But Becca needed a part-time husband, so she straightened me out."

My back teeth start to grind. "Do you really think she's going to keep you now that she knows you killed Mia?"

There's an actual whimper. "No... You don't know about that, do you?"

"Of course I know. I found her murder board in the garage."

Craig leans back, his index finger tapping his thigh. He's rattled. "So you solved the puzzle lock? I have to say, Amy, I'm genuinely impressed."

"I watched you do a similar one a few months ago." I pause, then add, "I did many puzzles as a child too."

He stares toward the humming furnace for a moment. "Oh yeah. I forgot about that." His broad shoulders shrug casually. "But you can't do anything about it."

I wrap both palms around the heavy crowbar. The steel feels powerful in my hands. It's a sensation that triggers something primal.

I need to bash him. Need to hurt him.

"Really? You don't think I'm going to stop you from killing more women?"

His mouth shifts, as if he's running his tongue along the back of his teeth. Then he huffs, "You can't prove anything about Mia. It was an accident. People die in car accidents all the time."

Oh no. My grip shifts on the weighty bar of steel.

Craig doesn't know that the police are aware Mia was murdered. And they're connecting the rest.

And I don't know how the murderer in front of me will react when I tell him.

44

AMY

The furnace finally clicks off, and we can hear a child's excited squeal of delight from outside the tiny barred-up window. "Pizza is Asher's favorite food." Craig's voice is a calm murmur. "Becca doesn't let him have it very often. Her personal chef is here, so they're using the outdoor oven."

A wave of longing to hold my own son sweeps through me. He needs me to get through this. It's impossible to guess how dangerous Craig and Becca might be if they were to gang up on me. So I'm going to have to maintain the upper hand.

The cloying mustiness of the mechanical room is wearing on my nerves. Plus, the bare concrete floor is chilly on my socked feet. "How many women did you rob?" I sweep the crowbar slowly in front of his face. "How many did you drug and kidnap?"

"Not a lot." His gaze is moving around too much. He glances at the tall shelf filled with cleaning supplies, a small toolbox, spray cans, a few baskets full of odds and ends, plus a mop leaning against the wall. "Not all of them were kidnappings. A few were simply clever thefts, and the women didn't notice until hours or days later."

"I'm going to stop you from hurting anyone else." My voice feels strained, like I can't seem to get enough air in. This dark, musty space is starting to get to me.

"You're not going to go to the police." Craig flashes a charming smile. "You can't. You don't have any evidence."

I'm supposed to keep a poker face. I'm supposed to keep playing all of my cards close to the vest. Instead, a hysterical laugh bubbles out of me. "Evidence?" I sputter. "I have all of your brainstorming boards. Or murder boards. Whatever you want to call them. I have photos of the ones from Becca's garage, and the originals from your garage."

"*Our* garage."

"Absolutely not."

He snorts, his hands slowly sliding higher up his legs. "You think any cop is going to believe you? No way. They'll find out that your husband has been with another woman, and they'll think that you're jealous and insane."

Swallowing hard, I find it difficult to admit he has a point. I would definitely sound like a lunatic.

"Plus," he says, slowly leaning forward. "All of the robberies were of your customers. You don't think that's going to look suspicious?"

"Bastard." I poke him sharply in the forehead with the curved end of the crowbar. Just enough to make him jump. "I said, hands on your knees."

He sits up straight, but his weight is shifting to his feet.

"I will knock you out in a heartbeat." My voice is flat. "I don't care if all the cops in the world come rushing here. In fact, I'll call them myself."

"No!" He cringes back into the chair. "Don't do that. Please. Becca would kill me."

It's hard to concentrate while watching the man I loved changing personalities several times a minute. Is he actually out of his mind?

"Elevated people always reach a compromise," he states with a hopeful glimmer in his eye. "Don't you want to compromise?"

"Now you're regurgitating Becca's woo-woo mantras?"

We hear her laughing outside the window, then Asher's squeal of delight. "Maybe in a few days, we can make pizza with our Asher," Craig says hopefully.

Stepping back, I kick the door wide open, but keep my body blocking it. "You will never see my son again."

"*Our* son."

"Not on your life." I snort. "*Your* life. You don't really exist. I've looked you up. There is no mention of you online, and you're already married to another woman. Therefore, you're not my husband, and you have absolutely no legal tie to my son."

He flinches back hard, as if I poked him with a taser. "Amy, honey, you can't—"

"I can and I will. Now get back on track." The crowbar is getting heavy, so I switch most of the weight to my left hand to shake out my right shoulder. "Why are you robbing women instead of getting a real job?"

He rolls his eyes, pouting. He looks so childish. Like he's forgotten how to be the Craig he's always been for me. Maybe that's a good thing.

"Those women aren't doing anything productive with the money," he says. "They spend a criminal amount of money on trinkets. It's ridiculously easy to drain their accounts when they disappear for a little while. People just assume they've gone on a shopping spree, and all those jewelry and designer goods are easily pawned."

"Theft is theft. It doesn't matter who it's from."

"But women like that are soulless," he says gently. "They came from money instead of making their own. Unless they're creating something of substance, they can't be redeemed."

"Oh, my..." The realization almost makes me dizzy. "Becca really has brainwashed you, hasn't she?"

He smirks, still looking so strange without his normal button-down shirt. The t-shirt makes his neck seem skinny. How have I never noticed that before? He's also paler than I remember. "I've always been searching for something. Becca has given me guidance. Purpose. Plus, my first child."

"You're a puppet." I refuse to feel even the slightest bit sorry for him. "You did all of her dirty work. When the police begin to investigate, you're both equally liable."

He snorts. "Don't be dim. The incidents were in very different areas. In different ways. And the women had almost zero connection. There's no way they'll put it together."

"Echo Radcliffe was just found dead. Leah Kline is missing and presumed dead. Investigators are putting it together. They also know something else."

Craig is perfectly silent, his vivid eyes looking darker in the dim light. Then his head drops, and he's blinking strangely. Is he finally worried?

"All of the incidents happened on Mondays." I pause to let that sink in. "The news is calling you the Monday Maniac."

An odd noise circles us in the tight space. Craig begins to

sway forward and back in the chair, his hands in fists, bouncing on his knees, like a toddler starting a tantrum. I've never seen him this utterly frazzled.

My husband has always been cool as a cucumber. I've never seen him angry. Never seen him frustrated.

I've certainly never heard the thready high-pitched whine rattling his throat like this.

Which means I really don't know what lengths he'll go to if he tries to leave this room without telling me everything I need to know.

A young woman's life might be on the line.

And now, maybe so is mine.

45

AMY

It's difficult to shove down the revolting realization that my husband doesn't really exist. Not the way I saw him. Somehow, I must have been lost in love. Lost in what I wanted to see.

Deep breath. I am going to take care of this. I just need to stay in the moment.

If Olivia, or any other girls, have already been taken, I'm the only one who can save them. And it's getting late.

"Hey," I say gently, waiting for Craig to meet my eyes. "I'm sure you've memorized her schedule. Where is Olivia right now?"

"She's on her way to–" He stops short, looking up at me in shock. "Dammit, Amy, I almost told you." His face freezes, then he gives his head a shake and smiles sweetly. "I really do love you, you know."

My stomach clenches. "Do you actually think that matters now?"

His eyebrows knit together. "Yes." His voice is scratchy.

Wounded. "It's the one thing that Becca didn't plan for or anticipate. Our love."

"I was just supposed to be a baby machine to give you an extra son?"

"It's very important to me to continue my line. So, at first, yes." His grin is disarming. "Along with your client files, of course."

Stepping back, I lean against the door frame as it strikes me that these women are in danger because of my records. My business. I'm never going to know exactly how much of this is my fault. But I have to keep him talking.

"Honey," I start slowly, "I know that Becca pressures you quite a bit." He nods quickly, his eyes furtively flicking to the window. "She must need an awful lot of money to keep you so busy."

The chair creaks as he shifts his weight. "It's not just the money."

"Then what is it?"

"It's a challenge." His face lights up. "Figuring out their lifestyles, guessing or cracking the passwords. Draining just enough of the accounts that it looks frivolous. Taking just enough of their possessions without making it obvious that there's been a theft, unless a full-on robbery will sell the story better in that case."

His eyes sparkle. "Some of the girls really have their guard up, so it's tricky to charm them away for a quick drink. But there's always a way."

"And you always manage to figure out the way?" I ask as gently as possible. "You don't have to hurt them?"

His beautiful lips snarl into a frown. "It depends how much of a rush Becca is in for the money. Sometimes I have to hurry a job along more than I want to. Especially with the extra projects I have to work into my schedule now."

"The ones that you're planning in my garage, that Becca doesn't know about?"

His jaw and fingers tighten. "I can't believe you told her about that. You have no bloody idea how much trouble I'm going to be in. It's going to take a long time to calm her down, which is going to mean even more jobs." His eyes narrow. "It takes a lot of time and planning to trail these girls."

"Focus, honey. Where is Olivia now?"

"Why are you so fixated on her?"

"Because her board was the only one with a date. Tomorrow. Which means you have something planned, don't you?"

I hate to admit there's a strange satisfaction in watching Craig squirm. Fingers digging into his knees, ankles turning outward as he shifts. The backs of his hands bounce, then his shoulder drops as if a shiver ran through him.

"You know that I can't tell you about her." He looks up at me through his lashes." People going through episodes of change and growth don't have to explain themselves or their processes."

"Stop repeating Becca-speak!" Lunging forward, I use the crowbar to give him three sharp raps in the forehead. "Tell me if Olivia is alive."

Staring into his eyes, I know it's the truth when he mutters, "Yes. She's alive."

"Where is she?"

His head tips back and forth, sing-songing, "Magician secrets."

I honestly think he's losing it. Is it possible that there is a Becca-Craig, and an Amy-Craig in his addled brain, and trying to combine the two is making him snap?

Or. Something falls into place. There might be another one, as well. Crazy-murderer-Craig.

"What do you think Becca will say when I point out that all of the girls on the boards at my house are prettier than the girls at her house?" I drawl casually.

His cheeks pale, hands clutching together. "You can't say something like that. She will freak out."

"I can and I will"

"You know, Amy, you've always been so smart. You always make things work. So we're going to work this out. I know it."

"You're not going to make up excuses as to why the new batch of girls are prettier?" I lean in slightly. "And... younger?"

His left eye twitches slightly. "What do you mean by that?"

I've touched a nerve. Craig has never been good at confrontation. Those intense hazel eyes are too expressive. Too revealing. My suspicion is now confirmed.

"You need all of that extra money for Becca's business." I keep my voice slow and even, stepping forward with the crowbar firmly gripped in my hands. "But you suddenly need even more money, don't you? Another big, expensive life change is on the horizon."

His Adam's apple bobs as he swallows hard. There's a slight shimmer of perspiration on his brow. "What... I don't know what you're talking about."

It's a dark, sick thrill to realize I've finally put together an answer to why he's been such a psycho. Why he would need a lot of extra cash fast and couldn't tell Becca about it. Why he suddenly flipped from just robbing easy targets to robbing women he might need to murder. "Oh, yes, you do. It involves a young, pretty girl. And the situation might end up costing you a fortune. Yet you don't want your two families to suffer, do you?"

He leans back again. "You have no idea what you're talking about. You're just trying to get me to incriminate myself."

"Oh, that ship has sailed."

Taking a cautious step closer, I keep the heavy bar of steel between us as I raise an eyebrow.

"You didn't think I'd find out you knocked up Penny?"

46

AMY

Craig lunges for me with raw madness in his eyes.

Terror surges through me like wildfire. He's already hurt me so much. That ends now.

Lifting the crowbar sharply, I shove it upward under his chin, knocking him back. "In your chair," I bark. He lurches back, the old chair creaking. "Your wife drugged me and tied me up. Shall I do that to you?"

His energy snaps from rage to meek in a blink. It's as if he flipped a switch. "No," he sulks, rubbing his chin. "How could you hit me, Amy? You know I love you. This is all just a big... you know. Misunderstanding."

"Hands on your knees and sit up straight."

I wait until he's settled and looking straight at me before asking, "What do you think Becca is going to do to you when she finds out you got Penny pregnant?"

I stare in fascination as Craig's expression blanks while his shoulders shake. "How did... you can't think... Um, that's not true."

To be fair, I was only maybe fifty percent sure until this

moment. For such a conniving person, it's comical that he doesn't realize his face is an open book. "Of course it's true. Penny can't lie to me either. She's been sick and dizzy with an alleged stomach flu for a few weeks, which started about a month after you two had been getting quite close."

"Don't tell Becca!" His legs press together, fingers digging into the top of his thighs. "Please. I'll do anything."

Wow, he is seriously terrified. *Good.* "Where is Olivia?"

There's a grinding sound from the back of his throat. "You know I can't tell you that."

"Saving her is more important than your money problems. Do you have her holed up somewhere? Or are you planning to kidnap her tomorrow?"

"She's a bitch. You've said so yourself. Why do you care?"

"Because civilized people have a basic concept of right and wrong!" I snap, louder than intended. We both look toward the window as there's another round of laughter outside.

"Craig, you are running out of time. After dinner, Becca is going to come back down here. If you don't tell me what your plan with Olivia is, I'm going to tell her about Penny."

His face pales instantly. "Let's make a deal."

My feet are chilled on the rough concrete, and the crowbar is getting heavy. He can't see me fidget. I'm the person in control right now. "No deals. Tell me now."

Craig's hands rise slowly. "Let me get something out of a secret compartment behind the furnace."

Allowing him to move might not be smart. Yet I'm so curious, I can't help it.

Stepping directly in front of the door, I raise the crowbar. "Move at an absolutely glacial speed, and keep your hands where I can see them." It's a relief that he obeys. Of course, who knows how much practice he's had obeying Becca and her whims?

He moves slowly toward the furnace, then pokes a screw in the drywall behind it. He lifts a panel, lowering it to the floor to reveal a hidden safe. He blocks the number panel with his shoulder as he enters the code, then opens the door.

My blood feels overheated, pumping too fast. The safe isn't big enough for Olivia's entire body, but he might take out a finger. Or a map to where she is.

He pulls out some sort of tray, then turns toward me. "I've kept... um... souvenirs from every... target."

I was not expecting this. Please, please, please don't let this be what I actually think it might be.

Staring slowly upward, I can see it in his body language. He's proud of this collection. Thrilled to be sharing his treasure. He sees this secret stash as a personal triumph.

Craig is positively beaming as he holds out what has to be his serial killer trophies.

47

AMY

Craig holds up a velvet board covered in earrings, as if expecting me to be thrilled.

Diamonds, rubies, emeralds, sapphires. Large gold hoops. Tiny, dangling, elegant crystals. They sparkle in the dim light, as I stare in disbelief. The collection is larger than I could possibly have expected.

Trying to blank my face, I ask, "Where precisely did these come from?"

"I keep the earrings that they're wearing when they... You know."

Oh no. No. No. No.

When he robbed them or when he... No. There are dozens of pairs. He cannot have killed this many women. "When *what*?"

He shrugs, casually tilting the velvet board slightly as one large diamond stud rolls toward the raised edge. "You know. When they... *Left.*"

Craig pokes at a pair of beautiful ruby teardrops. "Sometimes they're just small, everyday earrings," he says casually, as if he didn't just confess to being a serial killer. "These ones would look nice on you. Becca doesn't know about them. You can have all of them if you help me."

Dammit.

"I knew you'd keep trophies," I breathe, staring in horror at his offering. "I wasn't sure if the murder boards themselves counted as trophies because the girls never touched them. But that's something they were wearing. Definitely trophies."

He looks at me in confusion, then bursts into laughter. "Oh, my... You mean like serial killer trophies? Like their hair or something? No, this is totally different. This is just for money. Like a nest egg."

I stare in utter shock at the board, then up to meet his eyes. Once, I thought I knew this person as a kind, sweet man. Now he is an absolute psychopath. Which means I cannot predict any of his behavior at all.

He must see my expression switch to utter disgust. His eyes drop, locking on a point on the floor as he mumbles, "I'm not... I'm not a..."

"Craig, this is evidence. Do you understand that?"

He inhales sharply, stepping back. "Amy, we've always been a team. I need you to be cool about this."

His mannerisms and emotions are careening all over the place. It's absolutely disturbing to see this impostor of my husband. As if an alien were wearing my Craig as a skin suit. The Craig I thought I loved never really existed.

Which means I'm going to be dealing with a lot of emotions down the road. Now is not the time to give in to them. However, he probably expects me to be emotional. To be weak.

"Hey, honey," I begin slowly, forcing a gentle smile, "the

only way to get me back on your team is to tell me where Olivia is right this second."

"I want to work together. I really do. But I can't," he says sadly.

"Of course you can. Then we can be a team again." My smile falters. "Becca doesn't need to know about your souvenirs, or about Penny and your baby on the way. We're both very smart people. We can figure out a way to get plenty of money fast without having to hurt anyone."

"Why do you care about them?"

It's sickening that he would even ask such a question. The Craig I knew showed empathy toward everyone. Everything. He taught Asher that we don't bash toys around because it hurts them. Showed him how to scoop a spider into a cup and take it out to the back garden instead of squishing it.

I have to stop thinking of him as someone I know. And since Craig's plan is definitely going down tomorrow, I am the only person who can save Olivia. If it's not too late.

"I care because hurting people is wrong," I say simply. "That's not the kind of world we want our son to live in, right?"

"Don't be so naïve." He shakes his head sadly. "Life has winners and losers. I need to be a winner, and I need that payout tomorrow. End of discussion."

The slightly dusty air feels thin. As if there isn't enough oxygen. There's something wild lurking in his eyes. True crazy. Unhinged. He thinks he's correct to do these things.

Craig sets the tray back in the safe, but leaves it open as he turns toward me. There's been too much familiarity here. I need to take control again before he does something dangerous.

I use my most commanding tone to bark, "Back in the chair."

"No."

There's another round of laughter from just outside, then I hear Becca call out, "If you're finished, we can go for a few laps of the garden before your bedtime."

Craig shifts his weight from one foot to the other. "Jackson takes care of Asher's bedtime routine if I'm not around. She'll be coming soon."

I watch as his gaze darts around the room. Following his line of sight carefully, I see him contemplate the mop and broom. The row of cleaning fluid bottles. The odds and ends of hardware supplies in baskets.

That bastard is trying to solve a puzzle right now.

My guts and brain finally coordinate and snap to the answer. "You're supposed to take me out down here, aren't you?"

His chin jerks up. "Of course. But I was hoping I could get you to join us."

"Sure. I'll join you. If you tell me about tomorrow's plan right now."

I detest how sexy he looks as he runs a hand through his hair and smirks at me. "Come on, Amy. I've made a few mistakes, but I'm not that stupid."

"Then I'll tell Becca everything. See if she can talk some sense into you."

His eyes blaze. "You wouldn't dare."

For the first time ever, I see genuine fear in his eyes. Across his entire face. It's a lightning-bolt moment as we both realize that I am deadly serious.

And if he makes a single move...

Emphasis on the *deadly*.

48

CRAIG

My mind is swimming. I need to stop that immediately.

I'm not supposed to let my thoughts swim for too long, or I get groggy. Like Becca is always harping at me, I get sloppy. Yet sometimes my thoughts tangle and swirl, and unless I have a puzzle in front of me, I don't know what to concentrate on.

Shifting my feet, I try to sit up straighter while keeping my body relaxed. This piece of junk old chair is not comfortable.

Wait. At the moment, Amy is the puzzle.

Focus up, man. There's no reason to fear Amy, no matter how hard she glares at me.

I will definitely get out of this. I always do. Every single time.

People have always underestimated me because I look so innocent. There's something about my eyes that just makes everyone trust me. Plus, I've got an unusual reserve of pure charm when I need it. Obviously, I've used the hell out of this power since I was a child. Back when everyone said I was a sweet little scamp who deserved a cookie.

Since then, I've also apparently deserved two wives and a hot young side piece. I flirt with every target to get them to trust me implicitly. Even if they aren't interested in dating me, they're interested enough to chat. To learn more about me.

People just believe me when I tell them I've gone to Harvard, or own a tech company, or that I'm the solution to whatever problems they have. I'm just a middle-of-the-road guy who just wants to help. Yet when I hit that charm button, I can become captivating.

Now it's time to help myself out of this ridiculous jam. I'll need my focus tomorrow for the job.

It's difficult to keep a slight hint of fear in my eyes as Amy stares down at me. I'm not afraid. I'm freaking ecstatic. I love that Penny is pregnant. Having as many children as possible is the only real legacy I'm going to have in this lifetime.

I hope it's a girl. Becca will kill me if I name her Piper, but maybe something else cute like that. Peony. Or... Poppy. Or maybe something serene, like Fern. Or...

Wait. Wrong brainstorming. Focus up, man.

I've never seen Amy angry. Ever. Even when I messed up the groceries, or when Asher smashed her favorite coffee mug. She was mildly irked, at most. I didn't think she was capable of true anger.

I start to shift my weight again in the rickety wooden chair, then stop. She can't see me fidget. Can't let her know that I'm eyeing up the thickness of that mop handle and wondering if I can use it to knock out the wife I love.

"Honey, I–"

"Never call me that again," she snaps.

"Fine. You can't really hurt me." My eyes open wide as I smile gently. I should tell her that I love her. Explain how much I love our son. Then I see a certain hardness pass through her expression. It's as if... she's pulling on a new personality, just like I often do. Which means pure emotion isn't going to work.

"You need me, Amy," I murmur softly. "You haven't found all of the planning boards."

"Yes, I have." Her beautiful lips are confined to a firm, straight line.

I'd love to jump up and kiss her. She's not as classically beautiful as Becca, but I've always thought that Amy was sexier. There's a wildness about her that runs to her core. She doesn't let it out very often, keeping a quiet, reserved aura around her like a safety blanket. Yet I can tell it's hiding deep inside her. I've always known it was there.

I should keep her talking. "Really? Where?"

"In our, sorry, *my* garage. The large boards and the filing cabinet. The same here in Becca's garage."

My elbows twitch back toward my body – an involuntary reaction to shield myself. Becca's fancy breathing exercises are no help now, as I start to actually panic. Has Amy seen... no. She couldn't have.

Her teeth grit together as she notices my reaction, and she raises the crowbar with one hand. It would take the slightest movement for her to bash in my skull, the weight itself pulling the bar down hard. So I remain perfectly still as she pulls out her phone and flips through photos.

Oh no.

She stops, and I already know which board she's staring at, her pupils growing wide as her hand quivers slightly. She squints, zooming in. Then her expression falls completely, a neutral mask taking over her pretty face.

"Me," she mutters flatly. "It's true. The two of you planned me."

My mind races with excuses and comes up blank. There's nothing I can say to make this better. Knowing that I hurt her is going to haunt me forever.

Her thumb slides around to various parts of the photo, as her fist tightens on the bar of steel. Then her jaw tightens. "I was going through the boards of missing women, and the ones with recent dates. I missed your brainstorming board for me." She swallows hard. "Apparently, my job was perfect to help your thieving, conniving plans." Amy shoots me a glare so vicious I jump back in my chair. "There's more of *her* handwriting than yours."

I wait while watching her take a slow, deep breath. It's not like she's calming herself. It's like... I'm not sure what this is. As if she's fighting something inside her.

"You don't have to worry about me getting caught, if that's what's upsetting you. I was always extremely careful. They didn't have a single personal detail about me. Any time I met with someone, I used my real first name instead."

Oh no. From the blaze of raw fire across her pretty features, that was the wrong thing to say.

"Which is?"

"Nicholas. That's why that name was totally off the table when we were choosing—"

"*Silence.*"

Her tone is quiet. Sharp. Kind of eerie.

There is a light in her eyes. No... a darkness. Something has changed. Clicked. Like the last piece of a puzzle snapping into place and revealing the true nature of the solution.

Amy always flushes when she's nervous. The base of her throat should be beet red at a time like this. It's not. Her skin is smooth and pale. Not even blotchy.

I look up into the lovely face of my darling second wife, and my blood runs cold. A few minutes ago, I was positive that I'd seen every side of this woman.

This is new. Like a totally different person standing in front of me. I've never witnessed rage so utterly icy.

This woman is capable of anything.

Now I am truly afraid.

49

AMY

There's more rustling outside the small basement window, pointing out to both of us that time is running out.

Craig's eyes narrow. "Last chance, Amy. Are you going to drop this?"

"Absolutely not." I hesitate just long enough to take a full breath. "If you tell me what your plan for tomorrow is right now, I won't hurt you."

He flinches back as if I'd slapped him. "Amy, you wouldn't—"

The furnace kicks back in, and Craig uses the split-second distraction to lunge at me, his hands reaching for my throat. I half-expected him to try to push me away from the door at some point, but I can't believe he'd actually attack me.

Spinning fast, I use the crowbar to block him, shoving my entire weight against him so that he stumbles back toward the chair.

I raise the steel bar up as if I were about to take a mighty swing with a golf club, then freeze. What do I think I'm going to do, brain him? I can't do that to my husband. Even though he's not really my husband at all.

Craig fakes a weak punch toward my head, then kicks the front of my shin, causing me to stagger to the side. I take a split second to focus, then crack him hard at the top of his shoulder, right at the acromioclavicular joint to do the most damage.

He drops with a shuddering groan, clutching his arm. "Honey, how could you?"

I smack him on the other side, clipping him just above the bicep, hoping to hit the nerve for maximum pain. "Just tell me everything about Olivia, and we can be civilized again."

He looks up at me with those beautiful caramel hazel eyes. "You'd never really hurt me, Amy. You're a nice girl. Exactly what I need for balance, and you make a good mother for my son."

The second I raise the crowbar again, Craig sweeps his leg hard and lightning-fast, catching me in the ankle and making me stumble. In a blink, his entire weight is on top of me, smashing me onto the concrete. The crowbar falls out of my hands with a loud clatter, rolling halfway under the furnace.

He pins my shoulders down as he straddles me, his weight crushing my lungs. His fingers digging into my scapula change absolutely everything.

Somehow, I have been holding onto the belief that he would come around. Come to his senses. Some tiny part of me still believed that Craig would give his head a shake and turn back into the rational, kind, smart, and balanced man I knew.

Now he's gone. Or he never existed. It doesn't even matter now.

But now, with Craig's snarling glare and his merciless grip on me, it hits me like a lightning bolt that I'm in danger just as much as those other women. I apparently know nothing about him.

However, Craig thinks he knows everything about me.

Nothing could be further from the truth.

"I wanted to keep you around," he growls, reaching for the chair with one hand. "You're an amazing mom for Asher. And great company. I didn't want it to turn out this way."

"What are you going to do? You can't knock me out with sedatives. I don't have anything worth robbing."

Oddly, his expression turns completely neutral. "All I have to do is obey what Becca said," he says serenely. "She told me to come down here and take you out. As usual, she was right."

"What?" I struggle, but he's just too heavy.

"I tried to reason with you. Tried to bribe you. I told you about the jewelry, and I wouldn't even share that with her." He leans close to breathe into my ear, even as I try to push him away. "You would've been such a good assistant if you joined me."

"Never." I twist and shake between his legs, but between him and the concrete floor, there's nowhere to go.

His grin is changing. As if an inner viciousness is finally sneaking out. "It's something I'm really good at, Amy."

"What is?"

"Manipulating these empty-headed women. Controlling them like puppets." His wild eyes are no longer sexy. They're manic. "Now that Becca has given me focus, it's so easy. Plus, the planning part is truly fascinating to me."

Becca controls Craig, Craig controls other women to earn his power back. In a way, it makes some sort of demented sense.

There's a tap at the window as if someone kicked it. Craig's head twitches up, his chin lifting, and I realize it's my only chance.

Yanking the old leather belt from my back pocket, I jerk and spin, surprising him enough to knock him to the side. My hands are a lightning blur as I circle his throat with the belt, twisting it tightly and pulling hard.

He's so surprised that I manage to flip him onto his front, grabbing his right hand and twisting it straight up his back while heaving on the leather strap.

He begins to choke, sputtering hard as he partially turns toward me. "Need... something."

Without losing my grip, I try to steady him. This is not the time to lose focus. I'm ready for this.

"Tell you..." he chokes. "Important."

It takes me a moment to squirm around until my knee is pinning his wrist into his back so I can fist his hair with one hand and grip the belt with the other. I loosen it just enough that he can speak.

"You're already in this too," he croaks.

"Because I'm your fake wife?"

He turns a bit more to face me. The way his eyes are twinkling so sweetly fills me with revulsion. I loathe the way that he thinks I'm still attracted to him, even though he's pure poison.

"Because, honey, you're the one who chose each victim personally."

50

AMY

My hands twitch so hard I almost drop the belt. Regaining my composure, I twist the knee that's digging into Craig's wrist, wrapping the belt around my forearm to yank it tight around his throat in a blink.

"What the hell are you talking about?"

"You're the one who always chose my targets."

"What do you mean?"

His charming smile is unnerving. "Your customers who were polite were simply robbed. They woke up dizzy, then walked away. Embarrassed and afraid to tell anyone about the ordeal, but fine." The creep has the audacity to laugh. "The ones that you said were unbelievably nasty to you are the ones that I... you know. They had to go."

I swear my pulse stops for a solid ten seconds. "Wh-what do you mean?"

He blinks in surprise. "I can't let someone who was cruel to my darling wife just walk around in this world. They're not allowed to be happy after behaving like that. After upsetting you so much. I love you."

Son of a... I don't want to know this. I don't want this to be my life. Don't want this moment to be happening right here under my hands that are seconds from squeezing the life out of the man I was madly in love with just a few days ago.

"How could you do such a thing?" I gasp. "How could you do something like that to innocent women?"

He snorts. "Not innocent. Useless. Money is all they could ever be good for. Becca needs the money. Well, and now Penny, too."

My mind is racing as I yank harder on his hair. "All of your focus is on Becca. Everything she needs. What about what I need? What about what our son needs? You didn't even care that Asher wasn't in a good school. We wanted him to be an engineer, since he loves building so much."

His neck cranks around a bit more as his eyes lock with mine. "Amy, honey, Asher would never go to university with you as a mother. You don't have the money or the drive, sweetheart. And I don't think your Asher is smart enough to get into engineering."

Time stops.

A few dust motes sail away from the furnace vent. I see the grain in the wood in the creaky chair beside us. The faint green gleam of the small blowtorch in the open toolbox. Smell the hint of bleach and vinegar, and some chemical pine fragrance of the cleaners.

Craig's hips shift, his free hand useless at this angle. He still thinks he's getting out of this.

He dared to insult my son?

My hand twists Craig's head to grind his nose into the concrete below. His screeching whine is deeply satisfying.

Fortunately, it's quiet enough that nobody in the backyard can hear.

Time still feels altered. It's running at a quarter of the pace it's supposed to.

I can sense every single beat of my pulse as it throbs, sending waves of blood through my veins.

I've heard of people seeing red.

This isn't red. It's more of a swirling orange and black. There are gray smudges around the edges of my vision. Like I'm floating. My body knows what to do. My mind is taking a step back, simply watching what's going on as if I were comfortably settled in front of a movie. A slightly dull, badly lit movie that smells like dust, concrete and a whiff of bleach.

Working with leather for years has made my hands, wrists, and forearms incredibly strong. Craig wrestles like a demon for several minutes as I find my footing to hold him in place. Wedging my sock against the furnace, I bear down hard.

My focus narrows in. Craig can't draw a full breath with both compressed lungs and a leather strap compressing his carotid arteries. While grinding his nose into the floor, I pull even harder. At this angle, it will only take ten to thirteen seconds. My hands clench with a savage force, as if it isn't even me. As if I were overtaken by another entity. My gut knows the correct thing to do.

Craig's movements gradually cease, his body slowly growing limp as if deflating. Once he's unconscious, I compress the jugular vein and the trachea. Luckily, the furnace shuts off in time for me to clearly hear the fluttering, unsteady rasp of Craig's breathing as it eventually stops.

The silence is bliss.

51

BECCA

So much for my media cleanse. Not that I need to be one hundred percent honest with my followers anyway. My authenticity comes from the soul, not minuscule details.

Well, I wasn't taking any content in today, therefore keeping my mind refreshed. Yet there's no way I can resist posting these stunning photos of the gorgeous pizzas Chef Timothy has created.

It is the impeccable aspirational lifestyle moment that I need to be known for – the back garden with fairy lights glowing, my adorable son enjoying gourmet pizza, and the lavish greenery and roses all around.

I tell my viewers that I convey everything about my world. I'm an open book, sharing this incredible life experience to inspire them. That my universe centers on perfect motherhood.

There's no reason for them to know that my husband is in the basement killing his other wife because she's veering out of her lane.

I certainly can't have that odd mousy woman ruining

everything we've built together. Well, it's mainly been me doing the building. Craig just supplies the money. Amy had been supplying a detailed list of wealthy contacts who are easy targets, but Craig has certainly gotten hold of her database by now.

Glancing toward the basement window, I wonder what's taking him so long. Knowing how sentimental he is, he's likely making teary goodbyes, or trying to talk Amy into being reasonable. I have a feeling that he really does love her. Not like he loves, obeys, and worships me. Yet there is certainly some fondness there. Craig's a very caring man.

A sudden dark thought creeps through me as I watch Asher running in wide circles across the grass. I should have looked into Amy's mother. Will she keep the other Asher now that Amy is gone? Or put him up for adoption when Craig disappears from their lives? She'll have no real name or way to track him.

And there's no way in hell I'm letting that brat live here with his father. What a nightmare. He's probably never even worked in video before. I don't have the bandwidth to train someone from point zero, and there's no way to explain where he came from.

Plus, Craig might have to go underground for a bit while this Monday Maniac crap blows over. Although, as I've learned quite well, once the media gets its filthy hands on a shocking alliterative term, they'll drag it out as much as possible for as long as possible.

It's been a weight on my chest from the second I realized that Craig's work has been noticed. I shouldn't blame Amy, since she's just the one who told me the news. Yet I feel like everything that has gone sideways is her fault.

Fine. I roll my shoulders back and smile. I'll simply use

the angst in my blog posts. Everyone has a stressful nightmare weekend now and then, and they don't need to know
all of the details.

"Mommy, are you going to eat some more?" Asher chirps.

"I already had a whole slice." I smile, rustling his hair.

"Yeah, but I had two slices and Jackson had three."

"Very observant, buddy." Jackson reaches out to pat
Asher's shoulder. "You're getting really fast at noticing
numbers."

My son stares at me until I give him a better answer.
"You need more food because you are a growing boy. Jackson
needs more food because he's a big, strong man." I shrug.
"Mommy has to stay delicate so that she fits into the sample-
size dresses that one of her contacts is hopefully going to
send her in a few weeks."

"Really?" Jackson flashes me a grin. "That Alice Blue
group, or whatever it was?"

"Yes. I'm meeting with their people in a couple of weeks."

His dark eyes glow with pride, and I'm dazzled all over
again by how breathtakingly sexy he is. Not only is he fabulous with Asher, he understands my lifestyle completely.
Plus, he pays attention to details about the real me.

I always felt that Craig was more focused on Asher, my
house, and planning his targets than actually seeing me for
the woman I am. A man who doesn't see the real you is not a
man worth having. I did an entire "Becca Gets Honest" series
about that a few months ago.

"It's a shame that PR chick had to leave before dinner,"
Jackson says as he wipes Asher's mouth with a linen napkin,
laughing at the way he squirms. "This is the whole lifestyle
thing that she's going to be representing, right?"

My shoulders tighten. "PR chick?"

He looks at me blankly. "Yeah. Catherine York from Avenue PR. You were having tea with her earlier."

The tiny bit of pizza I ate threatens to come back up. I swallow hard. "I didn't introduce you. How do you know her name?"

He frowns. "She got the dates wrong and came for your appointment yesterday. I wasn't going to say anything. She seems really sweet."

I thought Amy had just been sneaking around the back-yard and garage. Not introducing herself to Jackson and trying to pry her way into... My fists clutch at my dress as I barely suppress a scream.

Screw Amy and her revolting fake sweetness. It kills me that she just pranced onto my property, speaking with my child and poking around. How did she become such a liar? Craig always went on and on about her being so sweet. Whenever he hauls her corpse up from the basement, I might actually kick her a few times just to vent some frus-tration.

"Right. Thanks," I murmur.

Sometimes, I wonder how much Jackson really knows. I've caught him reading childcare books. He's also become quite talented in gauging my moods, knowing when I'm in the headspace to interact with my son and when I cannot handle that high-pitched voice.

He doesn't know who Amy is. Didn't ask any questions when I sent him to take photos of Amy's house to see if there really was a garage just like mine.

He doesn't know everything, but does Jackson know too much? And if he does, is he wise enough to stay silent?

52

AMY

It's like watching a documentary close up.

No control. No attachment. It's simply... *fascinating* as I observe Craig's body gradually becoming limp.

Every pore. The curve of his ear. Even his thick hair seems to go flat.

His legs twitch a few times, then he spasms as if trying to throw me off. He pushes back against my knee, and against the floor, but his hands are useless.

Only one thing will stop my hand from wrenching on the belt. More time to be absolutely sure.

Once Craig has been still for a full minute, I slide two fingers along his neck to check for a pulse. Nothing. Flipping him onto his back, I open one of his eyes to check for pupil dilation. Nothing. My hand lightly resting on his chest doesn't move. No breath.

He's gone.

When Craig watched the life drain from those girls, did he laugh? Did he get off on it? Did he enjoy this sort of power?

I feel sick.

Wait. No, not really.

Numb.

Yet somehow... stopping a murderer doesn't feel wrong. Not at all. I simply hate that I had to be the one to do it.

This is correct. This is the right thing to do. I know it in my bones.

Holding on for another full minute just to be sure, I take slow, deep breaths. Remaining somewhat detached is easier than I would have imagined. Craig did this many times, obviously. If I could ask him one more question other than whether Olivia is safe, I'd ask if he reveled in this moment. If he enjoyed his few brief moments of absolute power.

His body is now completely limp. I wait another twenty seconds, then jam the belt into my back pocket, and take his wallet – not for money, but for ID and clues I can use later. There's no phone on him.

It takes some leverage and a lot of muttered cursing, but I manage to roll him into the darkest corner near the furniture dolly. There's a very tall old metal shelf filled with cleaning supplies. Helping myself to a few alcohol-based cleaning wipes, I clean the crowbar, the chair, the doorknob. Anything I may have touched.

I keep listening for any noise from upstairs, but everything is nearly silent. I need to get out of this house full of cameras.

Mom doesn't even have Craig's phone number. My friends have never met him for more than ten minutes, and he's not on social media. Becca is the only person who can directly tie me to Craig. The only person between my escape from this entire disaster and my son being known as the child of the Monday Maniac.

No. They're going to eventually find out about the killings. The Monday Maniac will bounce around the headlines for much longer.

How can I let poor darling Asher be burdened with that? It's bad enough he's losing his father. It's unsettling that I have no idea how much influence Craig has had over him. I might have some damage to undo to make sure that my sweet, clever boy doesn't go down a dark path.

Wait. Becca said that she's doing a media cleanse this weekend. Hopefully, that means that most of her cameras might be off. And Jackson doesn't know my real name. He doesn't seem bright enough to dig very deeply.

The only hope of my son having a normal life is to silence Becca.

This is the right thing to do. I feel the... correctness... right down to my soul. It's energizing to know that I am about to improve the world by erasing a negative influence.

Becca is also responsible for the kidnappings and murders of those girls. Yet this is her house. Her domain. Where she has curated and polished every inch of her space.

Everywhere but in this room. Which has plenty of interesting possibilities on these filthy old shelves.

53

BECCA

Grabbing my camera, I shoot some footage of the garden fairy lights with the last purple streaks of sunset behind them. Shooting B-roll for future inspirational moments always helps me calm down.

This has been a charming family dinner, yet I'm distracted. How can I truly focus when I know what is happening in the furnace room? I keep glancing at the faint glow of the dingy little window half-hidden behind a shrub.

Craig should have turned out the basement light by now. What is going on down there? He'd better not be trying to reason with her.

Although I am fully aware that Craig must kill Amy to get rid of her, it's unpleasant. Since it's happening in my house, I don't want to be left with bad karma, or dharma, or whatever. Maybe I'll have to sage the furnace room. At the very least, I'll be repainting and putting down fresh tile or something.

Naturally, I never wanted it to come to this, but since

he's crossed that line already, he might as well do the right thing and clean up his own mess.

Once Asher has finished his super-juice and Jackson has inhaled another slice of pizza, we leave the dishes for Chef Timothy to take care of. That's why it's such a treat to hire him. He simply scoops everything into bins and disappears in his van within five minutes. I definitely feel like royalty having people serve me.

Craig doesn't know that I've been hiring Timothy more often, which is one of the many reasons I need him to take on some extra targets. The food just looks so much better on camera.

I walk with Asher and Jackson through the house, making sure they don't go anywhere near the basement door. I listen carefully, but the downstairs is dead silent. That's a good sign. Hopefully, Craig has accomplished his task and just has to wait until the coast is clear to get rid of the evidence.

I spend a little time with Asher, helping him choose which of his squishy toys will be his story-time partner, then Jackson settles in to read with him.

I made sure that Asher is fine with either Craig, myself, or Jackson reading him to sleep. Many mothers get their kid into a solid routine, then it's the only way they can function. But sometimes I need to do live broadcasts precisely at his bedtime. I can't change the country's algorithms just to suit one six-year-old's story time.

I'm not sure why I grab the camera again from where I left it on the hall table. Sure, I haven't taken any good footage downstairs lately, and I do have to remind people how large the house is. Yet now is not the time for a shoot. Naturally, I won't create evidence of what's going on downstairs. It's more of a reflex when anything new is happening around me.

Hopefully, Craig has cleared up his mess, and I can take some shots to brainstorm how to update that ugly furnace room. It was genuinely embarrassing to have Amy see the one ugly room in my home.

Not that it will be a worry ever again.

Listening at the door, I still don't hear anything. My shoulders sag as I realize what else I'm going to have to take care of tonight.

Amy was blabbering on about Craig planning extra projects on his own. That's simply impossible. And yet... Would Craig disobey me? Would he actually go off the path we planned so carefully?

He lives such a frugal life in his tiny studio apartment filled with books, brain teasers, and notebooks. I've made him swear up and down that he will never keep any of his planning evidence there, because I simply can't trust him. The minimalist life keeps him calm. Stops his impulsive, wild side.

Why would he suddenly need a lot more targets? I hope it was just for the money. But why? And what was that nonsense about him possibly killing one of the girls? Nothing brings attention to a news item like a murder. He knows that. We've discussed it, along with all of the other rules and regulations about his "job".

I sincerely hope that he hasn't completely gone off the rails, because training another part-time husband would be exhausting. Plus, he really does seem to be a good influence on Asher.

The basement door opens with a faint creak, drawing my attention down. My fresh pedicure looks perfect with my skirt swirling around as I slowly descend. Since I have the camera in my hand anyway, I aim toward the polished wooden steps for a few shots.

Once this revolting mess is all cleaned up, I'll start planning a before-and-after reorganizing and redecorating of the furnace room. Everyone loves a makeover, especially when the starting point is truly hideous. That will actually be brilliant content for around eight weeks from now.

Plus, hopefully, that will remove the bad vibes of what is inevitably happening in there at the moment. Or has happened.

Swinging the door to the furnace room open, I peer into the dim light.

Shit.

It's too quiet. Not just still... there's a feeling in the air. Like the silence after a war in the movies. The room feels hollow. Airless.

Everyone knows that I detest not knowing what's going on. I must have control at all times. Now I feel lost, looking around slowly and not wanting to see anything that I find.

In the corner, almost lost in shadow, is a big lump with an arm stretched out toward the light. It doesn't move at all. Doesn't even shift with the person's breathing.

A shiver runs through me. That lump is not unconscious. It is dead.

Well, that must be Amy.

Wait.

I nearly drop the camera as I realize I'm staring at Craig's watch.

No. Not Craig. I still need him.

Rushing to his side, I'm halted right in front of the big

metal supply shelf. *Ow.* What the hell? My feet are stuck to the concrete floor.

"Stop moving. It will make it worse."

I whirl toward the voice behind me, almost falling over as my feet twist. Waving my arms frantically to hold onto my balance, I let go of the camera, and it tumbles from my hand and smashes across the concrete.

"No!" I choke back tears. "Do you know how long it took me to find the perfect lens for that? They only make those ones in Japan!"

Amy's standing very still, with the strangest expression I've ever seen. Her eyes are flat. As if she were concentrating on a math exam. Does she not realize that Craig is dead on the floor beside us?

"What?" I snap. "What's going on?"

She silently nods toward the workbench. There's my giant can of superglue spray with the red plastic cap sitting beside it. The cap was cracked when I bought it, so it must have been damaged. The one time I tried to use it, the spray nozzle was broken and flooded out into a horrible puddle. Nearly ruined my art journaling project.

Looking down, I watch in horror as my skin stretches every time I try to lift my feet. There's no way to move without ripping my soles right off.

I'm completely stuck.

With my dead husband in the corner and his other wife behind me.

In the basement, where nobody can hear me scream.

54

BECCA

I am in serious trouble. Quick... *think.*

When we were at the school event just the other day, it seemed like Amy had the potential to be one of the women who looked up to me. Someone who would subscribe across all platforms, join the email list, and become a true fan.

My inspirational angels, I call them. Heck, I've talked many of them into starting several new accounts to help me boost my numbers.

There are so many women in the world who need guidance. They don't have the money or time for a therapist, so they turn to people like me. Can I conjure up that sort of energy so that Amy will stop glaring at me and realize we should be on the same team?

Manipulating my own energy is something I'm usually pretty good at. I just don't know how to maintain any focus with Craig's lifeless body on the floor in front of me. A chill runs through me, and not from my feet on the bare concrete.

I did like Craig well enough when he behaved himself. I mean, we were only intimate a couple of times, and I hate to admit it, but he was very affectionate. Not a hottie like Jackson is by any stretch of the imagination. But a solid B+. And he did give me a child with those amazing eyes that show up so well on camera.

Now the man with whom I traded a son for consistent money is dead. How? It must have been some sort of hideous accident. There is absolutely no way this mousy, crafty Amy had anything to do with it.

For the moment, I'm going to have to concentrate on myself and find a way out of this. Holding out my arms to keep my balance, I try to lift each foot again, but the super-glue seems to be setting in.

"Amy," I begin, using my sweetest tone, "there's apparently been some sort of accident... Did the glue spill?"

"You know it didn't." She closes the door, then walks around the puddle of glue.

Dragging the chair a few feet to the side, she sits directly in front of me, blocking most of my view of... of the... *body*. A tremor runs through me. This is too real. Too intense. How could I have ended up in this position?

Okay. Breathe. Just keep her talking.

"What did you do to Craig?"

Amy smiles slightly, but her eyes are vacant. "Don't you think a more pertinent question might be, what am I going to do to you?"

Nodding slowly, I hold out my hands palms up. "You're absolutely right. Focus on the present. The now. This moment is all we truly have, right?"

Amy leaps to her feet and slaps me so hard my teeth rattle. Then she sinks back into the wobbly chair as if nothing happened.

"I don't need your guru mantra speak right now." Her voice is faintly deeper. Emotionless.

Opening and closing my jaw slowly, I rub the skin with my palm. It burns something fierce. "That had better not leave a mark, you bitch!"

"That was your one warning. I need to know if Craig had set any plans in motion for Olivia. She hasn't posted anything on social media for hours. If he was planning on killing her tomorrow, he might have her locked up somewhere today. I need to know where that is right now." Amy's eyes narrow. "If another woman goes missing, it's another case that could lead the cops back to Craig. Which would be bad for both of us. I will not have my child brought into this lunacy."

"I don't know about Olivia!" I snap, still rubbing the side of my face. Dammit, she got me right on the most sensitive spots of the cheekbone and jaw. "That isn't one of the girls we planned to target. I don't know who she is." My eyebrow rises, and I can't help but snarl, "Except that she's obviously one of your precious clients."

Amy doesn't seem flustered in the slightest. Until I notice the tiny flutter in her fingers. Good.

"Yes. You and Craig used me for my client list. And Craig used me because he wanted another child, and you didn't."

"Well, not so soon."

"You need a lot of time between your textbook-perfect two children for your body to bounce back. I get it."

"Of course. I'm going to be getting fashion sponsors soon." It's unnerving, the way she's staring at me so intently.

She pulls out her phone and thumbs through some photos before holding one up to me. My arms fly out to steady myself as I wobble. It's one of the planning boards from my garage. Dammit. This freak has solid evidence.

I'm at a severe disadvantage. Except that she's not an aggressive person. Would she even have the nerve to go to the cops? I doubt it.

Uh oh. My legs are shaking from the weird angle of my feet, but now my entire body starts to tremble. I do a lot of Pilates, but I don't know how long I can stand like this. "So there's just as much evidence at your house. See? We're in this together, Amy. We're both going to be in trouble if anyone finds these."

"Oh, no. Not me. Just you."

She holds up the phone again, zooming in on the murder board from my garage. Then she flips to my blog post from last week, where I was filming myself writing in my dream journal.

It's the same paper. The same purple ink. The same handwriting. The cops wouldn't even have to call in an expert – my beautiful penmanship is quite distinctive. It should be. I spent a lot of my time and Craig's money on those courses.

I'm intrigued as Amy pulls the phone away and sits back in the chair, crossing her legs. She's sitting a bit taller than she did when she first came into my kitchen. It's almost as if she's smug about how the tables have turned. "Okay. So you have the upper hand. What is it that you want?"

She runs her hand through her long brown hair, smoothing it back. Taking a good look at her stylish black pants, her businesslike navy shirt, and tiny gold earrings, it hits me. "When you left the house this morning, you were on your way to a meeting. Where was it? Is there anything I can help with?"

Her smirk is slightly crooked as her head tilts to the side. "I was on my way to the police, actually. To have you and Craig locked up. Mainly, to save Olivia's life. Or kidnapping. Or at least confirm that she's not in danger." She stands up, walking slowly toward the large worktable at the back of the room.

Amy casually picks up a blowtorch.

My pulse hammers in my throat. She's not screwing around.

That damn handyman asked to leave a bunch of tools here since I call him every few weeks. Obviously, that was a terrible mistake. How much of my stuff has she been through? But she's likely just trying to scare–

The torch bursts into flame, and my breath freezes in my lungs. Have I severely underestimated this woman?

"That's not going to work," I mutter quickly, holding up my hands in defense. "I think superglue can only be removed with acetone. There's nail polish remover upstairs. If you let me call for Jackson–"

"Oh, no, we won't be involving him. He's not a murderer. This is just about you and me." Amy circles slowly to the side, toward Craig's lifeless body.

"And trust me, this isn't to free your feet."

55

BECCA

I shriek as the flame of the blowtorch comes much too close to my hair.

"Careful!" I whimper. "You'll melt the shine gloss."

"What do you think this is for, *Becca?*" The way Amy says my name is different. Almost like an insult. Or as if she's teasing me.

Her entire demeanor has changed. I have no idea how to read her anymore.

Shame on me. I should know better than to underestimate anyone. I first had her pegged as a quiet little mommy at home, and a calm, industrious craft person at work. Yet here she is, casually tossing the small propane tank of the blowtorch from hand to hand while taunting me.

Who is this woman?

I'm in serious trouble. This entire enterprise with Craig was so that I could control everything. Especially him, and through him, our finances. Now, apparently, I've lost him, and everything is about to fall apart.

My eyes are drawn to Craig's pale, motionless hand.

"Was it self-defense?" I whisper in a shaky voice. "Did he attack you?"

"It doesn't matter now. He's gone. You and I are having a conversation." Amy moves around again to stand directly in front of me at the edge of the glue puddle. I want to ask her if I can use the chair, since my legs are vibrating from being unable to move my angled feet. Plus, the concrete is cold against my bare skin. The chill is starting to spread up my legs.

"I was always taught to look friends, colleagues, and opponents straight in the eyes." She smiles coldly. "Which are you... *Becca?*"

"I hope I'm a friend. Or at least... a colleague, of sorts?" My words are too fast. Too high-pitched. "We've apparently lost Craig, but that doesn't mean that we can't work together. You have that wonderful shop, and I do all sorts of promotions. We could help each other."

"I don't want to be involved with the kind of person who sends her husband off to rob and kill young women. Not professionally, and not personally."

"There's no direct evidence that he's killed anyone."

Amy sighs heavily, dragging the chair to center it directly in front of me before she sits. Thankfully, she turns off the blowtorch. "Mia Harrington was killed. He made it look like a car crash, but the authorities have figured out that she actually died earlier than that. He had a murder board with all of her details in my garage."

Her chuckle is dark and gritty. "I know you're not a math wizard, but I'm sure you can put two and two together."

My eyes snap closed while I curse under my breath. Hopefully, being somewhat honest with Amy might be helpful. "Craig has been... unstable for the past month or two," I admit.

"Yeah? How so?"

"Um, usually it was me who was fixated on getting as much money as possible as quickly as possible. Then he suddenly got frantic about it." Straightening my shoulders, I take a deep, cleansing breath and lift my chin. "But apparently he's gone, so we need to move on."

"Yes. Let's." She crosses her legs casually. "You are going to tell me what I need to know. If you don't, I will take this blowtorch and scorch a line down the side of your face." She grins wickedly. "Maybe I'll do some spiral patterns like in your inspirational doodles."

My choked cry rings out around the room. "You wouldn't."

"I think you know that I would."

My stomach roils as if I need to be sick. But if I bend forward, my hands would land in the slightly glistening patch of superglue in front of me. My feet are burning, the muscles in my ankles and calves locking up.

I've worked so hard for years to be an influencer. A momfluencer. An inspirational guru to busy working women. There's no way they would look up to me if I looked... Good grief, what would I even look like with deep singes across my skin?

"Here's the deal, Becca. Your entire existence is wrapped up in being on camera. Putting yourself on display."

She waits for an awkwardly long time until I murmur, "Yes. That's true."

"And yet, you judge these rich girls for having more money than brains, and not doing something productive, *blah blah blah.* Meanwhile, they're only freaking twenty-two or so and haven't figured out their lives yet."

Amy leans forward, pointing the nozzle of the blowtorch at me. "Did you have your entire life figured out by twenty-two? Or even by twenty-five?"

"No. No, I didn't," I sputter, feeling like a child who has been caught in a lie. "You're right. That was judgmental of me. Not the kind of vibe I'm going for." Clearing my throat, I bend my knees a few times, attempting to unlock my quickly stiffening legs. "We're supposed to lift other women up. So..." I hesitate for only a blink. "So I will stop with all of the targets. I won't steal from wealthy women anymore. I'll simply work on my brand deals and try to be a better mother."

Although I'm sure that Amy can see right through my phony smile, I try it anyway. "Does that sound fair?"

"It would be a start... if you could tell me about Olivia."

"I really don't know."

Amy lights up the blowtorch again, bringing it so close to my face that I feel a nauseating wave of heat.

"I'm telling the truth!"

My shriek is so loud that Amy puts a finger over her mouth, walking around to shut the door behind me. "We don't want your sweet boy to be disturbed." Amy raises an eyebrow, pursing her lips. "Or your son, either."

My breath is speeding up as my hips begin to shake. Is that stupid glue toxic? My legs and feet are both burning now, and I don't know how much longer I can remain standing with this much pressure on one ankle. Stiffness is setting in and starting to ache deeply. It doesn't help that my terror is obvious from the way my hands and fingers can't stop twitching.

"Jackson reads to Asher for about half an hour after his bath. He'll be coming downstairs in another ten minutes or so."

"He's only been reading for about two minutes." Amy snaps the torch off and tilts her head toward the furnace vent. "When it's not turned on, that old thing conducts sound through the vents pretty well. I heard him take Asher out of the tub." She jumps to her feet again, pacing slowly around me in a circle.

"Amy, please." She's intentionally making me dizzy, and I've hit a point of desperation where I'm not above begging. There's no way I can pitch forward without my hands landing in the glue. I'm helpless enough already. "If you're not going to help me escape, at least let me sit on the chair. Otherwise, I'm going to fall."

"That would certainly scuff your perfect camera-ready face, wouldn't it?" She pauses just to my left, her eyes meeting mine as if she's trying to look through my soul. "*Becca,*" she spits, "what if Craig has Olivia tied up somewhere? What if he was supposed to drain her accounts tonight, then deal with her in the morning?"

"He never drains accounts on the weekends," I blurt out without thinking. "Monday mornings are the best time, because nobody in the banks wants to be at work and their eyes just skip over everything." Of course, I should not have said that, but I'm getting seriously dizzy, and my entire body is beginning to cramp. My feet feel like blocks of ice, yet my skin is on fire where the glue has latched on.

Somehow, I know that my feet will be ruined. Do they even do plastic surgery on feet? I'll never be able to wear sandals again because of the scarring. Patches of my flesh are going to be stuck to this floor when I get some help. *If.* If I get help.

"Good. Then she's probably still around. I just need you to tell me if Olivia is still in any danger now that Craig is gone."

She says that so matter-of-factly that my breath seizes.

"Look, I–" My left knee wobbles as I turn to face her as much as I can. My arms windmill as I try to keep my balance, and she jumps back, raising the blowtorch and firing it up.

Geez, that woman moves fast. Her reflexes are instant. She's like a ninja in sensible slacks.

"If you try to reach for me, I'm burning your face off."

There's no reasoning with her. There's no way out of this.

"I'm not, I swear. I just don't want to fall. *Please.*"

As Amy studies me, I also feel like I'm studying her for the first time. She's no longer meek and timid. It's as if a switch has been flipped inside her, revealing another side. I had no respect for the other version of Amy. Yet if she weren't trying to torture me, I'd have to admit that this one kind of kicks ass.

Except that it's my yoga-toned ass she's kicking. And I have no way out.

Amy snaps the blowtorch off again, setting it on the workbench. Then she picks up her phone, aiming it toward me, as if taking a photo.

"You're about to tell me everything. Or not only will I scorch your face, I'll take video of you confessing everything and post it online. You'll never have a following again, and the police will be up your ass incriminating you for all of Craig's crimes."

My breath is a wheeze, not just from the dusty air down here. The unstoppable flood of panic tightens my lungs and squeezes my chest. My eyes fall closed as I try to think of any way out of this, but there are no other options.

Even if I do escape relatively healthy and unscarred, if I don't have my fledgling media empire, what am I?

Just another fussy housewife with delusions of grandeur.

Nodding, I bend my knees a bit more to maintain my balance, clasping my hands in front of me.

"I'll tell you everything I know. I swear."

56

AMY

What a strange sensation. Like I'm floating. Or flying.

They say that flying dreams represent being repressed and held back in your waking life.

I've always been held back to some extent. Mom made sure that I was good. Calm. Normal. Always making sure that any trace of my father's influence was either erased or deeply hidden.

I made sure that I was steady. Steady employment, growing as I opened my own shop. Being a good wife for my husband. Dedicating myself to being a great mother for Asher.

This is the first time I've felt absolutely wicked. Yet... *Righteously* so.

It feels *incredible*.

Like raw electricity is pounding through my veins as I toy with Becca. She's certainly not the polished princess now. Hearing her grovel is the sweetest music to my ears. I'm inhaling her pleas like fresh mountain air. I'm absorbing her terror as it feeds my soul.

So many years of suppressing my urges to right the world's wrongs, no matter what. To allow my inner vigilante to scream in triumph.

Today is a strangely glorious day.

I know that good will prevail over evil. Because I have taken charge.

As I look deeply into Becca's navy blue eyes, I see the faint, barely perceptible outlines of contact lenses. Of course, she's even cheating with her eye color. I can also tell that she's barely holding onto her own control.

"You don't respect these women because they come from money," I drawl slowly. "You don't just think they're wasteful. You're jealous. You don't like the divide between the high class and..." I raise an eyebrow, already knowing what she's about to say, more or less. "Wherever you came from."

"That's none of your business," she snaps.

"At the moment, everything is my business, unless you'd like to resemble a slice of toast." I chuckle cruelly. "Oh, wait. You're a fancy woman. How about crème brûlée?"

She snarls in a manner that would definitely not be appropriate on her Meditation Moments page. "Sure. My parents were crackheads. Losers. No drive." She straightens up a bit. "I came from absolutely nothing and am creating my own world purely through my own ambition. A truly aspirational life."

"Oh, that's it," I nod, taking a step backward, since her energy is becoming erratic. "You think you're better than your low-class family. But you also think you're better than high-class people who haven't worked as hard as you do."

"Precisely."

"Becca, what you don't seem to understand here is that I'm now on a mission." I resume slowly pacing in a circle around her to make her feel more unsteady. Weaker. "I have committed myself to saving Olivia. Craig made his choice and wouldn't help me. You have to understand that you are next, unless you help me find out where she is right now."

Her mouth falls open, and snaps shut three seconds later. "I honestly don't know where she is."

"Then you need to tell me where Craig may have stashed her, or keeps the information regarding his plans."

She stares down at her feet, which must be absolutely aching by now.

"Does he have any planning boards at his apartment?"

Becca snorts. "No. That's his serene, blank thinking place or whatever. I don't trust him to keep anything there. And yes, I go there to check from time to time."

"Good grief," I mutter. "You two are quite the obnoxious pair." I stop pacing and stand directly in front of her. "What about his car?"

"It's at his place. He always walks here – it's only five blocks away."

I didn't find a phone when I checked Craig's pockets. But there was a charging station upstairs, with some cables beside an outlet, at the end of the counter.

"His phone is up in the kitchen charging right now, isn't it?"

Her eyes grow wide, and she realizes she's giving herself away. After a few seconds, she nods. "Yes. But you don't have–"

"Of course I know his password. It's the number in the album title from that seventies prog rock band he loves."

I almost snicker at the way she pouts. Then Becca's eyes narrow. "You figured out his puzzle locks. You know his password. You know so much about him, and you didn't even know he had another wife?"

My entire back stiffens. The pain from my molars grinding centers me. She's correct. Which I detest.

"I was focused on my business. I wasn't looking for absolute insanity." There's no way to tell her that I've always been focused on keeping all of my paranoid thoughts under control. Anxiety causes me to second-guess myself.

But I've had enough of that. My true self has been unleashed, and it's not going back in the box.

We're running out of time. I need to get this over with before Jackson comes downstairs. I likely have less than three minutes.

Becca places a hand on her hip, her body language changing, followed by her voice. "I've already given you everything you want," she says. "You've apparently taken Craig out of the equation. Which is a shame, because I really wanted a little girl with his eyes. I'll just find another man to take over his position."

She's not lying. I can tell with dismay that this is the real Becca. Maybe. At least, one true side of her. This woman isn't just two-faced... She's kaleidoscope-faced. An unusual creature with no soul who will do absolutely anything to get ahead.

That makes her dangerous to a degree that makes it quite clear she can't be allowed to walk around in the world. She's just going to hurt more people. Not to mention what she might do to me.

Myself, my son, my mother, my business.

If this bizarre woman can't be trusted, there's only one thing to do.

57

AMY

The only other times I've ever been this laser-focused were at my sewing machine with a backlog of orders and a tight deadline. I've always been able to kind of dissociate to get an impossible job done.

Strangely, even though my hands are slightly trembling, I feel like I know what to do. It's as if I've trained for this.

Or... been trained for this.

"Hands behind your back." My barked command makes Becca jump with a dramatic twitch.

She rolls her eyes but obeys, clasping her wrists behind her. Her legs are quivering, hips swaying backward as she tries to steady herself. If she weren't a murdering, thieving bitch, I'd almost feel sorry for how much pain she must be in.

"A few scars across your face could be leveraged into sympathy, don't you think?" I lower my voice for dramatic effect. "How you've overcome hardship."

I fire up the blowtorch, skimming it very close to her cheek. It ignites a wisp of her hair, the revolting scent making both of us flinch. "If there are any more details about Craig and Olivia, you have two seconds to tell me."

She's absolutely silent. So still that I wonder if her heart actually stopped. After three seconds, I bring the blowtorch near her ear. She squeals, flinching back.

"Olivia is probably fine," she insists quickly. "Craig has a system. He befriends the girls on Monday afternoons. Sometimes he'll take their purse or their wallet. Then he makes plans to run into them the following week – either accidentally or to return their stuff. He takes the girls mid-morning when people are busy and not paying attention. Then he drains their accounts, takes whatever he can easily pawn, learns any secrets that could be of use, then... leaves them in an obscure, camera-free location."

"So you know he's been killing them?"

Her eyes shift back and forth before dropping. "I didn't *know*. I... I knew it might be a possibility if something went terribly wrong, but I didn't know he crossed that line yet." A long, shuddering breath. "We discussed it once. Just as a contingency plan. He said that if everything went wrong and he absolutely *had* to do it, he would make sure it was painless and calm. But we agreed that releasing them was better. Drugged, but fine. Craig made it clear that if they said a word to anyone about it, next time things would be much worse. He also told them all of the info he had about their friends and families – if they went to the police, they'd be endangering everyone."

"You didn't think he'd move on to killing?"

"No! Certainly not with the girls we were planning here. So, you know... I was assuming he wasn't involved with those other incidents."

"No, they were the ones planned in my garage."

Another harsh wave of jealousy hits me as I realize he's put me in far more trouble than Becca.

Nice. Very nice, Craig. You asshole.

Glaring down at his motionless corpse, I barely stifle the urge to kick him in the side.

"You know why he suddenly needed more money – money that he kept from you – don't you, *Becca?*" I'm starting to love spitting out her name like an expletive.

"No." Her eyes actually fill with tears. It's gratifying to know that she might actually have real feelings in there somewhere. "Do I want to know?"

"I'm not sure. Do you want to know that he knocked up our nanny, Penny?"

Her eyes could not have been more shocked if I'd stabbed her.

It's the first thing I've said to Becca where I know I've actually wounded her. Something blossoms in my heart, filling me with joy. It shouldn't be so satisfying to know I've caused her pain straight to the core.

I pull out my phone one-handed and swipe to a photo of Penny and Asher.

Becca's face reddens, eyes bulging. "You put a hottie like that in front of my husband? You frikkin' idiot! You're supposed to pick ugly nannies or hot guys. What moron allows a cute chick with perky tits like that into–"

She squeals as the blowtorch drifts over the top of her hair, sending another scorching wave of stench floating around us as a few more wisps ignite.

"Fine," she snaps. "You put a hottie in front of him, and he knocked her up. I put you in front of Craig because you seemed sweet and docile, and have a perfect job to find the right targets. Now you're angry that things have come full circle?"

"Yeah. I was picked because of my job." That little fact makes me want to toast my initials across her cheek.

Becca grins cruelly. "One of my friends raved about your purse repairs, and I saw that your business was growing. Craig wanted another kid immediately, so – boom." She smirks. "It was almost too easy to throw him at you. To get him out of my hair."

"What hair?" I begin to lower the blowtorch, then yank it back. This is the time to be logical, not emotional.

It feels like something has been unlocked inside me. I already know what to do. As if the pieces are clicking into place of their own accord.

"I know you chose me," I murmur slowly, waving the torch past her nose, nearly close enough to singe her false eyelashes.

"I'm relieved to see you calming down." Becca smiles agreeably. "Your mellow temperament and ability to deal with anything are two of the reasons I chose you for Craig. We thought he should be with someone sweet."

I'm running out of time. My decision has to be immediate, yet ice-cold. My entire future hangs in the balance.

This crazy woman is never going to stop. She's already tested the boundaries, and knows how easy it is to cross over to the wrong side. She'll just get another guy to do her dirty work. Maybe Jackson. Maybe someone new. She is a manipulator and will do anything to get her way.

There is no reason for her to become civilized now. If the authorities get involved, she'll just hire a fancy lawyer who not only gets the case thrown out completely but grows her social media tenfold.

More publicity will turn this cruel menace into a monster.

"Those are beautiful earrings," I whisper softly, admiring the emerald teardrops.

"Thank you." She shifts uncomfortably. "Listen, can I at least have that chair, please?"

"You know, Becca... You're not the only one who had a messed-up childhood."

I sense the smile sliding across my face at the same instant I know in my gut what I have to do.

Make it look like a fascinating accident.

58

AMY

Turning the blowtorch off, I set it back in its place, then clean it off with an alcohol wipe. Becca would never touch that thing. I pace around, wiping my fingerprints from anything I may have accidentally touched again.

Then I stand in front of the tall metal shelf filled with cleaning supplies and odds and ends. It's a cheap version of an industrial shelf. The kind of thing that would break with just a bit too much pressure.

Becca shifts her weight, bouncing her knees. She's going to collapse soon. "What are you doing?"

"*Silence.*" My businesslike voice booms in this small space. There's no time to speak with her anymore. It's time to get the job done.

The focus overtakes me, just as Dad always taught me. It's as if all of his lessons were designed for this specific moment. Most people know not to mix bleach and ammonia, but chlorine bleach also reacts with any acid. Like vinegar, that the little organic princess has a huge bottle of.

Dousing a thin towel in water, I make a quick mask for myself. Luckily, there are cleaning gloves, which I wear as I splash the bleach around. It just takes a few moments to calculate how much force it will take to cause an open bottle of vinegar to pitch forward from the top shelf. I set the open bottle of bleach right beside it for good measure.

I place Becca's shaking arm in place and tip the shelf toward her. She needs her right hand to balance, as her legs are quivering. One slip and the frame and supplies will topple directly on top of her. The open bottles are already trembling.

"What are y–"

"*Silence.*" My cold gaze is as effective as a slap. "If bleach is mixed with an acid, like vinegar, it creates chlorine gas. A super-high concentration, maybe if splashed down the front of your dress, would be fatal within minutes. So you'd better hold still."

I quickly scurry, slipping several nearby items into my pockets. I can't resist. My body and mind are firing on pure adrenaline, making everything crystal clear.

I think only of Asher as I conjure the strength to roll Craig onto a furniture dolly. The basement storm door creaks like crazy as I pry it open. Luckily, it opens at the side of the house, mostly blocked by shrubbery.

It takes most of my strength to drag the body out to the ravine at the end of the yard to deal with later.

The body. Of my husband. I'm so numb that reality feels like it's ten feet away, just out of reach.

Three slow, deep breaths. Time to fix everything up. I know in my heart that I've got this.

Analyzing the room again, I pause to check Becca's

angle. She's already faltering, with the bottles slipping to the edge of the shelf. I need to get out of here fast before her trembling arm fails and everything topples over her.

"I can't hold this," she gasps. "Where are you going?"

There are so many things I'd like to say to her. *"I'm going upstairs, and you're going straight to hell,"* comes to mind.

Instead, I simply stare at her quaking arm and unsteady knees while I take another slow breath.

Then I paste on a bright smile, and stroll upstairs to the kitchen as if I'm completely comfortable there. I grab my purse and coat just as Jackson comes down to the foyer.

"Hey, where's Becca?"

My eyes dart toward the door to downstairs, as I shake my head slightly. "She called me to come back another time, because she had a great idea that could be leveraged for sponsored posts with a cleaning supply company. She was rambling about doing a makeover of the furnace room."

I grimace slightly. "It was kind of impossible to explain that painting an ugly room sage green isn't what they're looking for. Then she freaked about some of the supplies in there looking sloppy." I shrug sheepishly. "I'm sneaking out, since I have another appointment."

He nods, running the hand with his hippie bracelet through his hair. "I understand completely."

"She was in a mood," I whisper.

His eyelids drop halfway, and he looks exhausted. "I understand that too."

"Thanks. Bye." I disconnect Craig's phone from the charging cable on the counter, drop it in my purse, and stroll calmly out the door.

Jackson comes to the front window to watch me pull out.

I give him a halfhearted wave, taking one more look at the positively gorgeous house.

Then his head snaps around to look behind him.

As if he's just heard a huge crash.

59

AMY

What a long, bizarre day.

The drive to Mom's to pick up Asher was nice to decompress. Flipping the radio around, I found some bouncy pop rock on a station with no news.

Thank goodness.

Exhaustion tries to seep into my bones on the way home, but it's not time yet. Glancing in the rearview mirror, I see Asher is napping in his car seat. I was talked into staying for dinner when I picked him up, and we all had too much lasagna.

It was as if Mom could tell I was rattled, because she wouldn't leave me alone for one second to check Craig's phone. She's always a little overprotective, so I've learned how to adjust my expressions and tone and project the moods she needs to expect from me.

I don't think of it as dishonesty. It's simply giving Mom the version of me that she would rather deal with.

Now that Asher is sound asleep, I'm unable to wait

another second. I pull over into a strip mall and park at the very end, near a convenience store.

My breath is slow and steady as I dig the phone out of my purse. The password is still the one I had accidentally noticed him use thousands of times. Yet it had never occurred to me that I might ever use it to unlock his phone. Until this weekend, I've never snooped in his things. I've never had a reason to.

Of course, until this weekend, I had no idea that Craig had another wife.

How could I not have seen it? It's because I wasn't looking. Everything was fine, and I never questioned it.

I was far too trusting. Letting my guard down should never have been an option.

From this second forward, I will question everything. Nothing will ever get past me again.

I scroll through Craig's phone, glancing briefly at the texts from Becca, where she orders him around like a servant. It points out yet again that the version of him with her was extremely different from the Craig who lived with me.

I guess we all have many versions of ourselves.

There's also a string of messages with Penny. I don't want to read the details. I really don't. Yet I skim quickly to get the gist of it. Their relationship turned from friendly and flirty to intimate about three months ago. It was just a month later that she told him she was pregnant.

My finger taps on the steering wheel as I stare into space for a moment. That sounds rather quick. Suspiciously too quick.

Flipping through the rest of the phone, I find no work

contacts. No business colleagues. No friends. Just me, Becca, Jackson, Penny, his doctor and dentist. Also, no apps beyond weather, maps and notes.

The only notes look like they were copied and pasted from a variety of websites. My skin crawls as my eyes drift over the pages of rambling. It's total raving lunatic nonsense about how having as many sons as possible is the only mark of a true man. How important it is to create a "legacy" so that a man will have mattered here on Earth.

It's the phone of a true psychopath. An actual serial killer. Holding my stomach firmly with my left hand, I apply slight pressure as my dinner kicks hard, trying to come back up.

After an undignified burp, I go into Craig's notes app. There it is. "Project OR". Just a few notes about Olivia's schedule, and where he had planned to meet her tomorrow.

The plan was simple, under the guise of returning her purse. Meet up after her nail appointment, since that would be convenient for her. The location was a generic coffee shop, which seems harmless. However, the parking lot backs onto an industrial area with its own parking area.

He was going to drug her coffee, walk her to the back lot to get her purse, and throw her in his trunk. Then take her keys and move her car to the back of an abandoned factory behind the dumpsters. It would be days before anyone noticed her car there.

Which means there would be no exact time for the police to search for clues.

Meanwhile, Craig simply drives off in the opposite direction with Olivia in his trunk, and does... whatever he wants with her.

A shudder runs through me as I realize I was living so close to true evil for so long.

I grab my own phone and check online for Olivia Rhodes. She posted a photo with some friends just half an hour before Craig arrived at Becca's, so she's probably fine.

Finally, a real sigh of relief flows through me. Olivia is more than a customer who sends a huge amount of business my way through referrals. She's a young woman who is still figuring the world out, and deserves to have a full chance at that without it being cut short by a madman.

Even if she's occasionally a bitch, she doesn't deserve to die.

Selfishly, I know that another murder would have the potential to bring police scrutiny my way. Now they'll have no more leads and nobody to search for.

Flipping through the rest of Craig's notes, I see more initials match the girls from the murder boards in my garage who have disappeared. I'll have some more work to do, double-checking everything.

I toss the phone into the side pocket of my purse, then put it back on the seat beside me. It was a close call when Mom tried to pick it up for me and move it to another chair back at her house. I caught her just in time.

The plastic bag filled with Craig's trophy earrings sitting in the bottom is pretty heavy. Mom would have been suspicious.

Just in case my plan didn't work out, I couldn't allow Becca to keep Craig's trophies. It felt wrong. Disrespectful to those poor dead girls.

There's nothing I can do about them now. But at least I am absolutely positive that I did the right thing by removing

Craig and Becca from the world. They would not have stopped for anything.

I, however, have already stopped. Just two... incidents.

Now I'm done forever.

Turning smoothly back onto the street, I set the radio to a murmur.

"Thank you for listening to WBLW — your top hit songs and the news every fifteen minutes. Bad news for people with businesses down on Barrett Street. Crews have finally fixed that nasty broken water main, but need an extra day to put the street back together now that the rain has stopped. They ask that people avoid the area until Tuesday morning, and assume that stores will be closed until then.

Dave will soon be telling us about the balmy, sunny week we have in store. But first, police have been called to the house of a local social media influencer who has been found dead in a freak accident in her own basement. Her nanny said that she was organizing a shelf full of cleaning supplies, and must have climbed–"

Asher calls out to me just as I'm turning the radio off. "Mommy?"

"Yes, honey?"

"Is your shop on Barrett Street?"

"Yes, it is. You remember the signs?"

"Yeah." His eyes are wide as they meet mine in the mirror. "What if you can't go to work this week?"

I grin. "It means I'll be the one picking you up from kindergarten. Then you and I are going to spend the whole afternoon together. We can go to that big park by the lake, and maybe get lunch down at–"

"Jimmy's!" he chirps, then laughs.

It's a tiny fifties-style diner, with servers who are all

grandma types who keep sneaking him cookies while fussing over "their little man". It's his favorite restaurant, but we don't get down there very often. That's going to change.

I've always thought that I was putting Asher first, yet I've had to work too much to really make that happen. Now that I don't have to worry about Craig's schedule and anyone else, I'm free to put me and my son first.

The way it should always be.

60

AMY

MONDAY

Asher is going to remember this day for a while. He kept calling it the best Monday ever. I stroke his sandy hair, stifling a laugh at finding actual sand in it. He lies across me on the couch in his clownfish pajamas, sound asleep after having insisted that he wanted to watch another episode of *Dance Dolphins*.

I'll wait another ten minutes until he's really out before moving him.

Slowly reaching for the remote, I switch to the news. They've been replaying the same story that I caught this morning, adding details as they develop.

If only Becca knew how famous she was going to be for another few days before disappearing forever. There were even news crews in front of her house at three in the morning when I snuck through the ravine to wrap Craig's body, load him back onto the dolly, chain him to it, and throw the whole thing in the river.

There's a deep spot where I know he won't be found for years, if ever. With no ID, no family looking for him, and apparently no job or connections beyond his two wives and their nannies, that case will fade away quickly.

While I wait through the weather segment, I check Olivia's feed, where she posted an angry rant several hours ago. *"Ladies, beware of weird men who seem sweet then disappear. Was supposed to meet up with a nice flirty man who apparently found my purse, then he never showed up! It was a birthday gift from Mom! Then my friend, who was with me when I first met him a few weeks ago, is pretty sure he's almost forty! Yeah, right, buddy. I'm not in need of a sugar daddy!"*

If Olivia only knew what she may have actually dodged.

An influx of sunshine icons overtakes the TV screen, parading across the entire week. Then I turn up the volume as a stone-faced middle-aged man in a stylish gray suit fills the screen.

"Local rising social media presence Becca Roberts was found dead in her basement, where she appeared to have attempted to climb a shelf. The vinegar-based homemade glass cleaner and bleach-based tile cleaner exploded right under her nose, where she was confined due to a fallen metal shelf and a broken can of superglue. She was discovered by her nanny shortly after the incident, but had already inhaled the fumes and passed shortly after. She'll be remembered as an inspiration to local women. Coming up at ten, we have footage of the new Barrett Street sidewalks, where a local daycare has drawn adorable designs in the new concrete frontage. Over to you, Claudia."

"I know a girl named Claudia at the park Penny takes me to." Asher's eyes open slowly. "She wears a pink jacket. It's too bright." He makes a sour face.

"You've never liked neon colors except for fish, have you?"

His head shakes as I pick him up, carrying him to bed. "Well, it doesn't matter what she wears, as long as she's nice."

"Yeah, she's nice," he drawls. "Can Penny take me there this week?"

"I don't know yet. If she's still sick, I'll pick you up after kindergarten, and you'll be coming to work with me."

I set him in bed, and he sits right up, glowing with excitement. "Really? Can I help?"

"Yes. I'm going to need you to sit at the front counter and color or read. When customers come in, you'll say hello to them, then you'll call for me."

I shouldn't have told him this right before he falls asleep. He grins from ear to ear, practically bouncing. "Can I work the money card thingy?"

"No, but you can watch me do it." He laughs at my wink. "Maybe you can do part of it with me if you go to sleep right now." Asher dives under the covers as I tuck him in, already faking a snore, then giggling at the shocked face I make. "Goodnight, honey."

"Goodnight, Mommy." He grins, gripping the edge of the blanket and his fish stuffie. "Thanks for beach park day."

"You're welcome. Sleep tight." I turn off the light, leaving the door cracked exactly one inch to let in a faint beam from the hallway.

I'm overcome by how lucky I am. My son is polite, well-rounded, and clever. Now that the bad influence is out of his life, all I need to do is get him into a great school.

With this bizarre weekend behind me, it will take some time to get back on track.

As always, I've done most of the planning already.

Starting with removing absolutely any elements that could possibly interfere with our incredible new lives.

No matter what it takes.

61

AMY

TWO DAYS LATER

I switch the van into a lower gear at the bottom of a long hill, surprised at how sluggish it is. It's not like the dead weight in the back is exceptionally heavy.

There's very little traffic, and the greenery all around is quite charming. The view is a little better, since this vehicle is higher.

Maybe it was studying Craig's murder boards for so long, but today's project was almost too easy. People really are predictable, and searching for the easiest way to get through their day.

Flipping the radio to an oldies station with my gloved hand, I keep the volume high enough to keep me company on the drive, but not high enough to become a distraction.

There's still some mental untangling to do. It's only been forty-eight hours since the evening I'm only mentally referring to as "that incident", and I've already shaken off most of the stress.

Yet there were still a few last details to deal with. Any

loose end will eventually unravel. I know that through my work, and I certainly know that through my life.

A slow sigh rattles through me as I take a long curve, slowing down to avoid a pothole. I don't quite trust this weird old van of Jackson's. The brakes are soft, and the suspension is questionable.

Which, for my purposes, is absolutely perfect, as I drive him to a certain road that curves out over a lake. There's a precarious railing that a van might happen to accidentally sail on through.

It's going to look like Jackson was headed to visit his uncle, like he often does this time of year. He looks like such a hippie type that it's easy to assume he was smoking up on the drive.

Who would ever think that someone drugged him and brought him out here? Who would guess that someone forced smoke into his face until he inhaled enough for it to pick up on a drug test, then set him behind the wheel?

In just an hour or so, there will be nobody left to place me at the scene of "the incident".

62

AMY

ONE WEEK LATER

Clearing out this stupid garage has been tricky. It's not just throwing things into a bin. This process has been fraught with too many decisions that make my skin crawl.

I haven't used the baby monitor in ages, but dug it out so I can hear if Asher wakes up while I'm out here. It's only nine o'clock – not an unusual time for someone to be puttering around in the garage. Yet I don't want to risk any surprises.

The boards at Becca's were cleared out and destroyed in a bonfire a mile away from her house. A few of them were so artistic and creative that I have to admit, I was almost tempted to take a photo first. But all USB keys were destroyed in that fire as well.

Yes, burning plastic is technically bad for the environment. I'll plant a few trees in the spring to make up for it.

After making absolutely sure that each target on every board has been verified to be either safe or already dead, I tear every photo, board and note into chunks, dropping them all into a large metal garbage can. There's too much to burn all at once. I have some fallen branches that need to go as well, so it should be easy to burn everything down over the next few evenings.

I almost wish I could invite Mom over for a glass of wine by the fire, but she would definitely ask questions. This is the wrong time to be anywhere near anyone nosy.

She's been concerned about me since I mentioned Craig was on an extended trip. I'll be confessing soon that he left us, yet I need a little more mental distance before I can deal with that.

My shoulders sag as I stare down at the pile of shredded pictures revealing glamorous eye makeup here, a diamond necklace there. Young, energetic, and so much potential. It turns my stomach to think that some of them will never discover their purpose in life.

The women who are safe will never know how close they came to–

"Hi there!"

I startle at the loud voice, clutching my chest as Fiona backs away with her hands in the air. "I'm so sorry, Amy! I saw the light on, and... you know. Wanted to say hi."

My heart rabbits as I try to haul in air. That woman is going to kill me someday with her constant intrusions.

Then the rattled feeling inside me shifts. Instead of flushing with heat, every part of me runs ice-cold.

Nothing has ever stopped this pushy woman. Not ignoring her calls. Or telling her I'm busy. Or, apparently, a closed garage door that she didn't even consider knocking on.

It's not just intrusive. Or maddening. Given what has gone on around here lately, it has become seriously dangerous.

I cannot possibly live like this anymore. Especially now

that I have things to hide in order to keep my child safe. Keeping prying eyes away is now self-defense.

There's no point in telling Fiona that I've outgrown this so-called friendship, since she's never listened to a word I said and doesn't even believe in things like manners or common courtesy.

Our entire friendship flashes before my eyes. Have I ever reached out to her? It's always been her coming at me, over and over. Like a prolonged smiling attack.

Fiona steps right in, twirling her lucky silver key necklace. "What are you up to back here?" Her eyes grow huge at the pile of chunky, shredded photos and prints. "Oh my God – is this the other woman? Was Craig having an affair?"

Her laughter is pure delight. "I knew it! I knew a guy who looked like that would eventually..."

That shrill voice turns to static in my ears.

I take a few steps back toward the toolbox.

Necklace or not, sadly, Fiona's luck has just run out.

63

AMY

THREE DAYS LATER

"You're looking a lot brighter, Penny."

She smiles faintly, then drops her eyes to the ladybug keychain in her hand. "Yeah. It's been a rough few months, but my stomach has settled."

She had kept up the ruse of "stomach problems" for another few days after Craig disappeared, until it became apparent he was never coming back.

It didn't take much detective work to skim her socials and see that she'd been out drinking with her friends several times a week while pretending to Craig that she was pregnant. A short stomach flu probably gave her the idea to fake a pregnancy, and she ran with it.

I detest how delighted Craig was in his messages with her. How many promises he made, vowing to be a great father and keep the child healthy. How he would make some sort of arrangement with me in just a few more weeks.

There was a lot of venom in the way I finally smashed the hell out of his phone before pitching it into the river.

That's another few trees I'll have to plant in order to apologize to the environment.

Knowing Penny was never pregnant was a huge relief on so many levels. Having a kid on her own would be a difficult challenge at her age. Sure, part of me was furious that she would fake such a thing, and that I jumped to that conclusion so fast. I'm still relieved.

A dark part of me doesn't think that Craig deserves any more sons.

I have to admit, Penny was really good at feigning illness. Plus, she must have used a bit of gray makeup to make herself so pale and sickly when she managed to drag herself here. Who knows what she said to Craig?

I discovered that you can buy positive pregnancy tests online – one of those bizarre facts that I wish I could scrub from my mind.

A sexy older man banging the hot nanny is not that much of a surprise these days, unfortunately. Yet the fact that she fabricated all of that to trap him into being with her? I almost respect her hustle. Just not the carelessness of forgetting to cover her tracks.

I don't know what kind of situation she had with Craig. Did he claim to love her? Did he actually love her? Did he plan a future with her?

Penny seems to be dealing with his disappearance quite calmly. Yet I've learned that her reactions are absolutely not to be trusted. Actually, nothing about her can be trusted. She had been plotting some kind of permanent connection to my husband.

Not to mention, she knows every detail of our lives. Which means she is extremely dangerous.

Yet I need her to say a friendly farewell to my son, so that he has closure.

"Are you excited about school?" I ask her.

Penny's smile lights up her eyes. "Yes. But I'm going to miss this little tiger!"

She kneels down for a hug. "Goodbye, Ash—" He gently smacks his hand over her mouth, making them both laugh. "Um thorry," she mumbles against his palm. He removes it so she can try again. "Goodbye, Jace."

I asked him if he'd like to go by his middle name when he starts school this fall. Turns out my son thinks Jace is much cooler. It's bad enough that he looks like the other Asher. I don't want him to be mistaken for him.

Partly because that could bring up questions that have no safe answers. Mostly because I don't want to ever have to think about the night of the incident again.

"Bye, Penny. I hope your school is nice."

She straightens up and smiles. "It will be." She accepts the envelope with her most recent earnings from my hand and stuffs it in her purse, as her ladybug keychain dangles from her hand. Penny gives me a strange glance, then her eyes become cloudy as she leaves without another word.

Jace frowns. "Mommy, is she gonna happy-cry or sad-cry?"

"I think it's both, honey. Sometimes when people move on to new things, there's a whole bunch of emotions. You're happy about the new things, but you're still sad the older things are over."

I plop onto the couch, resisting the urge to help as Jace climbs up beside me. Wow, he's getting so big. Almost as big as Becca's Asher.

I checked up on him – he's now living with Becca's parents in Ohio. I feel like that's a lot healthier than having the poor boy trained and posed for the cameras like a show pony. Her parents are the furthest thing from crackheads – tending to their farm where their only social media is a one-page website asking people to drop by on Saturdays to pick up fresh corn, potatoes, beets and spinach.

. It doesn't surprise me in the slightest that Becca lied straight to the end. Everything about her was polished and manipulated. It's comical that she promoted organic, natural living while she was fake through and through.

Her followers posted lavish messages about their sorrow for a few days. Since then, it feels like they've all moved on already.

Jace leans over the coffee table and goes back to coloring a page filled with bright fish. I asked him last week if he missed playing puzzles with his dad. He simply shrugged with a strange expression and said his dad was weird with puzzles, and that he got kind of angry and quiet sometimes.

Then he gave me that adorable smile and said he'd rather read a book with me. My heart couldn't have swelled more.

I told him that Craig was traveling for work, and Jace hasn't asked about him since then. I feel like that's a sign they never really bonded. Which makes sense, since Craig seemed like he wanted to crank out children as some sort of genetic permanence, not to be a great father.

I watch as Jace skims his blue colored pencil lightly across the waves around the orange fish. It seems like he's already moved on.

Will we move on?

Maybe that's the answer.

I have the money now. No husband making wild

excuses. My mission to get my son into the best possible school suddenly has a simple answer.

It's just a shame I didn't think of it before the new installation in my closet. That's fine. It's the one thing that can be moved safely.

64

AMY

TWO WEEKS LATER

"Hey, honey, I have to get ready. Do you think you'll have that page finished by the time I get back?"

Jace has been fixated on his coloring lately, using his fancy new colored pencils. I think it might be his way of adjusting to the calmer energy in our home now. He looks up at me with those big hazel eyes. "I'm not gonna rush and wreck it, Mom."

He's been calling me Mom sometimes instead of Mommy. It's taken a great amount of control to not comment on it. He's probably picking it up from some slightly older kids at the park. It's simply a sign that my sweet boy is growing up. Which is natural, even though it's like a gut punch.

"You're right. Just take your time."

In my bedroom, I brush my hair, switch to a nicer shirt, then add a slim copper and crystal choker. My throat hasn't flushed in weeks. Not sure if it's because I am no longer worried about money all the time, or that I've... Okay, it sounds like one of Becca's fluffy sayings to think that I've "stepped into my power" or whatever. It's just nice to be able to wear necklaces again.

Should I wear a jacket to appear more businesslike? Once I slip it on, it's obviously too formal. I hang it back up, and can't resist letting my fingers trail along the top of the small standing safe I've had installed in the closet.

It's been several days. I'm allowed a thirty-second peek once in a while. As long as it doesn't become a habit or compulsion. The inability to control compulsions is likely what led to my former husband's demise.

My fingers whirl the dial around a few times in each direction, then the door silently glides open.

My breathing instantly becomes smooth and deep as I gaze at the top row of carefully arranged objects. An old, worn black leather belt missing a buckle. A large chunk from a red plastic superglue cap. A blue and red string hippie bracelet. A silver key necklace. A ladybug keychain. Neon green gardening gloves. A hammer.

The feelings that overcome me should not be mine. It wasn't my choice. All I ever did was defend myself. Then I was forced to kill killers. And those who had the potential to hurt me. And those who got too close or nosy.

I was only protecting myself and my son. That's all.

Staring at these objects makes me feel peaceful. It's like listening to rain on a mellow Sunday. They feel tranquil.

These aren't... you know. *Trophies*. That's ridiculous. They're just... well, tiny mementos, I suppose. Of the times when I was correct in my judgement.

Deep satisfaction rolls through me in warm, rolling waves. I did the right thing. Every time. The right thing.

Nothing will ever harm me or my child.

This is why I will always do what is right.

Glancing at the bottom row of beautiful earrings, I smile. Selling one pair at a time in random nearby cities is the perfect way for Craig to support us without even being here.

I shut the safe door and spin the lock before I can let the feeling of intense tranquility wash over me for too long. I need to keep my wits about me to make sure I'm always making the best decisions.

And to make sure that nobody ever hides anything from me again.

Strolling to the dresser, I put on my lucky emerald teardrop earrings and grab my everyday purse on the way to the living room. Glancing inside at my fraying gray leather wallet, I wonder if it's time for a new one. After all, the bank cards inside now access...

My chin lifts, shoulders dropping as I turn toward the living room. "Ready to go?"

"Yeah." Jace drops his colored pencils into the plastic bin and hurries to the front hall to pull on his shoes. "Where are we going?"

"We're meeting with a nice lady named Tara. She's a real estate agent. What do you think about living in a bigger house, with a bigger backyard? There's a huge garage at the side that I could fix up to be my workshop, so I'll always be around. It also means you can go to St. Mary's Elementary – it's an amazing school."

"Do they have more blocks and building stuff there?"

"They sure do, honey."

A smile touches my lips, then my heart, as I take my son's hand on the way to the car.

Life is back to the rhythm I cherish – my son, my work, my home. That's all.

The End

THANK YOU FOR READING

Did you enjoy reading *The Secrets Between Us?* Please consider leaving a review on Amazon. Your review will help other readers to discover the novel.

ABOUT THE AUTHOR

After a few detours as a graphic designer, webmistress, painter, and rock singer, Cyan is now focused on writing novels that examine the fragile, resilient, and twisted parts of the human mind. (Honestly, most of us are barely held together with emotional duct tape!)

She enjoys reading psychological and domestic thrillers, sci-fi, spec fic, and bizarro comedy fiction. Cyan lives in southern Ontario in a beautiful little town by the river, with a cute guitarist husband and not quite enough house plants.

Please visit Cyan on her website:
cyanmichaels.com

Made in the USA
Monee, IL
30 October 2025

33286061R00194